THE ADVENTURES OF HERMES, GOD OF THIEVES

100 Journeys
through Greek Mythology

MURIELLE SZAC

translated by
MIKA PROVATA-CARLONE

PUSHKIN CHILDREN'S BOOKS

Pushkin Children's Books
71–75 Shelton Street
London, WC2H 9JQ

Original text © Editions Bayard 2006

English translation © Mika Provata 2014

First published in French as *Le Feuilleton d'Hermès*

First published by Pushkin Press in 2014

0 0 1

ISBN 978 1 782690 30 6

Set in Berling Nova by Tetragon, London

Printed and bound in Italy by Printer Trento SRL on
Munken Print White 100gsm

www.pushkinchildrens.com

For Félix-Hermes and Esther-Artemis

For Marie-Agnès

ΕPISODΕ 1

IN WHICH WE WITNESS THE
BIRTH OF HERMES

╔╗╔╗╔╗╔╗╔╗╔╗

The sun was only barely beginning to rise when Hermes came out of his mother's womb. He stretched himself, yawned and leapt right away to his feet. Then he ran to the entrance of the cave where he had just been born, in order to admire the world. "How beautiful it is!" he murmured.

It was indeed a very strange birth. Had anyone ever seen a child who had started to walk and talk the instant he was born? This child, however, lived in the land of the gods. This child lived in the beginning of time. In times of mystery when everything was possible. What Hermes discovered on this first morning of his birth was a landscape of rare beauty. The cave where he had just seen the light of day had been dug out at the top of a very high mountain. Fine grassy hills extended below his feet. It was the fourth day of the month of May, and spring was bursting. The child put his hand over his eyes to shield them from the rising sun. He looked for a long time at the small white blotches on the green grass:

they were flocks of sheep. He looked for a long time at the small purple blotches on the green grass: they were budding trees. A bird flew in the sky above, tracing great circles. A fine perfumed smell wafted in the air. Hermes suddenly felt the urge to laugh, to burst into laughter: this is how beautiful life seemed to him as it began.

It was then that a gentle voice called to him from inside the cave. It was Maia, his mother. She had long, silky hair and her gaze was sweet like honey. She smelt good, she smelt of mummy. Hermes went back inside the cave.

"Where is my father?" he asked.

Maia gave a strange smile. "He is everywhere and nowhere."

Hermes pulled himself sharply away from his mother and stamped his foot on the ground: "But I want to see him, I want to!"

"Everything in good time," replied Maia, running her fingers through her child's curly hair.

The sun was already high up in the sky when Hermes realized that he was hungry. His mother had fallen asleep and he had followed her in her slumber, nestling tightly close to her. Without a sound, he freed himself from Maia's arms and decided to go off in search of adventure. He really hoped that he would find on this beautiful earth something which would make him happy. Noiselessly, Hermes clad himself with a sheepskin; he slung a bag over his shoulder and left the cave. Then he scampered down the slopes of the very high mountain without looking back.

He was whistling gaily and walked at a brisk pace. All of a sudden his foot struck what he took to be a great green stone. The stone rolled some feet away from him. Hermes stopped and picked it up. It wasn't a stone, but the shell of a tortoise! "It might always come in handy," he told himself. And he slipped it into his bag.

A little farther, Hermes saw at the edge of the road some great shrubs with shiny leaves. A pungent scent which tingled his nose emanated from them. They were laurels, the sacred tree of the god Apollo. Hermes did not know this yet. But he liked the smell, so he broke off a laurel branch and slipped it into his bag. "It might come in handy," he told himself. A little farther still, Hermes came near a pond. A forest of supple stalks swayed around him. He thought that he could hear them murmur: "Good-day, day-good, good-day..." Since he was naturally polite, he returned the greeting to the long reeds. Then he slipped a few of them into his bag, saying to himself: "They may always come in handy." And he continued on his way. He was not yet very tall, and the forest of reeds concealed him almost completely. This is how he arrived unseen before a herd of cows. These cows were magnificent. They possessed long, curvy horns. Their skin glistened in the sun. With their heads held high, they contemplated the world around them with astonishing elegance. They were so white and so nobly proud that Hermes was certain that he had discovered the most beautiful cows in the world. He felt a great urge to play with them. He dreamt of climbing on their backs for a royal jaunt. He dreamt of sliding underneath their udders to drink their milk. Hmm, how good that warm and frothy milk must be! Hermes, who was getting very hungry, felt his mouth water at the thought. He threw a few glances all around but there was no drover in sight. No one seemed to be keeping watch over this herd. So he made up his mind to serve himself. Yet he had to show cunning. Hermes lay down for a few moments on the mound of cool grass in order to think. The butterflies flitted about him, the sun tickled his neck. What would be the best way to steal these cows without getting caught?

To be continued...

EPISODE 2

IN WHICH HERMES INVENTS FIRE

*Previously: On the very day of his birth, Hermes
runs away from the cave where he was born, in order
to see the world. He discovers the most beautiful
cows on earth. And he decides to steal a few...*

Hermes looked minuscule next to the immense cows of the herd he had discovered. He did not hesitate for an instant, however. He edged his way among the beasts and approached the one with the longest horns. He was convinced that this particular cow was the leader of the herd. He stretched one hand gently towards her; the cow turned her head around sharply. Hermes flinched: was she going to give him a good, hard blow with her horns? The animal's eyes were, however, full of kindness. Hermes raised himself up on the tips of his toes and spoke into her ear for a long time. What was said between the child and the animal has remained secret. Yet the cow nodded her head thrice to tell Hermes that she had understood well. Then she assembled fifty or so of the most beautiful cows of the herd, and walked them backwards out of the field. That's right—the cows were all of them walking backwards! Hermes was skipping with joy all around them as he guided them along the way. He was very proud of his ruse: in this manner, they were fleeing in one direction, while their hoof prints gave the impression that they were heading in the opposite one. Hermes could not keep from laughing, very pleased with the trick he had just played on the owner of the cows. Hermes could not help but wonder who could possibly possess such beautiful beasts. A thought crossed his mind: what if these cows were the property of a god? There was a good risk that his anger might be terrible...

As the way was long, Hermes decided to take shelter with his cows in the recess of a valley. A small brook snaked its way through the hollow of the valley. The beasts drank and the child began to skim stones. He was so absorbed by the small pebbles he was throwing against the surface of the water that he did not notice the passage of time. All of a sudden he shivered. "But what is happening? It is dark here and it is cold too," he murmured, bewildered. Night had fallen soundlessly, and Hermes was discovering it for the first time. Very quickly he began to feel anxious. No matter how wide he opened his eyes, he could see nothing in the darkness. He could just barely make out the outline of his herd, if at all. "But where has the light gone? Will it come back? I cannot stay in the dark, I am too scared, I really am!" He approached the cows in order to feel more reassured. The beasts had lain on the ground. The cow with the longest horns, however, was still standing. She was striking the rocky ground with her feet, staring hard at Hermes as she did so. She struck, and struck, and struck. All of a sudden a faint spark sprang from under her hoof. When he saw it, Hermes leapt to his feet. Right away he began to look for a tender piece of wood. When he had found it, he took out of his bag the branch of laurel that he had picked up along the way. He took it between the palms of his hands and began to rub the branch against the piece of hard wood. The child rubbed, and rubbed, and rubbed. He rubbed so very much that after a while a thin plume of smoke emerged, then a flame leapt up. Immediately he added some dry grass, then some kindling wood, and soon there were great flames dancing. Hermes had just invented fire! The fire drove away the cold, the fire drove away the darkness, the fire drove away fear. Hermes was happy. He had just created on earth the invention which would prove the most useful to men.

Since that morning, he had still not eaten anything except strawberries and raspberries he had collected along the way, and some bitter-tasting fruit he had picked off an almond tree. His hunger was once again making itself felt. He went to see the cow with the long horns. As though she had understood, the fine beast laid herself down. Hermes lay next to her and drank all of her milk.

Once he had drunk to his heart's content, Hermes resumed his way. A friendly moon had risen. Having reached the foot of the same mountain where he had been born that very morning, he hid away the stolen cows. He wished them good night, clambered up to his cave and slipped noiselessly into his crib. His mother Maia had, however, heard him. She had been waiting for him.

"Where do you come from in the middle of the night?" she said.

"You scold me as though I were a baby," protested Hermes, "but I am all grown up now."

Maia was about to reply to Hermes that one should not go too fast in life, but she stayed silent. Hermes was tired. As he had been talking, he had taken hold of a rag with one hand and his tortoise shell with the other. The great adventurer looked once more exactly like a baby. So Maia approached the crib and began to hum softly:

Sweet baby Hermes, you will be the one most loved.
Great cuddly Hermes, you shall never fear a thing.
Because you are the son of the strongest of the strong,
The son of the master of the living gods.

With his thumb in his mouth, Hermes murmured: "Mummy, who is my father?"

Maia leant down and whispered: "He is called Zeus, he is the king of the gods."

But Hermes did not hear her. He had already fallen asleep.

And he would do well to rest, for on the following day a great surprise awaited him...

To be continued...

ΕΡΙSODΕ 3

In which we witness Apollo's
enormous outburst of anger

*Previously: Barely born, Hermes has gone off to discover
the world. Along the way, he stole a herd of magnificent
cows and he has brought them back with him.*

When the sun rose up again, Hermes felt stronger and taller
still. Sitting on the ground by the entrance of the cave,
he began to play with his tortoise shell. First of all, he imagined
that it was a ship. He blew and blew, harder and harder, until
his tortoise ship keeled over. After that, he wore the shell on
his head like a hat. It had now become a crown. He imagined
himself king of the earth, ruling over all living things. The child
played for a long time like this. The more things he invented,
the more he amused himself.

This is how Hermes took out of his pocket some small bits of
twine. Seven short pieces of string. He attached the seven strings
onto his tortoise shell and tightened them well. Then he pulled
at one of the strings. A strange sound was produced, a sound

that no one had ever heard on earth. Something which echoed deep in one's heart. Surprised, the child plucked another string. Another sound was heard. As beautiful, but a little different, more low-pitched perhaps. Hermes was dumbfounded by his discovery. He began to strum the seven strings each in turn, faster and faster, and a melodious music arose from them. It was as though it had the magic power to render one happy. Maia, his mother, had come nearer. She was looking at him, deeply moved. And Hermes felt then the urge to cry out loud the joy which inhabited him. He began to sing in order to accompany the beautiful music. His song flowed like a torrent, untamed and strong.

He sang of the world's beauty, which had dazzled him when he had opened his eyes upon life. He sang of his mother's caresses and of her warm breath down the nape of his neck. He sang of the wind between the branches. He sang of the murmur of the leaves. He sang of the reflection of the sun on the ocean and of the sheen on the plumage of a field bird. He sang of the perfumes of the orange trees and of the tangy taste of lemons. He sang of the beauty of the fire he had invented and of the pallor of the moon which had provided him with light. He sang of bitter almonds and of the limpid dawn. He sang of the blackness of the night and of the absence of a father.

A tear was running from his mother's eye. Hermes had just invented the lyre, that musical instrument which soothes the hearts of men, but makes them heavy too. He had just offered music to the world, for ever.

All of a sudden, a shadow masked the sun. A huge man

stood on the threshold of the cave. He carried a silver bow over his shoulder and his tunic left one guessing at the magnificent body underneath. It was impossible not to be awestruck by his beauty. Hermes did not waste time in examining him, however. He hurried to the depths of his crib and bunched himself up into a ball under his blanket, like a baby.

"You little brat," cried the man, "you had the nerve to steal my herd of cows!" His wrath was terrible. His voice resonated in the cave.

But Hermes was not going to let himself be intimidated: "You don't know what you are talking about! I was born only yesterday! How could I have gone out to look for your horned beasts?"

The handsome young man seized him by the scruff of his neck and hoisted him out of his bed. "Out of your crib with you, you rascal!" He shook the child up and down, but he did not succeed in appeasing his fury.

It was then that Maia cried out: "Would you dare to hurt your own brother?"

Surprised, the young man let go of little Hermes, who fell down on his bottom. Maia hurried to take Hermes in her arms.

"You are Apollo, isn't that right? The great Apollo, god of Light and Beauty?" said Maia.

"Yes," the young man said, puffing himself up like a peacock, for he was flattered that she had recognized him.

"Leto is your mother's name," Maia continued, "and Zeus is the name of your father, isn't that right?"

"Yes," confirmed Apollo.

"Then in that case Hermes is your brother, since you have the same father," smiled Maia.

Having crept inside the folds of his mother's tunic, Hermes was trying to keep out of sight. But what he had just learnt filled him with happiness. It meant that he was the son of Zeus, the god of gods! So he was himself a god! Before him, Apollo remained speechless.

Hermes, who did not know how to appease the wrath of such a powerful older brother, suddenly had an idea: "Let us not argue any more, brother, and let us go and see daddy, so that he can decide which of the two of us is right." The god of Light let out a sigh. But he had no reason to refuse. He agreed therefore to submit himself to the judgement of Zeus. And this is how Hermes went away to meet his father.

To be continued...

EPISODE 4

IN WHICH HERMES DISCOVERS
HIS FATHER'S PALACE

*Previously: Hermes has just discovered that he is the
son of Zeus, the god of gods, and that the herd of cows
he stole belongs to his brother, the god Apollo. The
two brothers have decided to ask Zeus to settle their
dispute. Here is Hermes, then, off to meet his father.*

The earth was dry and it crumbled under the steps of Hermes
and Apollo. A reddish dust enveloped them. The child was
very impatient to discover Olympus, where all the gods of the
universe lived. And he had great difficulty keeping silent.

"What does our father's palace look like?" he had asked
gaily. Apollo had not replied. "Is it far from here to Olympus?"
Hermes had enquired again.

"Be quiet and walk!" Apollo had grumbled. And since then,
the hours had gone by with no exchange of words.

Hermes was hungry. He thought ruefully of the beautiful
cow who had offered him her frothy milk. He missed her. He

19

would have given anything to be able to be next to her and talk softly in her ear, as on the day before. Keeping quiet was very hard for him. It was obvious that Hermes' presence bothered Apollo. Not only was he still annoyed about the theft of his herd, but the discovery of a new little brother vexed him.

So then, his father Zeus, the god of gods, had fallen in love again with another woman! And he had fathered with her a new child! This was not the first time, and Apollo knew well that it would not be the last either. Zeus fell easily in love. And no woman seemed able to resist his charm. In point of fact, Apollo's mother had not been Zeus' wife either... All the same, Apollo did not like discovering new brothers... From the corner of his eye he threw a glance at the little chap by his side, and his wrath flared up even stronger.

When it was time for lunch, the two brothers stopped to eat. Apollo took out of his bag a bowl full of a curious foodstuff. It was a kind of bronze-coloured broth. Its smell was deliciously sweet, and Hermes instantly felt his mouth water.

"Could you maybe let me taste a little bit?" asked Hermes.

"No," grunted Apollo, "this is ambrosia, a meal reserved exclusively for the gods."

Hermes was silent for an instant, then he replied in a small voice:

"But I too, I too am a god, since I am the son of Zeus. A small-sized god, but a god nonetheless..."

Apollo did not deign to reply to him. He had got to his feet, and had picked up his bag and his staff once more.

They finally arrived at the foot of a very high mountain, even higher than all the ones they had walked past on their way. A white cloud formed a cap on its summit. This cloud served to keep the palace of the gods hidden from view. The two brothers quickened their step as they climbed the mountainside. At the thought of discovering his father's house, Hermes had recovered in full his joyful impatience. When he reached the summit, he was dazzled by the sight.

The walls were dressed in marble, gold and precious stones. With each step, the child discovered a room even more beautiful than the one preceding it. Bowls filled with ambrosia were laid out on low tables. Hermes dipped his hand into one of them. The ambrosia was so delicious in his mouth that the child almost wept with delight. Magnificent atria accommodated fountains from which there jetted out an amber-coloured liquid with a bewitching smell. Hermes was fascinated by this golden-hued beverage.

"What is it?" he asked, forgetting that Apollo had ordered him to remain silent.

"You will know soon enough," replied the god curtly.

At that very moment, the double doors of the great throne room opened up. This was where the assembly of the gods was held. All the gods and goddesses were sitting in a semicircle around Zeus, the king of Olympus. And they all waited. Hermes shuddered. What would happen once Zeus learnt of the theft he had committed?

To be continued…

€PISODE 5

IN WHICH HERMES MEETS
ZEUS, HIS FATHER

*Previously: Hermes and Apollo have made a long
journey in order to reach Olympus, the seat of the
palace of the gods. Hermes is mesmerized by the
beauty of the place. He is preparing to meet Zeus.*

When Hermes entered the council hall of the gods, his
heart began to throb with great fast beats. He had just
caught sight of his father, sitting at the centre of the room.
So this was the man who had loved his mother to the point
of giving her a child. He wore a white tunic which fell down
to his feet. His long beard, his hair and his bushy eyebrows
made him look severe. Yet Hermes thought he cut a fine,
noble figure. He held in his hand an object which discharged
a blinding light: it was the lightning bolt of the thunderstorm.
"He is truly the king of kings," Hermes told himself proudly,
looking at the flashes of lightning which were the symbol of
his father's power.

"Good morning, Apollo," said Zeus, "who's that you've brought along with you?"

"It is your latest son," replied Apollo drily. "And I have come to complain because, barely born, this scallywag has already stolen from me an entire herd of cows!"

Apollo then told the story of the disappearance of his beasts. He recounted how he had picked up the trail of their hoof prints, how he had realized that the thief had made the cows walk backwards to cover his tracks, and how he had arrived in this manner at the cave where little Hermes was sleeping. Zeus listened to his eldest son with a faintly ironic smile on his lips.

At the mention of Maia, the child's mother, a tender glimmer flashed across his gaze. Hermes could not take his eyes off him. He had to win his father's favour, no matter what it took. He had to attract his goodwill. Get himself adopted. He made up his mind to soften his father's heart and he began to speak in turn:

"Dear daddy, you I love a lot. My brother Apollo, he is mean to me, he frightens me. You are not going to believe his story, are you! How could I, so very little that I am, steal fifty cows from him? I was born yesterday! Please, come to my rescue, you who are the king of kings. I am the weakest of all the gods, and you always stand by those who are weak..."

With his brown curls falling down his forehead, his bewitching smile and his sparkling eyes, Hermes was deploying all his charms. He spoke and spoke, with such natural eloquence that everyone suddenly saw the god of all the gods dissolve into hearty laughter.

Zeus knew very well that Hermes was the cow thief, since Zeus always knew everything. Yet the little fellow amused him, and he liked his cheekiness. Deep down inside he was not at all displeased to see Apollo, who was always so sure of himself, be the loser for once. Hermes could tell that he had found the right words to touch his father's heart. The only thing left now was to win over the other gods. He looked at the gods and goddesses surrounding the throne. He did not know any of them, yet they all cast a hard and severe eye on him. How dare he speak with such easy familiarity to the master of the gods?

Zeus took the floor just then and said: "I wish that you make peace between you. You, Hermes, you shall return Apollo's cows to him and you shall promise never to do this again. And you, Apollo, you will forgive him. Go, and come back fast."

Hermes was thrilled. He had managed to get out of this rather well, and what is more his father had invited him to return to Olympus as quickly as possible! Yet in the hall, the gods mumbled discontentedly.

In order to mollify the crowd, Hermes suddenly had an idea. Plunging his hand inside his bag, he pulled out the piece of reed that he had collected. He brought it to his lips and blew delicately into it. A pure, clear sound came from it. A sound so light, so melodious, that a joyful rustling murmur ran through the assembly. No ear had ever heard any music like it. It was like the song of a bird, one might say, a song of joy and deliverance. Hermes had just invented the flute. And his music had given birth to a smile on everyone's face. His music gently stroked their souls. Hermes had won.

Once Hermes had finished playing, Zeus clapped his hands. The young boy made a deep bow and left the council hall radiant, accompanied by Apollo.

Yet when he saw Apollo's disgruntled face, he could tell that the return journey was going to be anything but easy.

How was he going to get his brother to like him?

To be continued...

EPISODE 6

IN WHICH HERMES SEDUCES HIS
BROTHER WITH HIS LYRE

*Previously: Hermes has succeeded in winning the heart
of his father Zeus, and in charming the gods of Olympus
with his flute. Yet he still needs to win his brother over.*

The two brothers set out on foot and headed once more
towards the cave. Apollo had gone back to being sulky
and surly. He did not say a word, his forehead was stubbornly
hardened, his eye full of black anger. He was brooding over his
humiliation. How could his father allow himself to be so seduced
by this younger brother, who had dropped from the sky, that
he did not punish him? Was he to replace him in Zeus' heart?
Apollo was discovering an emotion unknown to him until then:
jealousy.

For his part, Hermes radiated with happiness. A single little
phrase had filled him with joy, the last one that his father had
uttered: "Come back fast!" He could not prevent himself from
taking out his lyre so he could sing. Sometimes in life we feel

so very happy that we feel the urge to dance, to cry out loud. Once again, Hermes let his joy burst out through his music. He sang of the beauty of the palace of Olympus. He sang of the happiness of knowing his father. He sang of the warmth there is deep inside one's heart, when we know ourselves loved. He sang of the strength and power of Zeus. He also sang of the good luck of having an older brother he could admire. Then his song became more melancholy. He sang of the beautiful cow with the long horns that he loved so much. And of Maia, his mother, left alone in the cave to wait for him.

Apollo had stopped walking. He was listening to his brother in hushed amazement. Hermes' song was so delicate that Apollo had tears in his eyes. It wasn't for nothing that he was the god of Music and Poetry, the protector of the Arts.

"You may be very little, my brother, yet you know wondrous secrets," he said to him. "Would you be willing to teach them to me?"

At these words, Hermes turned red to his ears. Was it possible? The great Apollo was asking *him*, a little two-day-old fellow, to teach him something he did not know?

He replied: "You are daddy's firstborn son, you are his favourite. And you know so very many more things than I do! But I would happily show you how to play the lyre, and I can even give it to you as a gift, if you would like..."

Apollo seized the lyre with trembling hands, plucked a string, then two. Hermes took his hand gently and guided the fingers along the strings. Little by little a melody rose from the lyre. Apollo was deeply moved. His anger had completely disappeared.

"To thank you," he told his brother, "I offer you my golden staff and name you herdsman of my cattle. In this way you can still see the beautiful cow with the long horns as often as you like."

Hermes was delighted by this offer. And as he was still just a very young child, he fell on Apollo's neck to hug him. Apollo was a little taken aback and recoiled instinctively. Then he clasped the child in his arms, and hugged him in turn.

The two brothers were about to start on their way once more when a great racket was heard. A jumbled noise of rustling, chafing and whistling coming from a thicket of dense grass by the roadside. They went hastily to see what it was, and discovered two long serpents wrestling ferociously. Jaws agape, fangs sticking out, tongues a-whistling, they sought to bite one another and they coiled and twisted in every direction. This fighting frightened Apollo, who only liked tranquillity and beauty. Hermes, for his part, was fascinated by the violence of the scene. He suddenly seized the golden staff that his brother had just offered to him and held it out towards the two serpents. Instantly the serpents ceased to fight, and they wound themselves in a double braid around the magic staff. Once united on the staff, their two heads found themselves facing each other, and they embraced one another. Hermes gave a little smile of satisfaction. He took the staff, now bearing the two reconciled snakes, and he decided that from that day onwards he would never be without it. Then he turned towards Apollo and said to him: "Shall we go then?"

That evening, the two brothers stopped to spend the night by a river. The day's heat had been intense, but night enveloped them in a cooling mantle. Hermes made a fire under Apollo's admiring gaze. Then he sat cross-legged by the fire and took out his flute again. He had hardly begun to play, and already Apollo longed to possess that instrument as well.

"Brother, what would you want in exchange for your flute?" he asked him.

Hermes thought carefully for a moment, then he said in a clear voice: "You know so very many things, you must surely know what will happen to me. I would like you to teach me how to tell the future."

Apollo seemed ill at ease. "Yes, I know, but I don't have the right to teach you that myself," he answered. "The women who taught me to read the future, they alone can teach that skill to you as well."

Hermes' curiosity was inflamed: "Who are they? Where can they be found? Can you take me to them?"

"Calm down, calm down!" said his brother, smiling. "The women who taught me to foretell the future are the Thriae, the nurses of the babies of the gods. They are three old women living on Mount Parnassus. Go find them and tell them I sent you. Perhaps they will agree to entrust you with their secret..."

Hermes set out instantly for Mount Parnassus. Was he going to be able to learn the secrets of the three nurses of the babies of the gods?

To be continued...

€PISODE 7

IN WHICH HERMES LEARNS TO
SEE AN INVISIBLE UNIVERSE

*Previously: Hermes has become friends with his brother
Apollo. Curious about the world he is discovering, he has
made up his mind to go to see the old nurses of the babies
of the gods in order to learn how to read the future.*

Hermes was thirsting to know the world. He left instantly
and headed towards Mount Parnassus, taking with him his
golden staff with the two intertwined snakes. He walked singing
all the way. He crossed the verdant plains, then the flowering
orchards. Trees with pink or yellow flowers intermingled on
the grassy meadows and this vision of nature filled him with
happiness.

Hermes soon arrived at the foot of Mount Parnassus. That
mountain was not as high as the mountain of the gods, yet it
was dark and cold, despite the springtime warmth. The more
Hermes climbed, the more the herbs and flowers became scarce.
Soon there were only stones.

A little brook appeared at the turn of the path. There, an old woman squatting on her heels was washing great white sheets, which served to swaddle babies. Her grey hair was done up in a tight bun. She had a beautiful face, still smooth in spite of her advanced age. Yet her eyes were unsmiling.

"What have you come here for?" she asked gruffly.

"I have been sent by the great Apollo, who loves you so very fondly, O nurse," replied Hermes, "I would like to learn how to foretell the future."

The nurse gazed hard at him: "Why do you wish to know what *will* exist? Do you already know how to see what exists around you?"

The young god hesitated and then replied: "No. Teach me."

The stern-faced old woman beckoned to Hermes to approach. "Look down into this brook and tell me what you see," she told him.

Hermes looked at the flowing water and replied: "Good nurse, I see nothing but water flowing on the pebbles."

"When you leave this place, you will see there a thousand hidden treasures," she said. She took the boy's bundle and led him to the cave where she slept.

Hermes stayed for seven days and seven nights with the first nurse, whose name was Antalia. And she taught him to open his eyes upon the world. She taught him to observe life under a blade of grass, to smell the scent of the flowers, to recognize the taste of honey and that of salt, to love the caresses of the sun and of the wind, to listen to the voice of the earth, to hear the murmur of the stars.

By the end of the seventh day, Antalia returned to the bank of the brook with Hermes and she asked him: "Look down into these flowing waters and tell me what you see."

Hermes squatted down on his heels over the brook and this is what he said: "I see the dancing and graceful curve of the running water, I see the golden flecks of sun reflected on its surface, I see the little silver fish huddling under this stone, I see the green seaweed rippling in the current, I see the insect skating on the surface, and I see the tracks of animals who have come to drink. I smell the fresh scent of the moss, and that of bluebells. I hear the music of the droplets as they strike against the rock. I hear the dragonflies skimming the water with their vibrating wings. I hear the song of the little frogs crouching behind the blades of grass." Hermes stopped for an instant. He dipped his fingers into the current and brought a mouthful to his lips. "And I find again the wholesome taste of the earth and the sun in the purity of this water." Hermes had found the key to an invisible universe. Only he who knows how to wait and how to see may enter it.

Antalia smiled at last and said: "Hermes, you now know how to see what exists around you. You may continue your way. Go and find my sister, farther up on the mountain, she might be able to help you." The young god thanked the old nurse warmly for all that she had taught him. He picked up his golden staff once more and left, impatient to discover all the other mysteries of this world.

To be continued…

€PISODE 8

IN WHICH HERMES LEARNS HOW
TO FORETELL THE FUTURE

*Previously: Hermes has met Antalia, one of the nurses
of the babies of the gods. She has revealed to him how to
see the unseen around him. Now he is off again to seek
out the one who will teach him to foretell the future.*

Hermes walked for a long, long time. As the path turned, he
suddenly met another old woman. She was hanging on a
washing line great white sheets which served to swaddle babies.
The wet sheets flapped in the cold wind, which blew very hard
at this altitude. This woman resembled the one he had just left,
but she was older. In her tight bun, the silver hairs were more
numerous than the black strands. She had the same beautiful
face as Antalia, but it was already lined with numerous wrinkles.
Her eyes were unsmiling.

"What have you come here for?" she asked gruffly.

"I have been sent by the great Apollo, who loves you so very
fondly, O nurse," replied Hermes, "I would like to know what will

33

happen to me. I would like to learn how to foretell the future. And I am also sent by your younger sister, who has taught me how to look at the present."

The nurse looked at him sternly: "Why do you wish to know what will exist?"

"So I may know who I am," replied Hermes.

"Do you really think that the answer is to be found in the future?" said the nurse.

Hermes replied smiling: "Teach me, and we will soon find out."

And so Hermes stayed seven days and seven nights with the second of the nurses of the babies of the gods, whose name was Roxanne. And she taught him how to foretell the future. Roxanne would toss small and smooth round pebbles into a great pool full of water. In their fall, the pebbles traced beautiful patterns in the air and then in the water as they sank down. By observing these patterns, the nurse was able to foretell all that should come to pass. On the first day, Hermes questioned her about his life later on. "You will be much loved by your father, and you shall have a fine place by his side," said Roxanne. And she added: "Your entire life you will be a great traveller and you will be immensely curious." On the second day, Hermes sought to find out what would become of his mother: "Maia will be proud of you all her life and she will be happy to know that you are among the gods of Olympus." On the days that followed, Hermes himself learnt to foretell what would come to pass by following the fall of the small and smooth round pebbles in the water. By the end of the seventh day, he had mastered the art of prophesying the future. And yet the young god was still not quite satisfied in his mind.

"Well, then," Roxanne asked, smiling, "are you now content? Do you know who you are?"

Hermes sighed and shook his head: "No, you were right, I can read the present and the future, and yet I still lack something. But I do not know what."

"What you lack," replied the old nurse, "is knowledge of the past. You are made of what you experience today, and of what others have experienced before you. In order to know who you are, you need to know where you come from." At these words Hermes' face lit up. Yes, that was it: what he sought was to know the origin of all things! "Continue on your way," said Roxanne. "Go and see my sister, higher up on the mountain, perhaps she might be able to help you."

Hermes thanked Roxanne for all that she had taught him, grabbed his golden staff and left. He walked for a long, long time. As the path turned, he came at last before the eldest of the three nurses of the babies of the gods. She was sitting on a small stool made of stone, and she was folding up great white sheets which served to wrap babies with. A faint gleam emanated from her wrinkled face. She had swaddled, fed and cradled the children of the gods for all eternity. Her arms were tired from having carried so many. Her hands were coarse from having caressed too much. Her voice was broken from having sung so often. Yet she was the living memory of the world. Her eyes had seen everything, since the mists of time. She was called Pausania. Hermes looked at her without saying anything. It was she who lifted up her head and said to him: "Come in, I have been expecting you."

Hermes threw himself at her feet. And, without thinking any more, he rested his head on the old woman's knees. "I beg you, tell me about the birth of the world," he murmured.

She laid her furrowed hand on the child's hair and asked him: "Are you quite sure that you wish to know all this, little one? It is a story where the forces of evil and of good fight against each other. A story from which one comes out transformed..."

Hermes shivered. "Yes, I do wish to know," he breathed.

The old woman gave him a faint smile. She raised her hand and made a strange gesture, as though to cast a spell on Hermes, who was at her feet. He sank immediately into a deep slumber. "Since you have wished it so hard," muttered the old woman, "you yourself will witness the birth of the world."

To be continued...

ΕΡΙSΟDΕ 9

IN WHICH HERMES WITNESSES
THE BIRTH OF THE WORLD

*Previously: Pausania, the oldest of the nurses of the
babies of the gods, has agreed to reveal to Hermes
the origin of all things. Here he is projected into the
past, ready to witness the birth of the world.*

When Hermes opened his eyes, everything was darkness,
a profound darkness. There wasn't the faintest glimmer
of light. He did not know where he was. He could hear nothing,
nothing except an immense silence. The young god was floating
in an endless vacuum. He could feel strange movements around
him, as though some form of matter were stirring in silence.
As though forces were growing restless in this emptiness where
he found himself.

"You are inside Chaos," a voice breathed in his ear. It was
the voice of Pausania. She reassured Hermes: "You see, in the
beginning there was nothing at all. Nothing except a gaping
hole—Chaos. And then, all of a sudden, we do not know how,

or why, goddess Earth emerged from the Chaos. Look! She is called Gaia."

At last, something stable and solid had just been born out of this vertiginous black hole. Gaia, streaming with light, was offering herself up as the solid surface of the world. Hermes could not take his eyes off her, dazzled by this apparition. He felt protected, he felt safe, exactly as when he was still in his mother's arms. Part of Gaia still remained plunged inside Chaos, yet the rest lifted itself upwards. She was the goddess of the earth, the mother of all things in the universe. Henceforth, all beings would have a place where they could put down their feet. She stretched herself gracefully. And it was at that moment that another god appeared above her.

"This is Uranus," breathed the voice of Pausania in Hermes' ear. "He is the sky!" Uranus looked powerful and protecting. Hermes saw him lie down just above Gaia, covering her entirely, like a lid. Uranus had just attached the sky for ever above the earth.

Hermes murmured: "But this earth and this sky are still empty, they do not resemble at all the earth and the sky as I know them!"

Pausania broke into a little laugh: "How impatient you are!" she replied. "We are still only at the beginning of the story... There is still someone very essential missing..."

Utterly absorbed as he was by the marvels taking place under his eyes, Hermes had not noticed the presence of another figure, who had also come out of Chaos just after Gaia. This was a very old man with a long white beard. Two silver wings were attached to his back. He was sitting very close to Hermes, and was watching fondly the meeting between Gaia-Earth and Uranus-Sky.

"How beautiful it is..." he said all of a sudden. These words made Hermes jump.

"But... but... who are you?" asked the young god, discovering his new companion.

"I am Eros," replied the old man, "I am the god who brings love. For nothing may be born without love."

Eros' voice was pleasant. The kindness which could be read on the old god's face inspired trust in Hermes. He looked once more at Gaia and Uranus as they were creating the world. Gaia had just given birth to the mountains, the hills, the valleys and the caves on the earth. Then she had fallen asleep. Leaning tenderly over her, Uranus caused a light, fertile rain to fall. This rain slid in every secret crack of the earth. Instantly, the grass emerged, the trees, the flowers and all of the earth's plants. The light rain which continued to flow gently on Gaia filled the ponds, the streams, the rivers, then the oceans.

Hermes, eyes glistening with excitement, asked Pausania: "But why did you tell me that the story would be terrible? What I see here is wonderful!"

"It is after this that it all becomes complicated," replied the old nurse in a dark tone, "yet you have had the answer to your first question. Now, you must go back home. Come and see me when you have more questions to ask me."

To be continued...

€PISODE 10

IN WHICH HERMES REALIZES
THAT HE IS IMMORTAL

*Previously: Thanks to Pausania, the old nurse
of the babies of the gods, Hermes has just
witnessed the birth of the world. Now he is
returning to Olympus to discover his new life.*

On the way back, Hermes whistled as he looked at the valleys
and the hills, the seas and the streams, the fields and the
woods that he crossed. The earth was magnificent. Thanks to
Pausania, he had seen all these landscapes being born. He loved
the earth all the more for it.

When he was back at the palace of Olympus, Hermes did not
see his father Zeus again right away. He had gone off walking
on earth, as he was wont to do. He was still not back eight days
later. While he waited for him to return, Hermes took the
opportunity to discover his new home.

The first to greet him was Hestia, the goddess of the Hearth
and one of the sisters of Zeus. She had neither husband, nor lover,

nor child. Her main task was to oversee the smooth running of the palace. Hestia had welcomed Hermes with her customary gentleness. "How tired you look, come and rest, I will lead you to your room," the goddess had said to him in her sweet voice. And Hermes had instantly taken a liking to her, like everyone in the palace. Hestia, with her round face, her discreet smile, her chubby arms and above all her sweet voice, looked as though she had been born to sing cradle songs. It was by her side that Hermes learnt the habits of the palace of the gods.

Hermes was rather fond of food, so he began with the palace kitchens. Hestia and the maidservants never said no to him, and readily offered him good things to eat. Yet it was especially around the mysterious fountains that Hermes kept turning. He loved to admire the amber liquid which flowed in great tides in the palace atria. The first time that he had dared slip his finger under the fountain, he brought it hastily to his lips. The taste was exquisite. He glanced about him: no one was looking. And so he plunged both his hands in the fountain and drank avidly in long sips. The beverage poured down his throat like a caress. As though it were a promise fulfilled. Hermes suddenly felt himself invincible. Soon afterwards he noticed that all the gods who lived in the palace served themselves drink from the fountains.

One day, he was gorging himself on the golden beverage when he noticed a young girl, looking at him enviously as he drank. She was one of Hestia's maidservants. He beckoned her to approach and come and drink with him. Yet she shook her head to say no, and ran away. Hermes came across the young maidservant several times, several times he offered to share with her the delicious drink, yet she always refused, and would run off without a word.

"Are you quite happy here, my nephew?" asked gentle Hestia one day. "Do you have everything you need?"

"Yes, aunt, thank you," replied Hermes. "But I would like you to explain to me what this strange beverage is, which flows from every fountain in the palace. And why your maidservants refuse to dip their lips in it."

A smile lit up the goddess' face. "You speak of our precious nectar. It is reserved for the gods alone; this is why my maidservants cannot taste it. It is the drink which renders us immortal."

Immortal? So then the gods themselves never died? Hermes was left speechless. And so he, Hermes, would never die either?

To be continued...

EPISODE 11

IN WHICH HERMES DISCOVERS
THAT HE CAN FLY

Previously: Hermes has made an astounding discovery: the gods never die, thanks to nectar, the drink of immortality which flows in the palace of Olympus. He is waiting for Zeus' return, so that he can find out what his fate will be.

Zeus came back on the morning of the ninth day. He immediately summoned Hermes to his apartments.

"Good morning, my son," said Zeus, "how do you feel in your new house?"

"Well, father, very well, but I missed you," murmured Hermes.

Zeus was taken aback and he was moved. Nobody spoke to him with familiarity, except his wife Hera. And no one ever seemed to be waiting for him to come back. The gods and goddesses were only too happy to manage without him on Olympus. Truth be told, the great Zeus felt very much alone here. He liked Hermes' tenderness.

"You are not too bored?" he asked again.

Hermes looked deep into his father's eyes: "To tell the truth, I find it difficult to stay in one place. Everything is wonderful here, but I would like to discover the wide world." Then he lowered his eyes and added: "And I would really like to be useful for something." Zeus was enchanted by the words of his youngest son. He suddenly had an idea.

Zeus leapt to his feet, rummaged through the contents of a chest and pulled out two golden objects which gleamed under the light. There was a flat hat, with small golden wings on each side, and a pair of sandals, also with little wings of gold. He held them out to Hermes.

"Wear this hat, put on these sandals, my son, and you will be able to go freely wherever you like." Zeus was thrilled with the boy's look of utter wonder. He went on: "I would like you to carry the messages that I need to have delivered everywhere in the universe. How would you like to be my messenger?" Zeus usually issued orders; he never asked for anyone's opinion. But he did not wish to force anything upon this prancing youngster. By way of an answer, Hermes fell on Zeus' neck, and placed a sonorous kiss on his father's cheek. Zeus was taken aback. He was secretly thrilled, but he did not wish to show it too much: "Good, good, now calm down, my son, calm down," he said in a voice which was meant to sound strict. "As of this moment, you must be available to carry all my messages, no matter where to, at any given moment, understood? Now leave me. But come again later and join me at five, at the small postern of the palace."

Skipping out of the room, Hermes discovered with delight that his new hat and his new sandals allowed him to take giant strides. He began to run laughing up and down the corridors of the palace at top speed. He was having so much fun hurtling down the staircases and speeding from floor to floor that he did not see a door open in front of him. It was still early in the morning, but Hestia was in a hurry. She was going to fill all the house lamps and was carrying for that purpose a great amphora full of oil. Arriving too fast, Hermes was unable to avoid the goddess, and he crashed into her. Taken by surprise, Hestia let her amphora drop. The vase smashed on the floor, and all the oil spread everywhere! Slipping on the oil, Hermes could no longer stop himself. At the end of the corridor there was a small balcony overlooking the valley. Unable to check his momentum, the boy stumbled into the void. Hestia and her maidservants screamed out loud and rushed to see what had happened.

As he was thrown out into the void, Hermes did not have time to feel his fall. A sudden sense of lightness took hold of him. The golden wings of his hat and sandals had begun to flap, causing him to rise gracefully in the air instead of falling down. "But... but... I am flying! *I am flying!*" he shouted. And he began to turn somersaults in the sky, while the women on the balcony applauded. Hermes would soon become the king of aerobatics in the sky. Yet, as he let himself be carried off by the wind, he tried somewhat anxiously to guess what would happen at five, the time of his appointment with his father.

To be continued...

ΕΡΙSΟΔΕ 12

IN WHICH HERMES UNDERSTANDS
THE ORIGIN OF DAY AND NIGHT

*Previously: Zeus has asked Hermes to become his
messenger. He has offered him a winged hat and
sandals, and Hermes has discovered that he can fly!*

At five, Hermes waited for his father at the postern gate of Olympus. That small door allowed one to leave the mountain without being seen by the palace inhabitants. When Zeus arrived, he was dressed as a simple wayfarer. Without his royal vestments, and above all without his thunderbolt, the king of the gods seemed less impressive. He put his arm around his son's shoulders, and they descended Olympus together. Hermes understood then that Zeus had not only chosen him to carry his messages across the universe, but also as his travelling companion, and this gave him immense pleasure. He began right away to tell him about thousands and thousands of things, and above all to ask him questions concerning everything that surrounded them. Zeus was amused by this endless curiosity, and he could not stop laughing at the young god's jokes.

Little by little, the light became weaker, and the glimmers of a magnificent sunset turned the sky red. Hermes stopped talking at last, in order to admire the sight. Then he knitted his eyebrows and murmured:

"But if you are with me at this moment, then it isn't you who commands the sun to set?"

His father replied: "I have entrusted this task to Helios. Follow me, the time is right, I will introduce you to him."

While they had been walking, Zeus and Hermes had reached the ocean's shore. Zeus pointed with his finger to a milky-white palace on the horizon. This palace seemed to stand on a golden cup floating on the surface of the sea. They approached. And the more they approached, the more dazzling the palace looked. It was so luminous that Hermes was blinded by it. They were about to enter when a blazing chariot drawn by four white horses descended from the sky. The sun was placed at the back of the chariot, and the charioteer was Helios. He held himself up perfectly straight, and he cracked his whip high in the air above the heads of his team of horses. Hermes thought he was quite magnificent. When the sun god crossed the gate of his palace, he met with another chariot, which was leaving it. This one was silver-coloured, and drawn by four black horses. At the back of the chariot was placed the moon. "This is Selene, the sister of Helios and goddess of the Moon. She is beautiful, isn't she?" murmured Zeus in Hermes' ear. The pale, long-limbed young woman had a serene and melancholy face. The chariot of Selene began to rise in the heavens. It was going to travel across the sky throughout the entire night. "You have not seen the most beautiful one yet, wait, I will introduce you to her," whispered Zeus to Hermes once more.

When he entered this palace so full of light, Hermes was very impressed. Helios came at once to greet them. Shimmers of sunlight still clung to his long golden cape. He yawned, and sparks escaped from his mouth. Since Helios travelled across the sky all day long, nothing of what took place on earth escaped his gaze. It was therefore in Zeus' best interest to treat him well. "Go and rest now, my friend," the master of the gods said to him, "we are just going to say hello to your little sister." Zeus and Hermes then entered a room of pink and purple hues. A woman was lying on a couch. As they approached, Hermes discovered a goddess dressed in a yellow gown, her face covered with fresh dew, her fingers a bright pink. Her long hair spread about her, forming a golden crown. Zeus looked at her fondly. "This is Aurora, the rosy-fingered goddess," he murmured. "She announces the onset of dawn, and takes out her chariot just as her sister sets the moon and before her brother raises the sun." They observed her for a long moment. The young beauty twitched in her sleep. A fresh smell of lavender and rose filled the room. They did not have the heart to wake her and they went out on the tips of their toes.

Now dark night had fallen, brightened only by the pallor of the moon that Selene was carrying across the world. Hermes was still dazzled by what he had just seen. In the darkness his eyes gleamed with excitement. Then, when they had reached the shore once more, he noticed a strange mountain, a mountain that spat out fire. A tremendous groan seemed to come straight from the earth's womb. Fiery stones and boiling lava spurted out from inside. Showers of red and yellow sparks burst suddenly in the night. And a thick smoke accompanied this eruption. It was splendid and frightening at the same time. Terribly impressed, Hermes gripped his father's arm:

"Daddy, what is this?" he stammered.

Zeus did not reply. Hermes felt the ground shake under his feet. Boulders of rock came hurtling down the slopes of that mountain, and went to throw themselves noisily into the sea. The water had turned red and it was scalding hot.

"It is a volcano," mumbled Zeus.

"But where does it come from? Who is causing such a frightful thing?" asked Hermes.

With a sudden, angry gesture Zeus prised the young man's fingers from his arm.

"That's enough for now, we are going back. You don't need to know all the mysteries of the earth." Zeus seemed to be very ill at ease. What was taking place under their eyes escaped his control. It did not take more to kindle Hermes' curiosity. He left his father straight away to go and ask Pausania for the key to this mystery.

To be continued…

ΣΡΙSΟΔΣ 13

IN WHICH HERMES MEETS THE
HUNDRED-HANDED GIANTS

*Previously: Zeus has shown Hermes how the sun and
the moon travel across the sky. But he refused to explain
the origin of volcanoes, those fire-spitting mountains.*

When he returned to Mount Parnassus, Hermes felt a joyful
excitement rising up inside him. Old Pausania did not
seem surprised to see him arrive.

He knelt beside her and asked: "O nurse, show me once more
the mysteries of the universe. What is hidden under the earth
behind the volcanoes?"

"In order to understand, my child, you must go back to the
time just after the birth of the world. Do you feel you are strong
enough to face once more that savage world? Are you ready?"

"Yes," murmured Hermes passionately, and he laid his head
on the nurse's lap.

When Hermes opened his eyes again, the valley in which he
found himself was calm and green with grass. One could hear

the warbling of the birds, the crystalline chant of a waterfall and the sweet murmur of the sea nearby. The air was filled with the scent of flowers opening their blossoms for the first time. The universe appeared to be in order. Calm and appeased, finally out of Chaos.

Then all of a sudden, *Braoum! Braoum!* The ground trembled violently under Hermes' feet. A great, dull sound was getting closer and closer... *Braoum! Braoum!* A little frightened, Hermes hid behind a great rock. He had hardly taken cover when three monstrous Giants appeared. They were horrible to look at. They each had fifty heads and a hundred arms. And they thrashed their arms all about them, hitting, knocking, pulling, throwing down everything that lay within their reach! At their passing, they left behind them nothing but ruins. Uprooted trees, trampled grass, torn flowers, stones flung in every direction. It was a gigantic mess. "I present to you Gyges, Briareus and Cottus, the hundred-handed Giants. They are the firstborn of Gaia and Uranus," whispered Pausania. The young god huddled close to her, much relieved to feel her beside him.

After having given birth, then, to the mountains, the rivers, the oceans, the plants and the animals, Gaia had continued to populate the universe by coming into union with Uranus. Yet goddess Earth had brought some terrifying creatures into the world.

Hermes cowered behind his rock, hoping with all his heart that he would escape the notice of the hundred-handed Giants. But the three Giants decided to stay right where they were. They had invented a new pastime. Each in turn seized a rock with one of his hands, and hurled it with all his might into the sea. Their arms were so powerful that as it sank into the tide, the rock caused waves many feet high to rise on the water surface. These waves overflowed onto the lands and gobbled up everything that had barely just hatched. The more the showers of sea spray rose high, the more the Giants laughed. The more the sea devastated the earth, the more the Giants rubbed their hands. Nothing gave them greater joy than to spread mayhem with these monstrous tidal waves.

Hermes was a powerless witness to the destruction of this terrestrial harmony. Every rock around him was flying into the ocean. Soon the rock sheltering him would suffer the same fate. Hermes had no intention of finding himself hurled to the very bottom of the ocean, clinging on to his great pebble stone. All of a sudden he had an idea. The Giants were as strong as they were formidably stupid. He took a stone and threw it in the direction of one of Gyges' numerous heads. Then he immediately hid himself behind the rock.

"Hey!" bellowed the Giant, turning towards his brothers Briareus and Cottus. "Have you gone mad, you two? What are you throwing stones at me for?"

"It isn't us!" rumbled the other two menacingly.

In no time at all, the three brothers began to pelt one another with stones. A gigantic fight flared up and they knocked themselves senseless. Gyges, Briareus and Cottus had passed out on the ground. Phew! Hermes could now come out of his hiding place. Not so fast! For here was Uranus approaching in his turn, exasperated by the cries of his three sons. When he discovered them lying there senseless, he struck the ground with his foot and the earth opened in two. An enormous chasm appeared. "This is Tartarus," murmured Pausania in Hermes' ear, "one of the deepest regions of the Underworld. If you were to throw an enormous rock down this hole, it would take nine days and nine nights for it to touch the bottom..." At that instant, Uranus took hold of his sleeping sons and he hurled them down to the bottom of the chasm one by one. The earth closed back again: the three Giants were the prisoners of the earth's belly.

It was these terrible monsters, closed up below the earth, who knocked on the walls of their underground prison, shook the ground and caused the mountains to spew. Hermes, however, would soon discover that other creatures, more frightening still, were also kept in the depths of Tartarus.

To be continued...

ϵPISODϵ 14

IN WHICH HERMES MEETS THE CYCLOPES

*Previously: Thanks to Pausania, Hermes has gone
back into the past in order to understand the origin
of volcanoes. He has discovered that hundred-
handed Giants were confined underground.*

I n this world at the beginning of time, Hermes went from
one discovery to the next. Hermes had been journeying for
a long while when he came near a black mountain. A cave had
been dug into the mountainside, similar to the one in which
Hermes had seen the light of day. Red and orange flashes of light
escaped from this cave, followed by showers of sparks. Hermes
approached quietly. The more he approached, the more he could
hear muted and regular noises. *Pang! Pang!* After each noise a
shock ran through the mountain. The little god felt very uneasy,
yet his curiosity was greater than his fear. At long last he reached
the entrance of the cave. Now that he was fairly near, Hermes
could also feel waves of burning heat coming forth. He looked
inside and what he saw made the hair on his head stand on end.

Three powerful Giants, their bodies half-naked, were bustling about before a gigantic forge. The first was blowing onto a great fire. The second held pieces of metal in the flames with great pliers. The third, armed with an immense hammer, was striking at the metal, which became malleable once it had been heated. His blows were so violent that the mountain quaked. Each time his hammer struck the metal, great showers of sparks spouted forth. The three Giants were sweating.

"Blow harder, Brontes!" cried one of them in a deep voice.

"Clench your pliers more tightly, Arges!" shouted the other.

"Strike harder, Steropes!" yelled the third in the midst of the racket surrounding them. The fire glow lit up the cave walls. Little by little, the fiery metal took the shape of a shield.

It was at this point that one of the Giants lifted his head in order to mop away the sweat running down his face. And Hermes discovered to his horror that he had but a single eye in the middle of his face—an enormous and monstrous eye which seemed sharp enough to see things very, very far away. "These are the Cyclopes, also the sons of Gaia and Uranus," murmured Pausania.

Suddenly there was silence. Steropes had paused his work. With one gesture of his hand, he had signalled to his brothers to stop working as well. The Cyclops began to sniff at everything, probing everything with his gaze, every nook and cranny of the cave. "I sense a strange smell," he rumbled, "a smell I do not recognize. Someone has come in here." Hermes was trying to make himself really small so that he might avoid detection. The Cyclops went towards the cave entrance where Hermes was hiding. His solitary eye swept across the tiniest crack in the rocks. Nothing could escape his gaze. Hermes was caught in a corner. When he discovered Hermes, the Cyclops let out a roar and pounced on him.

"What are you doing here?" he cried, seizing him between two fingers. "I shall roast you in our furnace for having dared to come here and disturb our work!"

Hermes shut his eyes for an instant. Then he mustered all his courage and, choosing his words with the utmost care, he gave the following reply:

"Dear and venerable Cyclops, I have come to admire your prodigious work. I have come so that I may tell everyone of the wonders that you create. I have come so that I may sing your praises everywhere in the universe." These flatteries, however, seemed to have no effect on the Cyclops, who was holding Hermes precariously suspended over the fire, ready to drop him at any moment right in the middle of the flames.

At that instant a thick fog invaded the cave, enshrouding everything in a grey veil. Taken aback and feeling anxious, the Cyclopes began to whimper like babies. For once deprived of their sight, they become fragile and defenceless. Steropes had set Hermes down on the ground once more, and he was desperately rubbing his eye so he could see something, anything. Suddenly a formidable force lifted the Cyclopes up in the air. They let out a great scream. The earth split open, and they were hurled to the bottom of a hole, together with the fire of their forge. Steropes, Brontes and Arges had just gone to join their brothers, the hundred-handed Giants, in the Tartarus.

Uranus, for it was he once more, had stopped his three other sons from causing damage on earth. Satisfied, the god of the Sky left the Cyclopes' cave. The fog melted away.

Hermes approached the chasm. There was but a narrow crack left. Hermes now understood that the red lava coming out of the volcanoes came from there. And that this lava arose from the fury of the Giants and the Cyclopes, who were shut up below the earth. He had had the answer to his question; he could now leave the past and return home.

To be continued...

ΕΡΙSΟΔΕ 15

IN WHICH HERA GIVES BIRTH
TO A MONSTROUS BABY

Previously: Hermes has discovered that the Giants
and the Cyclopes had been shut up in the bowels
of the earth at the birth of the world. And that
it is they who cause the volcanoes to spit. Now
he is off again and on his way to Olympus.

Hermes returned quickly to Olympus; perhaps his father needed him. By carrying the messages of Zeus, the young god knew everything, was involved in everything and was having great fun. Once his missions were accomplished, Hermes never grew tired of fluttering about in the heavens. He loved being carried off by the wind, or plunging into the clouds. He also did not hesitate to descend frequently down to earth to give his mother a kiss. He always became very emotional when he approached the cave where he had first seen the light of day. His mother Maia would appear on the threshold, and it would be as though a sun had risen. At such moments the messenger of the gods felt himself becoming a small child again, and he would run to nestle in Maia's arms. He would leave his head resting on his mother's shoulder for a long time. She was proud of him. After a final kiss, Hermes would return to Olympus feeling carefree.

When he had first arrived at Zeus' palace, Hermes had discovered right away that he had to be wary of the white-armed Hera, Zeus' wife. This beautiful yet haughty goddess always carried herself with her chin tilted upwards and her eyes launched flares, as though she were permanently ready to attack. Everything about her revealed her pride, her nobility, but also her hardness. Hermes often found her unfair towards the maidservants, whom she scolded for no reason. Each time a matter was discussed by the council of the gods, Hera always proposed some course of punishment. She never excused nor understood a wrong. She guarded her authority jealously. As a matter of fact, everything in her character was founded on jealousy. Hera envied the other goddesses, whose beauty might rival her own. She detested the children that Zeus had had with other women he had loved. And, above all, she hated the women with whom Zeus fell in love.

Hermes had been living on Olympus for quite some time, when Hera became pregnant for the first time. She waited for the arrival of this baby with immense joy, for Olympus was peopled with children that Zeus had had with other women. This time it was she who would bring a new god into the world. She hoped he would be more magnificent than all the others. She dreamt of a total triumph. The more her belly became round, the more her character softened. She had stopped quarrelling with each and all, and as the time for this birth approached, a joyful bubbliness reigned in the palace. "If he is a boy, he shall be called Hephaestus, the radiant one!" she declared some days before she gave birth to the child. Hera was sure that she was going to have the most beautiful baby in the universe.

The day of the birth had arrived. The entire palace was full of expectation for the happy event and Hera had been surrounded by people throughout the whole day. Poseidon, one of the brothers of Zeus, had come expressly from the ocean depths. A host of gods and goddesses had dropped their occupations in order to be present at such an exceptional occasion. Yet the baby took its time coming, and all had retired to their apartments.

In the middle of the night, great cries were heard at last. Yet they were neither cries of joy, nor those of a newborn: they were Hera's howls of rage. All the gods and goddesses rushed to her side. Inside her room, Hera had her back turned, and was looking fixedly out of the window. The nymphs who had helped the queen of the gods give birth to her baby were crying, crouching at the feet of the bed. Trembling, Zeus went closer to the bundle of swaddling clothes that enveloped the baby and which had been placed on the bed. He leant over it, separated the folds and recoiled, bewildered. An expression of horror appeared on his face. Poseidon approached in turn; he bent down over the child and burst into roaring laughter. He took the newborn and brandished it towards the crowd, without stopping his cruel laugh. The baby, a little boy, was revoltingly ugly. Instead of the most beautiful baby on Olympus, Hera had just given birth to a monster.

Hermes could not lift his eyes off the little deformed body. A heavy silence had succeeded the offensive laughter of Poseidon. Suddenly, as though it had understood that it was not the baby everyone had desired, the infant began to cry. His wailings hurt one's ears. Hera then had a sudden fit of rage. She threw herself upon the child, seized it by one leg and hurled it through the open window all the way down from the top of Olympus, howling: "You are not worthy to live in our midst, Hephaestus!" No one had had time to make a single move to stop her. The misshapen baby had been excluded from the kingdom of the gods.

The gods looked at one another, but they did not react. Hermes had rushed to the window. He observed the baby's long fall with horror. He saw the baby disappear into the sea far down below. Tears welled up in Hermes' eyes. How *could* such violence, such wickedness exist? Without waiting a single moment, he left to go and find Pausania.

To be continued...

EPISODE 16

In which a conspiracy is plotted against Uranus

Previously: Hera has brought into the world Hephaestus, a baby so ugly that she has hurled it out through the window, all the way down from the top of Olympus. Having witnessed this drama, Hermes can no longer make sense of things. He seeks to find out where violence comes from.

When he arrived at the home of the old nurse, Hermes' face was clouded with torment. He recounted hurriedly to Pausania the scene that he had just witnessed. He spoke fast, now sitting down, now standing up, and getting more and more restive. To calm him down, Pausania said to him: "Didn't you learn from my sister Roxanne how to read the future? This is the time to use your knowledge." And so Hermes threw his little round pebbles into the water. He peered down to study the course traced by the pebbles, as Roxanne had taught him. And this is what he saw.

An image appeared at the bottom of the water, blurry at

first, then getting more and more focused. It was the image of a woman leaning over a child's bed. The woman was tenderly singing a lullaby. She was caressing the child's head softly. As the child turned around, Hermes discovered his face. He was a very ugly yet smiling creature. His eyes looked lovingly at the woman who was rocking him to sleep.

"Now you must sleep, Hephaestus my love," said the woman.

"Good night, Thetis!" replied the child, closing his eyes.

"You are a gift from heaven to me, my baby," said Thetis. "You did well to fall into the sea right next to my cave, my heart."

And she kissed him. Hermes observed closely the place where Thetis and Hephaestus were, and he understood that it was an underwater cave.

Thetis murmured: "I will take care of you until you no longer have need of me." Then the image dissolved.

Hermes lifted up his head again and his brow was no longer wrinkled with worry. "Hephaestus will be saved," he told Pausania. "And he will even be loved." The old woman merely smiled. *She* knew everything.

Hermes now felt reassured regarding his brother's future, but he was still left with a great question in his mind. How was such violence possible? What had happened then, after the birth of the world, for violence to be born? He beseeched Pausania to reveal to him the origin of violence. For the first time, Pausania hesitated. Then she agreed, saying: "Hermes, you are going to witness the first drama in the history of the world. Others have followed since. Yet this one is the beginning of everything. Be wary." The young god laid his head on the nurse's lap and closed his eyes.

When he reopened his eyes he was lying on a mound, on the bare earth. He could hear voices. He did not budge and he waited. The voices became more distinct. One, gentle and feminine, trembled with sustained anger:

"Why do you prevent them from seeing the light of day? Why do you prevent them from living in the light?"

The other voice, deep and masculine, replied, also with irritation: "That's enough! These children are monsters! They must stay prisoners underground."

Hermes understood that he was witnessing a discussion between Gaia and Uranus, between the earth and the sky who covered her entirely. Gaia was sighing: "You are unfair! The Cyclopes and the hundred-handed Giants are monsters, but not our other twelve children, the Titans and their sisters the Titanides. And yet you condemn them too to be stifled underground, inside me, since they have no space between you and me to see the light." Uranus did not answer. Suddenly she shouted at him: "The truth is that you are afraid of them, afraid that they might take your place! That's why you will not allow them to exist! But they will avenge themselves, Uranus. You cannot eternally prevent my children from seeing the light!" After this terrible threat, Hermes heard nothing more. He remained for a long moment with his face against the ground, then, tired as he was, he fell asleep.

That night, in the depths of the earth, there where the children of the earth and of the sky were being retained, a voice whispered in the ear of one of the sleeping Titans: "Oceanus, Oceanus, my son, you cannot remain imprisoned like this. You must rebel against your father." Oceanus, however, did not reply. The voice murmured next in the ear of a sleeping Titanide: "Thetis, Thetis, my daughter, you cannot remain imprisoned like this. You must rebel against your father." But Thetis merely shook her head and went back to sleep. Gaia, for it was she of course, spoke in this manner to seven Titanides and to six Titans. They all refused to rebel against their father. There was only her last-born left for her to question, the Titan Cronus. "Cronus, Cronus, my son, you cannot remain imprisoned like this. You must rebel against your father," she breathed in his ear.

Cronus opened his eyes and replied: "I am here, mother. What must I do?"

To be continued...

€PISOD€ 17

In which Hermes witnesses
the world's first crime

Previously: In order to find out the origin of violence, Hermes has gone back to the time when the world was born. He discovers a conspiracy against Uranus.

On the earth's surface, a paling moon lightened up the darkness. Hermes, lying on the grass, had heard the entire conversation between Gaia and her children. Now he listened to the noises of the night and held his breath. He did not sleep; he waited. Suddenly, a great scream tore through the night. A terrible scream. The scream of a wounded god. That of Uranus, being attacked by his own son, Cronus. In order to come out from under his mother, Cronus, armed with a sickle made of stone, had just separated Gaia from Uranus. The lid which spread over the earth was thus lifted. The children of Gaia and Uranus were going to be able to exist. For an instant, a deep darkness settled over everything. The stars and the moon became extinguished. Hermes could no longer see a thing. Then the stars and the moon began to shine once more. The sky had gone to affix himself for ever above the earth, but far, very far away from her. Uranus would never again be able to rejoin Gaia. There was now a space between them. Living beings would be able to exist within that space, with the earth under their feet and the sky above their heads.

Other screams had answered Uranus' scream, screams of triumph this time. The liberated Titans were hailing Cronus, the new king of the world. Thanks to him, they were finally able to see the day. Hermes could not refrain from shuddering. He had just witnessed the first drama in the history of the world. That night seemed endless to Hermes. He could hear the noise of the joyful feast held by the children of Uranus, celebrating their liberation. He could hear for a long time their laughter and their shouts of joy. Then the uproar ceased. Everyone must have gone to sleep. Cronus was getting ready to spend his first night of triumph—he had taken his father's place. Yet he was not going to be able to sleep at all.

Hermes had lit a fire to warm himself up in this world turned cold by the crime which had just been committed. At that very instant, three shadows emerged out of the darkness. They each carried a flaming torch. Wrapped in their long black wings, they glared hard at Hermes, looked at one another without a word, and shook their heads. No, this wasn't the one they were looking for. A gust of wind made their hoods slip off, and uncovered their faces. On their heads, vipers writhed in every direction. And their eyes shed tears of blood.

"I am called Megaera," said one of them.

"And I am Alecto," said another.

"My name is Tisiphone," concluded the third.

"We are the Erinyes. We were born of the blood of Uranus. We are looking for Cronus," they said all at the same time.

"I do not know where he might be," stammered Hermes. The three Erinyes nodded to him, then without a word they faded away into the distance. Nothing remained of their passage except an insufferable stench. Hermes decided to follow them from afar.

Cronus had just lain down. He had barely closed his eyes when a revolting smell invaded his room. Voices murmured in his ear: "Cronus! Cronus! You have dared to attack your father! Such a crime shall not remain unpunished! We are here to avenge him." The Titan leapt onto his feet, seized his sword and began thrashing about all around him. Yet there was no one there. He calmed himself down immediately and lay down once more, thinking that he must have fallen prey to a bad dream. He had barely closed his eyes again when the voices whispered in his ear: "Cronus! Cronus! You have committed the greatest crime of all! You are accursed! And you shall be killed by your own child!" Wild with fury, the king of the world sprang up again. He just had time enough to see three shadows disappearing, their faces contorted by grimaces, their heads swarming with hissing serpents. He woke everyone up, demanded that dozens of torches be lit and that every place be thoroughly searched. Yet the three shadows had vanished for good. Exhausted and anxious, Cronus lay down once more. He had barely closed his eyes when the voices returned: "Cronus! Cronus! Your crime is immense. We shall never leave you in peace!" Cronus was beating the air with his hands to chase away the three Erinyes. Losing all control of his senses, the Titan began to scratch his own face.

Dawn arrived, and Cronus had not been able to get even a moment's sleep. The Erinyes vanished with the first rays of the sun. Yet from then on they returned every night to remind Cronus of his horrible crime.

During that night, Hermes had seen the birth of crime and the coming into being of vengeance. The approaching dawn, however, had yet another discovery in store for him.

To be continued...

€PISOD€ 18

WHICH SEES BEAUTY BEING BORN

Previously: Hermes, transported back to the first nights after the creation of the world, has just witnessed the first crime. He has seen violence and revenge being born.

Once the Erinyes had vanished with the first rays of the sun, Hermes felt some peace returning to this still-early world. He looked about him and saw that he was on a precipice overlooking the sea. He decided to go and explore his surroundings, in order to stretch his legs a bit. This is how he came to a shore of perfect tranquillity. It was a world still pure and limpid. The white, soft sand made him want to take off his sandals. The water was calm. Hermes was skipping along the fringes of the white sea-foam, now with one leg in the water, now with one leg on the shore, when a tiny ripple travelled across the surface of the sea. He raised his head, looked and was left speechless with astonishment by what he saw appear. An enormous seashell emerged from the waves and headed slowly towards the shore. This seashell was so big that one might have thought it was a boat—an oarless boat, however, advancing simply by gliding on the water, as though carried by the waves. And riding astride this seashell was a woman of incredible beauty. Never had the earth seen anything as beautiful as this. The woman was naked, merely enveloped by her long hair, which was strewn with violets and which danced around her, forming a soft coat. Her skin was milky white. Her eyes sparkled like precious stones. And while she was approaching the shore, a host of animals began to follow her. Fish, sea turtles, but also numerous birds, who had rushed from the earth, accompanied her. Dolphins swam ahead of her, forming a queenly procession. The waves laughed as they looked at her. A crown of white sea spray framed her boat.

Before long the goddess—for it could only be a goddess—reached the shore. She first took a long piece of cloth handed to her by doves, and wrapped herself with it before descending from her seashell. Then she caught a wide golden belt carried by sparrows and she tied it around her waist. Once dressed in this way, she set foot on the shore. She yawned, stretched herself gracefully and suddenly became aware of Hermes' presence. "Good morning," she said, "what do you think of me?" Hermes, completely dazzled by this apparition, could no longer speak a single word. After some moments of silence the beautiful woman spoke again: "I am called Aphrodite. I was born from a drop of blood which fell tonight into the sea. It was the blood of Uranus, the god of the Sky. I am the goddess of Beauty." Once she had introduced herself in this manner, Hermes remembered that he had already come across this goddess once or twice in the palace of Olympus. Yet he had never spoken to her. She was said to be capricious and terribly vain. She wore a belt which had the power to make all men fall in love with her. "If you go near her, you will fall into the snare of her beauty, and you will never be able to escape from it. Beware!" his aunt Hestia had advised him. Hermes, however, could not understand at all why he had to stay away from her. In witnessing the birth of Aphrodite, Hermes had just discovered beauty. "How strange," he told himself as he was admiring Aphrodite, "the Erinyes, those horrid creatures of revenge, were born of Uranus' blood, and so was beauty..." Since the young man continued to remain silent as he contemplated her, Aphrodite pursed her lips in a disappointed pout and turned her back to him. She headed towards her seashell once more, which was still surrounded by a host of doves and sparrows. The goddess walked as though she were dancing. Flowers sprang up from the sand under her every step. She remounted her seashell and went away on the waves. Seeing her leave, the young god murmured simply "farewell". Yet he decided to go back right away to the palace—for he was eager to see the goddess of Beauty again, and as soon as possible.

To be continued...

ΣPISODΣ 19

In which Hermes forms a friendship with his sister Artemis

Previously: Hermes has witnessed the birth of Aphrodite, the goddess of Beauty. He returns to Olympus really hoping to meet her there.

Hermes thanked Pausania for this journey into the past, and again took the way back to Olympus. While going through a dense wood, he heard a groan. The young god left the beaten trail and went under the trees. Letting himself be guided by the moans he could hear, Hermes went far into the undergrowth until he came before a great pit. A little fawn had fallen down to the bottom of this pit. The animal was undoubtedly too weak or had been wounded in its fall, for it could not manage to get out of this trap alone. And its forces were waning.

At once, Hermes let himself slide down the pit. The fawn trembled as it watched him approach. But Hermes stroked its muzzle with his fingertips, and this gesture calmed the fawn's fear. He took the animal into his arms and got out of the pit as best he could. Once at the top, he heard a great commotion. There were dogs barking, horses stampeding. Hermes hid in the shadows with the fawn held tight against his heart. A company of riders emerged from the clearing and Apollo was at their lead. The god dismounted and approached the trap which had been dug in the ground. "Look! The trap worked but the animal has escaped! A curse on him who helped it!" he exclaimed. Then he reined up again and went off hunting farther away.

The clearing became silent once more. Hermes was doubly satisfied: he had saved the little fawn and he had played a trick at Apollo's expense. He came out of the undergrowth and set the fawn down gently on the grass. He was getting ready to treat its wounds when an arrowhead planted itself at his feet. Hermes jumped up, startled, searching with his eyes for the person who was attacking him in this way. Yet he saw no one. "Who are you? What do you want of me?" he cried. A rain of arrows was the only answer to his question, coming crashing down in a circle around him. Yet none of them seemed to have been shot to wound him. "Come on, then, reveal yourselves! It's not really brave to attack someone who is not even armed!" shouted Hermes again.

At that, a figure emerged from the shadows. Hermes had not expected quite this sort of apparition. Instead of a formidable warrior, as he had imagined, it was a frail young woman who was now walking towards him. She was wearing a short tunic held in place by a belt, and sandals strapped high up on the calf. She wore her hair up. Her face was pale and sad. She held in her hand a silver bow, and the quiver of arrows on her back was silver as well. As soon as she was just a few paces away from him, Hermes recognized her. He had already come across her in the corridors of Olympus, without ever having spoken to her. It was Artemis, the goddess of Hunting, the twin sister of Apollo. Secretive and silent, she lived among the animals and nature. She was their protectress. Artemis never smiled.

"Good morning, sister," Hermes said right away. "Why do you shoot all those arrows at me?"

Artemis did not answer his question. She too had just recognized the little messenger for who he was. She asked him drily:

"What have you done to this poor fawn?"

"I? I have *merely* saved its life, that's all!" Hermes exclaimed, as though this were a performance on a stage.

Hermes' tone and theatrical gestures amused Artemis. She broke into a tiny laugh, a silver-bell laugh. It was so rare to hear this goddess laugh that Artemis' attendants rushed instantly to her side. They were all of them delighted at this sudden gaiety of their goddess. At that instant, a great and beautiful doe came out of the undergrowth. The doe hastened towards the fawn and licked its muzzle. The doe looked at Hermes with gratitude. He had saved the life of her little one. This doe never left Artemis' side. She was her favourite companion. From that day on, the untameable Artemis would feel a deep friendship for Hermes. They returned to Olympus together. Hermes looked at Artemis and he thought that she too had great beauty. "She is not as beautiful as Aphrodite," he thought, "but there is nothing wrong with her. And yet she always seems so sad, as though she were carrying some wound inside her for all eternity." Hermes swore to himself that he would discover the secret hiding behind his sister's sadness.

To be continued…

€PISODE 20

IN WHICH ARTEMIS REFUSES TO PROTECT HERA'S NEW BABY

Previously: Hermes has just met his sister Artemis, the goddess of Hunting, protectress of animals. He now has a new ally.

T he days went by on Mount Olympus. Hermes was becoming more and more close to his sister Artemis. They would often get together in the evening on one of the terraces of the palace. The young god would huddle next to her and would tell her about his day's adventures. Artemis smelt the good smell of the tree leaves and of the undergrowth moss. Hermes loved to breathe in those perfumes. Sometimes, another smell, quite a different one, would mix in with the wild scents of the woods and meadows. A fragrance of honey and milk, to which was added a strange, tangy smell. A smell both sweet and pungent, which made Hermes want to laugh and to cry. Those were the days of birth-giving.

The first time Hermes had asked her: "What is that smell on you, my sister?"

And Artemis had replied gravely: "That of babies. Today I have helped a baby come into the world. Because I am the protectress of births. Didn't you know that?"

Hermes had not known it, and this new mission of Artemis' intrigued him a great deal. He questioned Artemis so very many times that she finally agreed to take him with her one day.

One night, Hermes heard a discreet light tap on his bedroom door. He woke up with a start. It was Artemis.

"What's the matter?" he asked, still half asleep.

"Get dressed and follow me. A birth is about to take place," Artemis answered.

This was enough to wake him up completely. All excited, he followed Artemis and left the palace. Soon they arrived at the doors of another palace. Soft music was coming from its interior. Maidservants came hastily to greet Artemis and Hermes, and led them right away to the bedside of the mistress of the palace. She was lying in an immense bed, and several maidservants bustled around her. Hermes approached the bed and recognized the young woman who lay stretched on it: it was Calliope, the Muse of Poetry. During the great dinners at his father's palace the Muses, who were nine sisters, sang and danced with Apollo. Each of them represented a particular art. Hermes loved above all to listen to the singing of Euterpe, the Muse of Music. But he also enjoyed a lot the poems recited by Calliope. He was deeply moved to find himself like this in Calliope's home, just as she was about to give birth.

Artemis had knelt next to the mother-to-be and had taken her hand. She spoke to her with great tenderness. Then she got up again and gave some orders to the maidservants. Right away, the maidservants placed great cauldrons full of water on the fire. When the water was boiling they dipped inside great white towels, then they took them out clean and steaming. Soon clouds of steam had filled the entire room. Hermes observed all this female activity with great astonishment. He looked at Calliope's belly, perfectly round under the blanket, and he felt himself growing more and more impatient.

The night progressed. Looking through the window, Hermes saw rosy-fingered Aurora driving her chariot. He suddenly heard a cry, a baby's cry, and this cry brought tears to his eyes. The door opened and Hermes edged his way to the bed. Calliope's face looked tired, yet radiant with joy. She held in her arms a baby all wrapped up in white swaddles and she was tenderly offering it her breast to suckle. Artemis too seemed exhausted. She was looking at the infant and at the mother without losing her usual expression of sadness. "He is called Orpheus," murmured the mother. Then she took her eyes off the baby and said to Artemis: "Thank you, thank you for everything." Artemis made a slight nod with her head and left the room. Hermes followed her.

This was how all births were protected by Artemis. One day, however, white-armed Hera was expecting a new baby. Everyone in the palace of Olympus seemed to have forgotten the tragic birth of Hephaestus. Hermes alone still gave some thought to that baby. While on his errands, he sought it with his eyes under the sea. But without success.

Once more Hera was announcing that she was going to have the most beautiful baby in the world and had every attention lavished on her. The entire palace was waiting for the happy event with impatience. One person alone refused to show any interest, and that was Artemis. So Hera brought her baby into the world without Artemis' help. The baby howled so loudly at its birth that Zeus called it Ares, the god of War. Artemis did not even come to see Ares.

Hermes asked her: "But doesn't this baby need your protection too?"

"If you had been born as I was born," Artemis answered, "you would understand."

Hermes knew nothing about his sister's birth. He questioned her about it, yet she refused to answer and walked away. What secret was Artemis hiding then?

To be continued...

ΕΡΙSΟΔΕ 21

IN WHICH HERMES LEARNS
ARTEMIS' SECRET

Previously: Hermes has accompanied his sister Artemis,
who protects all births. Yet she has refused her protection
to Hera, who has just brought a baby into the world.
This refusal hides a secret: the secret of Artemis' birth.

The mysterious words pronounced by Artemis had awakened Hermes' curiosity. The very next morning, he decided to question his aunt Hestia about it. He found her squatting on her heels in the kitchen, kindling the fire.

"I want to understand what makes my sister Artemis sad. Can you tell me about the secret of her birth?" he said to her.

Hestia replied: "What you wish to know might cause you to have doubts about your own father, my child..."

Yet Hermes insisted so hard that she began her story. "Do you know at all who the nymphs are? They are ravishingly beautiful young goddesses. They live in nature, in the midst of woods and meadows. They are beautiful and wild. Leto was a nymph. She

81

was the daughter of two Titans, Phoebe and Coeus. One day, she went to bathe in a small brook with her girlfriends. She was playing in the water and laughing a great deal as she splashed it onto her companions. She was laughing so hard that your father heard her from the heights of Olympus. He descended on earth right away, gently drew near and watched for a good minute, hiding behind bulrushes and reeds. He thought she was so very beautiful that he decided to draw even closer. Then he turned himself into a small quail. 'Oh, look at the pretty little quail,' exclaimed Leto. And she tried to catch the bird. The quail did not fly away, but it moved slowly farther away from the group of young girls. Leto followed it, without suspecting that she was in fact following the god of gods. Soon she had strayed so far away from the other nymphs that Zeus could now allow her to catch him. Leto took the little quail in her arms. And instantly, the nymph found herself changed into a quail in turn! In this way, Zeus was able to declare his love to her. The two quails remained together for a long while. And this is how two children were conceived. Zeus then flew away, and Leto turned back into a nymph."

Hestia fell silent for a moment, engulfed in her memories. Hermes hung on her every word as she went on with her story:

"As soon as white-armed Hera, Zeus' wife, heard the news, she flew into a violent rage. 'I forbid that any known place on this earth should receive Leto!' she yelled from the heights of Olympus. Your father did not dare to intervene and defend Leto, and so the poor young girl found herself rejected by all, not knowing where she could bring her children into the world. She was desperate. She sat on a rock facing the sea and began to weep. Fortunately for her, Poseidon, the god of the Seas, was moved by her tears. He laid his hand on the young girl's shoulder and said to her: 'Come, follow me.' Leto climbed onto the chariot of the god of the Seas, which was drawn by enormous goldfish. Once they had reached the middle of the ocean Poseidon clapped his hands, and a stretch of land suddenly emerged from the waters. An island with just a few pebbles, dry earth, a palm tree and a date palm. 'Here is an island for you, it is called Delos,' he said; 'you can take shelter here, my pretty one. It is not a place known to anyone, since I have just created it. Hera can do nothing against you here.' Leto had hardly set foot on the island when she sensed that she was going into labour.

At the foot of the palm tree, she first brought into the world a little girl. It was Artemis. Barely born, Artemis waited with her mother for the birth of her twin brother, Apollo. Yet nine more days had to pass before the boy's birth. When he finally arrived, seven white swans flew in a ring around the island. The twins had been born. Hera could no longer prevent them from taking their place among the gods. You see, Hermes, Artemis never forgave Hera for having persecuted her mother. Nor for having forced her to bring her children into the world all alone on a deserted island. So this is what makes your sister sad."

In the half-darkness, Hestia's face was just barely lit by the embers that she was stirring to stop the fire from going out. She let out a deep sigh. And in an effort to provide some excuse for her brother Zeus, who had not found a way to protect his children, she added:

"You must not hold this against your father. He too was cruelly persecuted when he was little..."

This made Hermes jump. Little? His all-powerful father had been little?

"O Hestia, tell me about the childhood of Zeus," he implored. Yet the goddess looked uneasy all of a sudden.

"No, no, no," she whispered, "one must not speak of such things. Above all, forget what I have just said. It's best for everyone that way." It did not take more than this to heighten Hermes' curiosity.

To be continued...

EPISODE 22

IN WHICH HERMES DISCOVERS CRONUS THE DEVOURER

*Previously: Hermes has learnt that his father
had been persecuted when he was little. He
is eager to discover Zeus' childhood.*

As soon as Hermes was able to leave Olympus, he went back to Mount Parnassus. Pausania received him with her usual gravity.

"Your desire to know the origin of everything is insatiable, my child," the old nurse said with a smile. "What do you wish to see being born today?"

"My father," replied Hermes, fixing her hard with his eyes.

She did not falter under the young man's piercing gaze, but her smile vanished. She sat on a stone outside her cave.

"It will be a tiring journey," she said simply. Hermes let his head rest on the nurse's lap. He closed his eyes.

When he opened his eyelids once more, Hermes was in a room where a woman lay asleep. It was the Titanide Rhea.

Beside her, a baby was wriggling gently in a cradle. Then the door of the room opened, and Hermes had just enough time to hide behind a curtain before he saw Cronus entering. The Titan had changed somewhat since he had taken over the place of his father Uranus. His face was hollow, his eyes swollen and red. "The Erinyes must be preventing him from sleeping every night," thought Hermes. Cronus seemed very agitated, yet he was trying to make as little noise as possible so that he would not wake up his sleeping wife. Suddenly, Hermes saw Cronus take hold of the baby with great caution, and—swallow it whole, in one go! Then Cronus tiptoed out of the room. At her awakening, the young mother discovered the empty cradle. "Hestia, Hestia, my baby, where have you gone?" she cried. But she could cry and call all she wanted; her baby had vanished for good. "Strange," thought Hermes, "this baby is called Hestia, like my aunt, the goddess of the Hearth and Home." Yet Pausania at that moment drew his head back on her lap. He felt himself overcome by sleep. Everything became blurred.

When he woke up, he was still in the same room. Rhea had just brought a second daughter into the world. This time, she was trying to stay awake to watch over her child. But she was too tired, and in the end she fell asleep. Hermes then saw Cronus come into the room, grab the child and—swallow it whole, in one go! Rhea woke up just at the moment when Cronus was preparing to leave the room.

"Where is my baby? Where is my little Demeter?" cried the wretched mother.

"I do not know," replied the wily Cronus, "I was only just coming to look at her myself."

Rhea began to weep noisily. "Strange," thought Hermes, "this baby is called Demeter, like my aunt, the goddess of the Seasons." Once more Pausania drew the young god's head back onto her lap. He fell asleep.

He woke up after the birth of Rhea's third daughter. The young mother had decided to stay awake no matter what it took. Cronus came to visit her and demanded to take the baby in his arms. Rhea held it out to him and, knowing the baby to be safe, she dozed off for a few minutes. Hermes saw Cronus swallow the baby right away, whole and in one go! When Rhea woke up, Cronus was groaning and he pretended to be searching everywhere for the baby, who had disappeared like the others. "Hera! Little Hera! Where have you gone?" he called out everywhere. Rhea, mad with sorrow, was beginning to suspect Cronus. Twice now the child had disappeared while its father was present. "Strange," Hermes told himself, "this baby is called Hera, like my father's wife." Then he fell asleep on Pausania's lap once more.

Hermes opened his eyes at the birth of the fourth child of Rhea and Cronus. It was a boy. Looking at Rhea's face, he understood that this time she was firmly determined not to let go of her child, not even for an instant. "Don't worry, Poseidon," she murmured to the child, "I am here, nothing will happen to you." It was then that Cronus entered the room.

"Give that child to me!" he demanded. Rhea refused. "*Give me that child!*" he yelled. And as she was still refusing, he snatched the child from her, and right there and then, before her eyes, he swallowed it whole, in one go! Rhea had now discovered the horrible truth.

"But why do you do this? Why?" the poor mother cried.

"Because I have been warned that one of my children would take my place one day!" he grumbled. "I killed my own father so that I could exist, I am not just going to sit and be dethroned by my children!"

Rhea wept, implored, yet the cruel Cronus remained unyielding. "Strange," Hermes told himself, "this baby is called Poseidon, like my uncle, the god of the Seas." Once more Pausania drew him back to sleep.

When he woke up, he witnessed the birth of Rhea's fifth child, a baby called Hades. Rhea was unable to prevent her husband from swallowing this baby as well. Hades went to join his brother and sisters in his father's belly. "Strange, this time the child bore the name of my uncle, the god of the Underworld," remarked Hermes.

At each birth, the young messenger of the gods had felt terrified by what he was seeing. When was all this going to stop? Until when would Cronus go on devouring his children?

To be continued…

EPISODE 23

WHICH SEES THE GREAT ZEUS BEING BORN

Previously: Hermes has just seen Cronus swallow each of his children whole and in one go, right after they were born.

O n the night when Rhea gave birth to her sixth baby, Hermes was still hiding in her room behind the curtain. Loud cries rang out: the child had just been born, and he was possessed of quite a voice! As soon as he heard the baby's wailings, Cronus had rushed to the room.

"Hand him over to me," he demanded of his wife.

"I will do, right away, I am just getting him ready for you..." she replied, bustling over the baby. She had her back turned on Cronus, who waited impatiently for her to finish dressing the child.

"You don't have to get him dressed, just give him to me as he is!" he raged.

Yet Rhea went on swaddling what Cronus took to be the baby. Hermes looked down to see the infant. And to his surprise, instead of a tiny face, he saw a lump of rock! In fact, the goddess had concealed the newborn under her skirts, and was bundling up a big stone in his place. In his impatience, Cronus did not even become aware of the treachery. As soon as she handed the stone to him, he swallowed it whole, in one go.

"By the way," he asked Rhea before leaving the room, "what was this one called?"

"He is called Zeus," replied Rhea. Upon hearing these words, Hermes leapt for joy: he had just witnessed the birth of his own father!

Rhea's trick had worked. Immediately, the goddess slipped out into the night, carrying her baby concealed in the folds of her dress. She went to knock quietly on the door of Gaia, the Earth Mother. It was she who had suggested to her how to save the baby. Rhea kissed her baby tenderly and told him: "You shall have a king's destiny, my son, farewell!" Then she entrusted him to Gaia's care. The baby looked at his grandmother. It was as though he could already understand all that was happening to him. A tender smile sketched itself on Gaia's lips. The child responded to her smile. "Let us not waste time," she murmured. "I shall take you where you will be safe from your father's appetite." And she went away in the darkness, holding Zeus tight in her arms. Hermes barely had time to cling onto Gaia, and he left with her into the night. After they had crossed the ocean, they reached the top of a mountain which was on an island called Crete. Everything had to be done fast, rosy-fingered Aurora could already be seen far in the distance. Some very beautiful young women came out of a cave and surrounded Gaia:

"Oh, how cute he is!" said one.

"He looks so sweet!" added the other.

"We are going to love him so much!" murmured a third.

"Thank you, nymphs," said Gaia. "Take care of him, and above all hide him well. His father must not find him either on earth or in heaven." Then, having cast a last glance on her grandson Zeus, she vanished into the night.

Hermes, who had been hiding up a tree better to be able to observe, saw the nymphs go and fetch an extraordinary beast. It was a great goat, who had on her forehead a single horn, long and twisted. This goat was called Amalthea. They brought her close to the baby, and right away he began to suckle greedily. Hermes was quite overcome to be watching his father as a newborn. The nymphs built a golden cradle for the child. And in order to be sure that Cronus would find his son neither on earth nor in heaven they suspended the cradle from branches between the earth and the sky. That's when Zeus began to cry. These baby cries could be heard far, very far into the distance... They risked being heard by Cronus! The nymphs summoned protecting spirits, who immediately began to clang their spears onto their heavy bronze shields, letting out wild cries at the same time, to cover up Zeus' own cries. There was no longer any risk of Cronus finding his son again.

"And now close your eyes," murmured Pausania in Hermes' ear. "The goat Amalthea was an outstanding wet-nurse to your father: the more he drank of her milk, the more he grew. We are now going to join him again after a lapse of twenty years." Hermes obeyed, and once he opened his eyes again he discovered a handsome young man, tall and strong, kissing one of the nymphs.

It was Zeus, about to leave those who had raised him with such care. When he went to bid farewell to the goat Amalthea, who had fed him so well, Zeus offered her a magic horn. It was a horn which resembled the solitary one that the goat bore on her forehead. "Take this horn, Amalthea, my good nurse," the young man said to her. "It will always be filled with delicious fruit, fragrant flowers, and all the good things that you'd like to eat. Thanks to this horn of abundance, you will never lack anything, just as I never lacked anything in your company." Then Zeus joined the shepherds of Mount Ida. There, he became one of them and began his adult life.

Hermes was thrilled to have witnessed his father's childhood. Yet he still could not understand what had given such fright to Hestia. What was there so terrible in that childhood? "You will understand later what your aunt Hestia did not dare to tell you," said Pausania to him. "It is now high time you went back to Olympus. Your brother Hephaestus needs you. You will return to your father's past another time—I will wait for you. Now go."

To be continued...

€PISODE 24

IN WHICH A MYSTERIOUS ARTIST
ENTERS THE PALACE

*Previously: Hermes has just witnessed his father's birth
and then his childhood. Pausania, however, has told
him that his brother Hephaestus has need of him.*

O
n his way back, Hermes wondered how he might be
able to help Hephaestus. He often thought of this little
brother whose mother had thrown him out of the window. He
had tried hard several times to find again the cave where the
nymph Thetis had received him, yet he had never been able to
discover its whereabouts. On that day, Hermes sat on a rock by
the seaside, all the while thinking of Hephaestus' disappearance.
The water was calm and pure, just barely disturbed by a light
wind which formed delicate ripples on its surface. His gaze
wandered in this way across the surface of the sea, until it was
caught by something shiny. With a flap of his wings, Hermes
swooped down upon the flash of light. It was a piece of jewellery,
a splendid brooch. "It must have been made by a craftsman of

exceptional skill," Hermes told himself. The brooch was placed on a bed of seaweed and it floated on the surface of the water. Hermes took it and returned to Olympus.

When he arrived at his father's palace, Hermes had attached the brooch to his tunic. This jewel did not pass unnoticed. No one had ever seen one as beautiful as this. The goddesses and nymphs pushed and shoved one another, the better to admire it. Hermes was flattered. White-armed Hera came by, however.

"Give me that brooch!" she cried.

"And why should I?" replied Hermes impertinently.

Scarlet with rage, Hera shouted: "Because I am the wife of the god of gods, and because no one has the right to wear jewels more beautiful than mine!"

Disgruntled, Hermes handed her the brooch. Then, the very next morning, when it was time for the assembly of the gods, a goddess appeared at the palace wearing on her head a magnificent jewel: it was a very finely chased diadem. It sparkled and every gaze turned towards its wearer. No one looked at Hera any more, despite her exquisite brooch. Furious, Hera leant towards her husband and asked him to summon the goddess to him. It was the nymph Thetis. She approached the throne.

Zeus questioned her: "Who is the artist who has fashioned a diadem of such beauty?"

"The same as the one who made your wife's brooch," replied Thetis.

"What is his name?" exclaimed Zeus. Thetis kept silent.

Hera lost all patience: "I demand to know his name, for I

wish him to come here and remain close to me so that he can make me the most beautiful jewels in the universe!"

With a small sidelong smile, Thetis murmured: "Are you quite sure, O goddess?"

"Yes!" replied Hera.

And so Thetis asked leave to absent herself, so she might go and fetch the artist who could twist the precious metals with such divine skill.

The crowd that had gathered in the great hall of the palace was waiting for her return with great curiosity. It surely had to be a god. Yet which god? Suddenly, the heavy doors were opened. A stocky, hunchbacked figure came limping forth. He was still young, yet a shaggy beard hid part of his face. He was extremely ugly. A startled murmur ran through the throng. How could this vile fellow be the one who had fashioned such graceful objects? The man approached the throne of Zeus and Hera and then went down on his knee. Only his broad, bull-like shoulders could be seen, and his great unkempt mane of hair.

"I am at your service, O king and queen of Olympus," he said. "My name is Hephaestus."

To be continued...

ΕΡΙSΟΔΕ 25

WHICH MAKES THE TRIUMPH
OF HEPHAESTUS COMPLETE

*Previously: The artist capable of creating the most
splendid golden jewels in the whole universe has
just been received on Olympus: it is Hephaestus.*

Upon hearing her son's name, Hera let out a scream and brought her hand to her mouth. Zeus, however, left his throne, approached the still-kneeling young man and gently raised him up.

"Welcome to my house, my son. You know how to work the metal as no other, and I therefore proclaim you the god of Fire and Blacksmiths. Come and live in my palace." Then, in a grave, emotional voice, Zeus added: "And so that I may be forgiven for not having known how to protect you from your mother's rage when you were born, ask me for anything you want, and I shall grant it."

Hephaestus lifted up his head. A smile lit up his hideous face. He had waited for this moment for such a very long time.

Tears of joy were streaming down Hermes' cheeks. He was happy to see his brother return to the family of the gods. And he waited with curious interest to know what he would ask of their father. Now Hephaestus was turning his villainous face towards the crowd of gods and goddesses. His gaze stopped upon Aphrodite, the goddess of Beauty.

"She is the one I want," he told his father. "I would like to marry her."

The gods' assembly broke into a murmur. What was Zeus going to reply to that?

The god of gods did not hesitate for a moment, for he had promised—and Zeus always kept his word. He beckoned to Aphrodite to approach. When the goddess was by his side, he took her hand and offered it to Hephaestus:

"Aphrodite will be your wife, my son, since you so desire it."

So the god who had been rejected on account of his ugliness was to marry the goddess of Beauty! Hephaestus was happy. With his eyes he sought the nymph Thetis among the crowd. She had been able to replace his mother. She had received him and cared for him in her cave. She had encouraged him to heat the metal, then smite it and twist it until he could give birth to these wondrous objects of silver and gold. She alone had believed in him, had had faith in him. She alone had loved him.

Thetis looked smilingly at Hephaestus. She was proud of him. She knew that from now on Hephaestus no longer needed her. She made a small sign of farewell to him. The god felt a momentary pinch in his heart, yet he was too happy finally to have been received in his father's house. He responded to Thetis' sign of farewell by sending her a kiss with his hand. Then he looked at Hera, his mother. There was no hatred in that look. Only love for the one who had brought him into the world.

Throughout that time, Hermes had been observing Aphrodite. What did she think of this marriage? The goddess' face showed neither anger nor opposition, it remained as smooth, as beautiful—and as cold—as ever. "Hephaestus will have no end of trouble with her," thought Hermes. He approached his brother, laid his hand on his shoulder and said: "I am happy to see you once again in our midst. I have looked for you for so very long..." Hephaestus was not listening, however. He had taken Aphrodite's hand and was gazing triumphantly over the assembly of the gods. Most of the gods present were lowering their heads. They were horribly jealous of Hephaestus, for many among them had hoped to marry Aphrodite, yet Zeus had always refused.

Hermes looked with astonishment at all these powerful gods obeying his father's will in silence. Why were they all obeying him, in fact? Why were they consenting to this marriage without saying anything at all? Yes, *why* exactly did Zeus command the gods?

To be continued…

€PISODE 26

IN WHICH ZEUS LEARNS THE
SECRET OF HIS BIRTH

*Previously: Zeus has agreed that Hephaestus, the ugliest god
on Olympus, can marry Aphrodite, the goddess of Beauty.
Hermes is asking himself why the gods obey his father.*

Hermes knew the way to Pausania's home by heart. He arrived at the cave of the old nurse of the babies of the gods towards the end of the day. He was impatient to decipher this new secret, yet he took the time to observe the colours of the setting sun, just as Antalia had taught him. The red hues were reflected on Pausania's face.

"O beloved nurse, I wish to see how my father became king of Olympus!" said Hermes, already laying his head on the old woman's lap.

But Pausania lifted up the young god's face between her wrinkled hands, and said: "Hermes, that particular journey is very long. It will last many, many days, and it is not without danger. Once again, are you quite certain that you wish to undertake it?"

A shiver ran down Hermes' spine, yet his eyes did not falter. "Yes," he murmured, "I *must* know."

"All right then. It will be as you wish," replied the nurse. She let Hermes' head rest on her lap. He closed his eyes.

When he opened his eyelids once more, Hermes was lying in a meadow, where a brook was flowing past. Tall heather tickled his face and kept him hidden from view. A young shepherd with a strong, athletic body had his back turned to him. He stood five paces away by the edge of the water, yet there was no risk of his seeing him because he was busy talking with a young woman. Her face was exceptionally beautiful. Yet what struck Hermes most were her eyes, which were as blue as the night. "Who are you?" the shepherd was asking the young woman. She did not reply, turning herself instead into a butterfly. The shepherd ran after her to catch her. Hermes saw her change into a titmouse. Then into a rabbit. Then again into a doe. The shepherd, who was falling in love for the first time, never stopped following her, laughing at all these transformations. Once the doe had changed back into a young woman, she consented to tell him her name: she was called Metis. She plunged her night-blue eyes into the shepherd's and told him these mysterious words:

"I recognize you, shepherd. And I know who you are even better than you know it yourself..." The shepherd, startled, replied nothing. Metis went on: "Your name is Zeus, isn't it?"

"But how do you know my name?" said the shepherd, bewildered.

"I know a great deal more about you," smiled Metis. "I know that when you were born, your father wanted to swallow you up

100

as he had swallowed your five brothers and sisters before you. And I also know how your mother and your grandmother saved your life by hiding you away here on this island."

When he heard these words, Zeus turned very pale. This woman knew his name. He could tell that she was not lying.

"But who is my father?" he asked Metis, his voice trembling.

"You are the son of Cronus, the king of the world," she replied.

Zeus sat down on the grass and took his head between his hands. He had just discovered the secret of his birth, and this awful secret left him sad and powerless. Metis went close to him and put her arms tenderly around his shoulders.

"Come, now, Zeus, son of the king of the world, you can become king of the world yourself if you wish. Do you know what now remains for you to do? You must avenge yourself against this terrible father."

Hermes saw Zeus lift up his head again, very slowly. His face was no longer sad, it was hard and tense.

"You are right. Will you come with me?" he asked Metis. The young woman nodded yes. And so they got up together and left for the harbour.

This is how Zeus and Metis boarded the first ship that was heading for the palace of Cronus, leaving the island behind. Hermes, of course, had slipped on board the vessel as well. Zeus' face remained preoccupied. He could not sleep at night. He kept thinking all the time about everything that Metis had revealed to him, and his anger against this cruel father who swallowed his children never stopped growing. Yet he did not know how to defeat him.

One morning he approached Metis, who was leaning on her elbows against the gunwale and was looking at the sea.

"Metis, I implore you, give me some advice on how to take my revenge on Cronus."

Metis smiled. This woman with the sea-blue eyes was the very essence of cunning and intelligence.

"Your father is unaware of your existence, since he believes that he has swallowed you," she answered. "There is no risk therefore that he might recognize you. Enter his service in order to get close to him. Once you are among his servants, you will be able to act." Zeus thanked her with a kiss.

When he arrived at the palace of Cronus, Zeus had no difficulty entering into his father's service. He had been working in the palace for some days when he came across his mother Rhea in a corridor. Rhea stopped, she looked at him briefly, and instantly a great smile appeared on her face: she had recognized her son immediately. She led him away from prying eyes and threw herself into his arms.

"Mother, I am happy to find you again," said Zeus, kissing her affectionately. "Yet I have come here to avenge myself against my father's cruelty. Will you help me?"

Rhea replied: "You may count on me, my son. I have been waiting for this moment for a long time."

Upon hearing those words, Hermes understood that another drama was unfolding.

To be continued…

EPISODE 27

IN WHICH ZEUS AVENGES
HIMSELF ON CRONUS

*Previously: Zeus has entered the palace of his father
Cronus as a servant. With the help of his mother Rhea
he wishes to avenge himself against his father.*

It was on a thundery night that Zeus and Rhea decided to act
against Cronus. That evening, the thunderstorm was terribly
violent. Cronus walked incessantly up and down in his room. He
was talking to himself and he took no notice of Rhea, who was
sitting in a corner of the room. His dishevelled hair, his puffed
face, his wrinkled clothes—everything showed clearly that the
Erinyes still came to visit him every night and prevented him
from sleeping. He was very agitated and he never stopped eating.
Several servants came and went in order to serve him enormous
dishes full of food, which Cronus never stopped devouring. Zeus
had slipped in among these servants. Hermes saw Zeus discreetly
hand Rhea a decanter of wine. With a quick movement, Rhea
dropped a powder into the wine. Then Zeus approached his

father and served him drink. Hermes was trembling like a leaf. Flashes of lightning illuminated the sky, and thunder rumbled. Cronus brought the cup of wine he had just been served to his lips. He made a wry face, as if the wine had a bitter taste, yet he swallowed the drink in one go. Suddenly Cronus began to convulse uncontrollably, seized by some great pain. He threw up an enormous stone wrapped up in baby swaddles. Then he also vomited Hestia, the first of the daughters that he had swallowed. He threw up Hades next, then Poseidon, followed by Hera and finally Demeter. The five brothers and sisters of Zeus had just been set free from their father's belly! For Rhea had added a vomiting powder to the wine Zeus had served him.

Cronus gave a roar of fury and threw himself out into the storm. His children went after him in the pelting rain. But he vanished into the night. The gods who had just been saved returned to the palace to celebrate their second birth. They could not stop embracing Zeus, swearing to him their total allegiance. Suddenly, a voice rose above the tumult:

"My children, you ought to prepare yourselves for battle. For your father will not give up like this. A war will break out." It was Rhea, who was trying to put them on their guard.

Zeus placed one knee on the ground, kissed his mother's hand respectfully, and asked: "Mother, what must we do?"

The goddess did not hesitate: "Set up your camp on one of the highest mountains that you can find and prepare your weapons. Cronus will go and fetch his brothers the Titans to fight you with. You, Zeus, you shall have to get out of the depths of the earth the Cyclopes and the hundred-handed Giants. Once these monsters have become your allies, you shall be able to win this war."

Hermes followed Zeus till they reached a very high mountain towering over the earth. As he approached, Hermes recognized Mount Olympus. "We are the Olympians from now on," said Zeus to his brothers and sisters. Then he welcomed the Cyclopes and the hundred-handed Giants. When Hermes saw all these monsters arrive, brought back from below the earth, he felt rather alarmed. Cronus, however, soon attacked the Olympians, accompanied by his powerful brothers and sisters the Titans. Hermes now found it quite reassuring to know that these monsters were on Zeus' side. Enormous boulders of rock crashed everywhere around Olympus. The earth never stopped trembling. The sky remained black, thick with the smoke arising from the terrible combats waged between old gods and young gods.

In the cave where the Cyclopes had set up their forge, Zeus and his two brothers, Hades and Poseidon, were holding a council of war.

"We *must* win," Poseidon was saying, "or else the earth will revert to Chaos."

"The brutal forces of Cronus will destroy everything if we do not stop him quickly enough," Hades was sighing.

"We need an invincible army in order to re-establish peace," Zeus was murmuring.

Hermes, who had slipped quietly into a corner of the cave, came nearer so he could hear them better. As he was moving towards the three gods, he passed close by the reddening forge. And what he saw caught his eye immediately. The Cyclopes struck and struck with all their might upon the burning metal. Showers of sparks burst forth. Under the hammer clangs of the Cyclops Brontes, a gigantic three-pronged fork was beginning to take shape. The Cyclops was fashioning a weapon. Once the fork had been finished, Brontes held it out to Poseidon. He bellowed: "Here is your trident, it will be the symbol of your power." The second Cyclops, named Arges, was almost done hammering the burning metal as well. He had wrought an enormous helmet. He handed it to Hades. Hades put it on his head and... he vanished! This helmet made the bearer invisible. He who put on this helmet disappeared instantly from the sight of others. Yet these were not the only surprises that lay in store for the three gods.

The third Cyclops, Steropes, was continuing to smite and smite a lump of golden metal. Little by little, in the heart of the fire, the burning metal was taking form. Hermes saw first one, then two, and then three long, sharp points emerge. "The thunderbolt!" he murmured in amazement. "He is forging the thunderbolt, my father's weapon..." The Cyclops bent one knee down on the ground, and then proffered the terrible thunderbolt to Zeus with the words:

"Here, this is what will make you everlasting master of the world."

To be continued...

€PISODE 28

IN WHICH HERMES SAVES HIS FATHER

Previously: Zeus and his two brothers, Hades and Poseidon, are ready for the oncoming battle. The Cyclopes have forged a trident for Poseidon, a helmet which makes one invisible for Hades and the thunderbolt for Zeus.

Never since he had been born had Hermes heard such an awful racket. And never had he seen such violence. The Titans and the Olympians were battling one another so ferociously that the mountains were crumbling down one after the other. Immense chasms opened in the ground. Hermes had the feeling that he was witnessing the end of the world. Zeus was hurling his thunderbolt incessantly against the Titans of Cronus. With all these bolts of lightning, it was as though the sky itself had gone mad. A rain of ashes was coming crashing down on the warriors. Finally, the hundred-handed Giants broke off enormous boulders of rock with which they pelted the Titans. Some rocks fell into the sea, forming islands. Others struck the Titans of Cronus. Little by little, the Titans were crushed under

107

the stones. Wearing his helmet of invisibility, Hades stole away from Cronus his last remaining weapons. The old god had been vanquished.

Zeus condemned Atlas, the eldest of the Titans, to hold up the earth and the sky on his shoulders for all eternity. The other Titans were imprisoned inside Tartarus, the very depths of the earth. And as the Cyclopes and the hundred-handed Giants threatened to go on fighting, Zeus sent them too for ever into Tartarus. There remained only the victorious Olympians. They chose Zeus as their king.

The new king would, however, have to triumph over one last and terrible obstacle before he could reign. Gaia, furious to see her children locked up in Tartarus again, sent forth the most monstrous of all her offspring. All of a sudden, the earth began to shake. Someone was approaching. Someone so enormous that each of his steps caused the ground to quake. Hermes was struck with horror. The monster that he then saw appear was more appalling that anything he had ever seen before. His huge black wings hid the sun. His head touched the stars. It was composed of hundreds of hissing vipers. His eyes launched flames and his mouth spewed forth flaming rocks. His body consisted of a multitude of serpent coils. This gigantic monster was called Typhon. Hermes had barely enough time to take shelter behind a rock. The monster had gone past. Typhon attained Olympus. Bewildered, the gods fled running, leaving Zeus to face the monster alone. Zeus tried to hurl his thunderbolt, but Typhon coiled his monstrous serpent's rings around the god of gods and stole from him the tendons of his heels. Zeus, vanquished and bereft of his tendons, was now unable to move. Typhon laid himself down before him and fell asleep.

Fortunately, Hermes was there. He had seen everything. He entered the palace of Olympus on the tips of his toes. In one of the rooms he found the helmet of Hades, who had dropped it in his flight. He put it on and became instantly invisible. In this way, Hermes approached Typhon without difficulty. The monster was clutching Zeus' tendons tight in his terrible clawed foot. Hermes gently loosened the claws and stole the tendons. Then, still invisible, he slipped quietly next to Zeus. The god sensed a presence, but he did not see his son returning his tendons to him. He realized immediately that he could use his legs once more and could stand up. He leapt to his feet, seized his thunderbolt and struck Typhon down. The sun reappeared the instant the monster was dead. A sudden gust of wind carried Typhon's body far away above the seas. And this is why terrible tempests are born sometimes in the ocean, arising from nowhere, and devastating everything in their passage. These raging and violent winds come from the body of Typhon. This time, the very last monster had been eliminated. Zeus would be able to build an earth governed by harmony and to establish order in all things. Hermes could feel his breast swell with pride at the idea that it was he who had saved his father.

To be continued...

€PISODE 2⁹

IN THE COURSE OF WHICH ZEUS
FALLS IN LOVE WITH EUROPA

*Previously: Hermes has witnessed the war of
the gods. It was Zeus who won the victory in
the end. And now he is king of the world.*

As he was returning home, Hermes could feel that he had
grown up. He knew now by what means his father had
conquered power. Zeus alone had known how to bring order
to the disorder.

Hermes was happy to find himself again on Olympus.
Zeus was leaning against the parapet of one of the terraces of
the palace when Hermes arrived. He was so busy looking at
something on earth that he did not see his young son come near
him. Hermes leant over to see what was fascinating his father
down below, and he too was seduced by the sight.

In the middle of a flowering meadow by the seashore, a group
of young girls were chasing one another, laughing. Their arms
were laden with spring flowers. One could see the purple of the

bluebells, the white of the daffodils, the yellow of the crocuses and the red of roses blending with the green, wavy grass—and it was a glorious image. One of the young girls attracted their gaze more than the others. She was wearing a long red dress, her hair was braided and she carried in her arms a basket glinting with gold. Hermes looked at his father and understood immediately: once again Zeus had fallen in love.

When Zeus finally became aware of Hermes' presence, he beckoned to him to follow him. The two of them descended on earth, and in order to approach the young girls without frightening them, they sneaked in among a herd of cows grazing nearby. Zeus turned himself into a splendid bull. He had a silver disc in the middle of his forehead, a horn in the shape of a crescent moon and his skin was a beautiful chestnut colour. The young girls were instantly attracted by the exceptional beauty of this bull. The one with whom Zeus had fallen in love approached the animal. She began to stroke it gently, to decorate its horns with garlands of flowers, and to hum in its ear. Her companions, seeing her go off side by side with the bull, called her back: "Europa, come back!" they cried.

Europa no longer listened to them, however. She had reached the seashore and was still playing with the bull. Hermes, who had assumed the form of a cow, was laughing inwardly at his father's ruse. He saw him lie down on the sand, in this manner inviting Europa to climb on his back. The young girl did not hesitate and she sat astride the bull. He dashed off immediately into the sea. He entered the tide and began to swim as fast as he could, carrying off Europa with him. They were getting far away from the shore and soon they were surrounded by a shoal of sea deities: there were Nereids, the deities of the Water, astride dolphins, and there were Tritons, who were half-men and half-fish, and who blew into great conch shells; even Poseidon escorted them, standing on his chariot, his trident in his hand.

"Where are you taking me? And who are you?" cried Europa in the bull's ear, a little frightened by these strange companions.

"Have no fear, beautiful child, I am the all-powerful Zeus, and I am taking you to Crete, the island where I was raised. You will be well received there," answered the god of gods.

Hermes watched this splendid procession spellbound. Europa's long red dress flapped in the wind almost like a ship's sail.

Soon the island of Crete came into sight. Zeus thanked all who had accompanied them and sent them back into the sea. He set Europa down gently on the sand and resumed his true form. Then he discreetly bid Hermes farewell, and the young messenger left his father to his new love.

When he reached Olympus once more, Hermes was astonished that the jealous white-armed Hera had not interfered. But she was too busy looking after her young son Ares, the god of War. Ares never stopped bragging. "I am the strongest. I am the best," he repeated all day long. This little upstart had managed to irritate all the gods and goddesses of Olympus. Yet the worst of it was that Ares tried to pick a fight with everyone. He bumped into people without apologizing, or he made fun of them, or again he insulted them. The moment he crossed paths with anyone, it always ended up in a quarrel.

Hermes detested Ares. He tried to avoid meeting him in the corridors, preferring to keep as far away as possible from his violence. "I have to show myself as canny as my father," he told himself. "He at least knows how to use his wits..."

To be continued...

ЄPISODЄ 30

*Previously: Hermes has seen how his father Zeus fell
in love with Europa and successfully abducted her. He
would really like to be as fine a seducer as his father.*

One day, while delivering a message to the river god Peneus, Hermes met one of his daughters, whose name was Daphne. This nymph had an artless and feral beauty. She ran about in the woods and the fields, a little bit like Artemis and her attendants. This was undoubtedly what Hermes liked in her. The young god became Daphne's friend, and would come to see her regularly. Daphne just loved living free. She was not interested in anything that nymphs and goddesses usually enjoyed. She did not comb her hair artfully, rather she just let it grow any way it liked. She did not wear long dresses with neat pleats, but donned instead short white tunics, held in place by a simple plaited belt. She wore no jewellery, she never made up her face and she dreamt of one love only: the love of freedom. "I want neither husband nor child," she had declared passionately to Hermes one day. "I love running alone in the wild too much for that." And Hermes, who really enjoyed Daphne's company, took good care not to fall in love with her.

Someone else, however, crossed the wild nymph's path one day. And this someone was used to being loved. It was Apollo. The first time he met Daphne, he had been out hunting. He had dismounted from his horse and had gone into some bushes. He was following a hare that he believed to have wounded. But instead of finding the animal, he came face to face with a little wild child who was holding up the hare by its ears.

"Hand me back what's mine. I am the one who killed it," said Apollo, reaching out his hand towards the prey.

"Not at all," Daphne retorted angrily, "you actually missed it! It was my arrow that killed it. Take a look!"

And she pulled out from the hare's body the arrow that had killed it. There could be no doubt: this arrow had come from the young nymph's own quiver. The god was slightly annoyed, yet he did not become angry. He was contemplating the nymph and he thought that she was gorgeous. With her hair in disarray, to which still clung pine needles and twigs, with her bare arms scratched by the branches and with her dark gaze, she was a picture of untamed nature. Apollo was instantly seduced. But the nymph had already gone away and vanished into the undergrowth.

From that moment on, Apollo wanted nothing more than to find the beautiful nymph again. He searched everywhere, questioned everyone, and finally he implored Hermes:

"My brother, go and find this nymph and tell her that I want her to be my wife."

Hermes agreed to bear this message to Daphne. She, however, burst into laughter:

"Apollo? Really? Well, you may go and tell Apollo that I have taken a vow never to take a husband, and that no one could force me to break this vow, not even he."

No one had ever turned Apollo down: he fell even more deeply in love with this nymph who could say no to him. He sought a way to seduce Daphne and he decided to abduct her. He therefore lay in wait for her in a wood where she was strolling alone, as usual. Then he approached her.

"Daphne, my beautiful Daphne, I am Apollo, and I lay my heart at your feet," he said to her. The young girl, however, took to her heels. Apollo chased after her, while continuing to shout words of tender love. Yet Daphne was exceedingly good at racing and the god could not catch up with her. In her flight, Daphne called Hermes to her aid.

"Go and warn Zeus," she cried, "ask on my behalf the protection of the god of gods!"

Hermes rushed to Zeus. Zeus did not want to anger his son Apollo—and yet he had to come to the aid of all those who asked for his protection.

Daphne could sense her forces weaken. Apollo was just about to catch up with her when she suddenly felt her feet push into the ground like roots; her body became covered with bark, her arms threw themselves up towards the sky like branches, and then were covered with leaves. She had just enough time to throw a smile of thanks to Hermes and to Zeus, before becoming completely transformed into a laurel tree. Apollo, seeing her changed into a beautiful tree of blue-tinted leaves, cried out: "O fairest of all young girls, I have lost you for ever. Yet the leaves of your tree will never leave my side. I shall make wreaths with them, which I shall carry constantly with me. I will offer these wreaths to all those who can recite beautiful poems and to all the victors. You, laurel tree, are now become my sacred tree." Hermes had the impression that he saw the tree's branches quiver, as though Daphne were accepting this tribute to her. She, the betrothed of nature, had been given back to nature.

Once more, Zeus had succeeded in provoking no one's anger. Each time that he was called upon to settle a dispute, he always found a skilled way to satisfy everyone. "But how does my father manage to possess this cunning and this intelligence?" Hermes kept asking himself. He resolved to discover how his father had learnt that particular art.

To be continued…

EPISODE 31

WHICH SEES THE EXTRAORDINARY BIRTH OF ATHENA

Previously: Hermes has great admiration for the intelligence of his father Zeus. He would like to penetrate its mystery.

Pausania was spinning wool when Hermes arrived at her cave. She did not lift her eyes from her work.

"You are already back so soon, my child," said the old woman. "Don't you know enough yet about the birth of the world?"

"O beloved nurse, there is one more thing I ask myself: how did my father come to possess such matchless cunning and intelligence?"

Pausania pushed her work away. The grinding of the wheel spinning the wool stopped. Hermes rested his head on her lap and his eyes closed instantly.

When Hermes opened his eyes again, he immediately recognized the place where he found himself: it was the seashore in front of Metis' cave, the Titanide with the night-blue eyes with whom Zeus had fallen in love as a young man. The day had barely broken; the beautiful Metis was lying on the sand still asleep. Hermes saw immediately from her round belly that she was expecting a child. Zeus, who was resting beside her, suddenly sat bolt upright. A voice had just awakened him; it was the voice of his grandmother Gaia, the Earth Mother. He rose to his feet and walked a few paces along the shore. "Be on your guard, Zeus, be on your guard. Metis carries inside her a girl. Yet on the day that she will bring a boy into the world, that boy will do to you what you did to your father Cronus, and what Cronus did to Uranus, his own father: he will take your place!" Upon hearing Gaia, Hermes shuddered. What was Zeus going to do? The god of gods went slowly back towards Metis, who was still asleep; he looked at her tenderly, then he lay down beside her once more.

Dawn came. Metis opened her eyes and smiled at Zeus. She was herself the very essence of cunning and she already suspected that something was not quite right. Zeus, however, asked her: "Metis, do you remember the day when I met you? You had turned yourself into a butterfly under my very eyes, then into a titmouse, then into a rabbit, and finally into a doe. Would you also know how to change yourself into a lioness?" Without replying, Metis instantly became a lioness. Her roaring and the stabs of her claws frightened Hermes, who was hiding behind a rock. "Well done!" exclaimed Zeus. "Well done! And would you also be able to turn yourself into a drop of water?" Metis did it right away. She had hardly turned herself into a drop when Zeus swallowed her! "I am really sorry, my dear Metis, but it had to be done," said the god of gods aloud. "I could not take the risk of you one day bringing into the world a boy who would dethrone me... and besides, I need your cunning, don't you see, to govern the universe. From now on, I shall have intelligence within me, since you are for ever inside me." Hermes at last understood why his father knew how to foresee everything, predict everything and master everything.

His father, however, who had sat on a rock, suddenly seemed to be suffering violent pangs of pain. He groaned, holding his head with both hands. The more time passed, the more the pain increased. The groans became screams. "Ah, it is too dreadful! It hurts too much! Quick, someone open up my skull to let this pain out!" Zeus was howling. Hermes did not know what to do. Zeus was all alone on that beach and the pain seemed unbearable. Hermes suddenly had an idea how to allay his father's pain. And there was not a moment to lose.

He ran back to Pausania. "Good nurse, I implore you: you absolutely *must* allow me to return to the past accompanied by someone," he told her.

"All right," said Pausania, "but your companion shall have to forget everything once he returns to the present."

The messenger of the gods then hurried to his brother Hephaestus to convince him to come with him quickly. He went back with him to the beach where Zeus was writhing with pain.

"Take your axe, my brother," Hermes said to him, "and go and split Zeus' head open to release the pain!"

And so the mighty god raised his formidable axe and cleaved Zeus' skull in two. At that very instant the earth shook and

Hermes and Hephaestus saw an extraordinary thing: a woman in full armour was coming out of Zeus' skull!

"Look," Hephaestus exclaimed, "it is the goddess Athena!"

The young woman wore a helmet and armour, and she bore a spear, all made of metal. She held herself straight and was casting a proud gaze upon the world around her. Zeus seemed completely relieved. He did not once look at Hermes and Hephaestus, but took the young female warrior in his arms. Seeing Zeus hold her tight against his heart, Hermes understood why Athena would always be the favourite daughter of the master of Olympus: Zeus had brought her into the world himself. Hermes and Hephaestus went discreetly away. Hermes had no idea that another extraordinary meeting awaited him.

To be continued...

EPISODE 32

IN WHICH HERMES MEETS PROMETHEUS

Previously: Hermes has understood where his father's
intelligence comes from: he has seen Zeus swallow
Metis, who is herself the essence of intelligence.
Shortly afterwards, he witnessed the birth of Athena,
who came clad in full armour out of Zeus' head.

W hat Hermes especially enjoyed were the great feasts on
Mount Olympus. Zeus liked to entertain guests, and
numerous gods, goddesses and nymphs were invited to his
table. Often, during those banquets, which could well last an
entire day, Apollo would sing, accompanied by his nine Muses.
Nymphs would sometimes dance. Hermes wandered about
everywhere, observing each guest and learning to recognize
them all. One day his attention was caught by a guest quite
unlike all the others. The newcomer wore his hair long, letting
it fall loose on his back. His face was full of nobility. His thick
black eyebrows overarched two piercing eyes which never
lowered their gaze. This guest was sitting on Athena's right,

and she never ceased to whisper in his ear. On the goddess' left side was another stranger, who behaved quite differently. He talked a great deal and was always restive; he would stand up, sit down again, laugh and clap his hands very loudly. Hermes slipped behind his aunt Hestia, who was organizing the order of the courses.

"Who is the guest with the very proud gaze?" he asked her. "And what is the name of the one next to him who will not sit still?"

Hestia leant towards him and answered in his ear: "He is called Prometheus. He is the only Titan to have chosen your father's camp at the time of the war of the gods. This is why Zeus receives him at his table. The nervy one sitting on his right is his brother Epimetheus. At Prometheus' request, Zeus receives him as well."

Throughout the remainder of the banquet Hermes did not stop spying on Prometheus' table. Everything that went on around the Titan astonished him. Athena's attitude, first of all, was quite startling. She, the goddess of Wisdom and Knowledge, rarely talked with the other gods. She had a passion for the science of the stars, for that of numbers, for medicine and for the science of thought, and she preferred to read or study. Even when she agreed to attend a banquet, she would always be seen talking to the owl perched on her shoulder, for she scorned her neighbours at table and did not speak to them. And yet here she was, engaged in a passionate discussion with Prometheus! Hermes could not hear their conversation, but he could see Athena's face becoming animated, he could see the eyes of

Prometheus sparkle. Hermes surprised them several times poring hard over a manuscript, scribbling mathematical formulae. There was no doubt: Athena had finally found someone who was intelligent enough to share all her knowledge.

Hermes noticed also that Zeus' attitude was different towards Prometheus. The complicity between his beloved daughter and this guest seemed to annoy Zeus. Yet when he spoke to Prometheus, he did so with great respect. And Prometheus responded to the master of Olympus without ever lowering his eyes. Never had Hermes seen Zeus show respect towards another person. Nor had he ever seen anyone address themselves to Zeus without bending their head low. Hermes was fascinated by Prometheus' pride.

His brother Epimetheus, on the contrary, never ceased to flit about like a butterfly all day long. He went from one pleasure to the next, skipped from one spectacle to the other, moved from one conversation to a new one, talking wild nonsense.

"He still has no more brains than a sparrow, that one," said a voice behind Hermes. It was his uncle Poseidon.

Hermes smiled timidly at the old bearded man. "You know them, uncle?" he asked in a small voice.

"Oh, do I indeed!" sighed Poseidon. "And if I were in your father's place, I would be wary of Prometheus. Do you know what their names mean? Epimetheus means 'scatterbrain, he who does not think ahead'. Prometheus, however, means 'the one who has foresight, he who thinks things out'. He showed us well enough the full extent of his intelligence when he had to make up for his brother's stupidity at the time he created mankind...

Prometheus, however, will not easily submit to authority. Zeus would do well to remember that..."

With these words, Poseidon walked away. Hermes was shaking with excitement. So it was Prometheus, and not his father, who had created men? Hermes left the palace immediately and set off towards Pausania's home.

To be continued...

ƐPISODƐ 33

IN WHICH HERMES WITNESSES
THE CREATION OF MAN

*Previously: Hermes has met a fascinating individual
called Prometheus. He has learnt that he was the creator of
mankind, and he has decided to witness the birth of man.*

ermes went to find Pausania as eagerly as ever. The old
woman was weaving with the wool she had spun sitting
by the entrance to her cave. Hermes watched for a few long
moments in silence the precise shuffling back and forth of
the shuttle on the weaving loom. It was a gentle and soothing
motion. He was thinking about what he had come to ask. It was
Pausania who spoke first:

"You seem very pensive, my boy," she said. "Are you afraid
of what you have come to seek today? You seem hesitant..."

Hermes lifted up his head and answered: "Nurse, O beloved
nurse, I am dying to witness the birth of the first man. But my
father, the god of gods, is absent from that story, this is what
troubles me."

Pausania gave one of her mysterious smiles: "Who knows, perhaps he is present in it, perhaps not. It is for you to find out!"

She had pushed her work away. Hermes laid his head softly on the old woman's lap and closed his eyelids. Once he reopened his eyes, Hermes found himself in half-darkness. He was lying on the bare earth, an earth of dry clay, hard and grey, which crumbled into dust under his fingers. Not far from him, a large form detached itself from the sky. His eyes became slowly more accustomed to the lack of light and he began to see better what was going on around him. The form was squatting down looking attentively at something placed on the ground. Hermes crept a little closer. From the broad shoulders, the long floating hair, Hermes recognized Prometheus. What the Titan was looking at was a round lump, a simple lump of black earth between his bare feet. Hermes saw him dip his hands in a jar full of water, then take the lump and begin kneading it gently. It seemed to consist of some of this hard and grey clayey soil mixed with a little water. Prometheus was concentrating hard on what he was doing. His movements were slow and certain. He pressed and squeezed the lump of earth for a long moment with his fingers, as though he were still thinking, then he began to stretch it and stretch it even more. Under his fingers, a body was taking shape. This body soon had a round head and four legs. Prometheus looked at it, not yet fully satisfied. "No, no," he murmured through his teeth. "This won't do." He shook his head, threw back a strand of hair which had slid between his eyes, and set back to work.

Hermes did not let those kneading hands out of his sight. He was fascinated by what was taking shape before him. Prometheus had taken hold of the body to which he had just given birth. With infinite care, he was setting it upright, was pulling it upwards. Two of the legs remained placed on the ground, but the other two were raised up. Prometheus sculpted those two forelegs and they became arms. Next, he tilted the head delicately upwards, and then stopped. "There," he said in a ringing voice, "you are the only living creature capable of looking at the sky. You are made in the image of the gods!" Throughout that time, his brother Epimetheus was also inventing new creatures. Zeus had asked the two brothers to create the earth's inhabitants. Epimetheus was to invent the animals and Prometheus was to create man. Zeus had entrusted them with a bag containing all that they were going to need so that these future living beings might be able to fend for themselves. Epimetheus had been hasty and had acted as usual without thinking ahead. He began by inventing a bird. Then he put his hand into the great bag and took out some feathers. "I give you these feathers so that you may fly," he said. Then he created a snail and he took a shell out of the bag. "I give you this shell so that you may hide inside it if you are attacked," he said. Then he created a hedgehog, drew some quills out of the bag and gave them to it. "I give you these quills so that you may defend yourself," he said. He then fashioned a lion and gave him claws and teeth; a serpent, and he endowed it with venom; a hare, to which he offered speed; a bull, to which he granted horns. Some animals received fur to fight the cold; others scales and fins in order to live underwater. After a while, Zeus' bag was empty. Epimetheus, very satisfied with himself, then went to see what his brother Prometheus had created.

He found Prometheus on his doorstep, squatting on his heels. Epimetheus leant over his brother's shoulder and discovered the creature to which Prometheus had just given birth.

"What is it?" he asked, rather startled.

"It is man," replied Prometheus, without taking his eyes off his creature. "And you? What progress have you made?"

"All done!" replied Epimetheus triumphantly. "I have finished everything, given everything away!"

Prometheus turned sharply round: "What? You have nothing more to hand out?!" he cried. "And man, whom I was charged to create, what have you put aside for his protection?" Epimetheus had forgotten to put aside anything whatsoever! Prometheus turned towards his human creature. He gazed at it, naked and defenceless as it was.

He bent down low and said: "Man, I offer you intelligence—"

"But you don't have the right!" cried his brother, scared. "We are not authorized to give what belongs only to the gods!"

Prometheus did not even spare him a glance. He continued to look at man with infinite tenderness. Then he said: "Be on your way, my son. And above all, always stand erect!"

To be continued...

EPISODE 34

IN THE COURSE OF WHICH PROMETHEUS
SHOWS THAT HE IS VERY CUNNING

*Previously: Hermes has just witnessed the
birth of the first man created by Prometheus.
And Prometheus has offered man intelligence,
which is reserved for the gods alone.*

As he returned home, Hermes' heart was still full with all that
he had just experienced. He now understood what it was
that had fascinated him so much when he had met Prometheus:
the Titan was the only one who had no fear of Zeus. Hermes
was troubled by this, but also secretly delighted by it.

When he arrived at Olympus, he found the palace in a state
of great unrest. At Prometheus' own request, the council of the
gods had been called up in all haste. Hermes slipped inside the
hall at the very moment when Zeus was asking Prometheus to
come closer.

"What do you want from me, Prometheus?" asked the god
of gods.

In a clear voice, Prometheus gave this reply: "O great Zeus, master of Olympus, the men on earth need food. If you will allow them to raise cows and to eat their flesh, they shall share with you every animal that is slaughtered. And wishing to honour you as highly as possible, they have charged me with the task of asking you to choose the cuts that you prefer. I have slaughtered a cow on their behalf and I have separated the cuts into two piles, which you can see here before you. From now on, every time that they slaughter a cow, they will reserve for you the share which you yourself will choose today, and they shall content themselves with the other pieces."

Prometheus stopped talking and allowed Zeus to observe the two piles. The first was irresistibly mouth-watering. It was covered with luscious white fat and bones stuck out. The second was altogether revolting. Pieces of gut and shreds of stomachs covered this pile, exuding a vile stench. Zeus did not hesitate for a second and pointed to the first pile with his finger. "Poor mankind," thought Hermes, "they will only be allowed the very worst cuts from now on..." Prometheus bowed respectfully. Yet Hermes had the time to perceive a mischievous twinkle in his gaze. Content, Zeus descended from his throne and approached the pile he had selected. Imagine his surprise when he discovered, underneath all that plump fat, a pile of bones, without the slightest shred of meat on them! The fine-looking pile contained nothing but bones. He turned towards the revolting heap next to it, pushed back the entrails with his sword, and discovered under that mass of gut all the meat! Astonished murmurs were heard across the hall, followed by some restrained laughter. The great Zeus had been utterly and completely fooled... From then on men would feast on the fine flesh of every slaughtered cow, while Zeus would have to content himself with the bare bones. He scanned the room with his eyes to find Prometheus, but the latter had disappeared.

A red glimmer flashed across the eyes of the master of Olympus. His wrath exploded. "He who dares to trick me must be punished!" he yelled. "If this is how things are, then I shall take fire away from men. From now on, I will never again send my thunderbolt to earth. The storm will never more burn a single tree. They shall be deprived of fire and be condemned to eat their meat raw. And I do not wish Prometheus to appear before me ever again." Zeus then left the council of the gods in a rage of fury. For the first time, and in spite of Metis' presence inside him, someone else's cunning had been stronger than his own.

The gods left the hall murmuring among themselves. Hermes came across Poseidon, who said to him in his usual surly tone: "You see, I was right when I told you that your father ought to be wary of this Prometheus." And yet Poseidon seemed to rather enjoy the god of gods' misadventure. Hermes flew away to reflect upon what he had just seen. He could not refrain from admiring the way in which the Titan had deceived his father. Yet he was deeply concerned about the future of Prometheus and that of mankind.

To be continued...

€PISODE 35

IN WHICH PROMETHEUS STEALS
FIRE FROM THE GODS

*Previously: Prometheus has managed to deceive
Zeus. From now on, mankind would not lack food. In
retaliation, however, Zeus has taken fire away from them.*

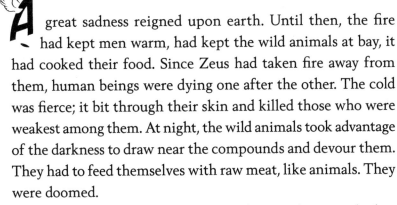

great sadness reigned upon earth. Until then, the fire
had kept men warm, had kept the wild animals at bay, it
had cooked their food. Since Zeus had taken fire away from
them, human beings were dying one after the other. The cold
was fierce; it bit through their skin and killed those who were
weakest among them. At night, the wild animals took advantage
of the darkness to draw near the compounds and devour them.
They had to feed themselves with raw meat, like animals. They
were doomed.

One night, when Hermes was not sleeping, he saw a shadow
slither onto one of the palace terraces. Another shadow came
out of the palace and joined the first. Hermes flew noiselessly
up to them and listened.

"How sad you look, my friend," a female voice murmured. "Things are not as grim as you say."

A male voice replied to her: "Alas, yes, things are very grim indeed! Men are dying one after the other. Soon there will be none left on earth!"

At these words, Hermes recognized Prometheus. He certainly lacked no pluck to dare return to Olympus in this manner! The one who had come surreptitiously to join him had to be Athena.

"But what would you propose to do?" Athena was asking. "It is very risky to go against my father's will..."

Prometheus whispered a few words into Athena's ear, but Hermes could not hear what he was saying. Then the two shadows separated and Hermes returned to his room.

On the following nights, Hermes wandered about the palace, yet nothing happened. One morning, he ran into Athena in one of the palace corridors and asked her with an air of feigned innocence:

"Have you any news of your friend Prometheus?"

The goddess hardly looked at him and replied drily: "Friend? What friend? You are talking nonsense, my poor Hermes."

He was beginning to wonder whether he might not have dreamt it all, when one night something happened. It was a night of black darkness, one of those nights when Selene, the goddess of the Moon, must have fallen asleep and forgotten to take the moon out on her chariot. Hermes, who was fluttering about the palace before going to bed, heard the leaves rustle. Prometheus had come to join Athena.

"Have you brought what we need?" Athena was whispering.

"Yes, yes," replied the Titan.

"Well then, follow me," said the goddess of Wisdom. She led Prometheus towards a secret door of the palace.

Athena pushed gently at the door and gestured to Prometheus to follow her. Astonished, Hermes saw the banished Titan enter stealthily into the palace. What was he planning to do? Hermes slipped in quietly behind them.

Once inside, the two conspirators headed towards the centre of the palace. They entered like shades the room situated at the very heart of the palace, the room of the sacred fire. Here goddess Hestia looked after the fire of the gods throughout the entire night. Her task was never to let it die out by stoking it up constantly with wood, and also to keep an eye on it. Prometheus had taken hold of a heavy jar, intending to knock Hestia senseless. Yet that was not going to be necessary: the goddess of the Hearth had fallen asleep. Prometheus immediately bent down over the fire, took out from his tunic a sort of hollow stalk, and slipped some embers inside the hollow. Then he went away once more, as silently as he had come. Hermes was relieved: Prometheus did not wish to take the place of the god of gods; what interested him was to save his children, the human beings.

"Thank you, Athena," murmured the Titan as they came back to the exit. "You have just helped me save mankind." Hermes looked at him for a long time as he disappeared into the night. The glowing red dot which the Titan had trapped inside the stalk allowed him to follow his course. In a single night, Prometheus went around the entire earth and lit fires everywhere. Wherever he passed, the shadows were repelled, light triumphed over darkness. In the early morning the Titan, exhausted, contemplated his work: everywhere in the world the fire that he had stolen from the gods blazed up to keep men warm and to give them light.

To be continued…

ΕΡΙSΟDΕ 36

IN WHICH PANDORA, THE WORLD'S
FIRST WOMAN, IS BORN

*Previously: With Athena's help, Prometheus has succeeded
in stealing fire from the gods so he can offer it to mankind.*

ever had Hermes seen Zeus so angry. When he had woken
up that morning, Zeus had discovered that there were fires
burning everywhere on earth. He had entered into a state of
mad fury and he had at first let out terrible screams of anger. Yet
towards midday silence had suddenly returned to the palace. A
strange jingling sound escaped through the door of Zeus' room:
Zeus was laughing! He had just found the way to retaliate against
this new act of disobedience on Prometheus' part. He instantly
summoned Hephaestus, Aphrodite, Athena and Hermes to his
side. When Hermes entered the council hall he felt very uneasy;
he admired the rebellious Prometheus and he also liked human
beings. The master of Olympus was sitting on his throne and he
was still in a villainous mood. He screwed his face into a smile.
Addressing everyone at the same time he said: "I intend to give

a nice gift to men; I wish to offer them the first woman. I would like each of you to give her the best quality that you possess." Athena frowned, as though she could smell a trick, yet Hermes took no notice. He was only too happy to see his father prepared to offer men a gift! Zeus turned towards Hephaestus and said: "My son, you are to go first. Take this earth, mix it with water, and fashion a woman for us."

Hephaestus rose heavily to his feet and did as he'd been told. He began to mould the wet clay into a woman's body. His fingers worked swiftly, kneading the clay and giving it nice curves. From time to time, Hephaestus would stop, take a quick look at Aphrodite, and then he would resume his task once more. It was obvious that he was using his own wife as a model in giving birth to the woman of men. Little by little, a splendid creature emerged from the lump of clay, a creature truly in the image of the most beautiful of goddesses. It was then that Aphrodite came forward and stood before the female sculpture of clay; she placed her hands on its shoulders and said:

"Since you resemble me, I give to you beauty and seductiveness."

Instantly, the statue became endowed with an irresistible charm.

Hermes approached in turn: "I give you eloquence and a taste for language," he said.

But Zeus interjected: "Don't you have anything else to add, something which is truly a part of your character, my son? Think well."

"Ah, but of course!" exclaimed Hermes. And, turning towards

the earthen woman, he said to her joyfully: "I offer you also curiosity, my immense curiosity."

A gleam of joy shone bright in Zeus' eyes. Unbeknownst to him, Hermes had just played his part in setting up his father's trap for men. Athena drew close to the future woman and offered her beautiful clothes and splendid jewels. Then she placed on her forehead a bride's headband and veil and took the opportunity to whisper discreetly in her ear:

"I also offer you intelligence. Above all, learn to make good use of it!"

To finish, Zeus rose to his feet and said: "You shall be called Pandora, which means everyone's gift, and you shall be the first woman of mankind." Then he breathed life into the statue. Immediately, a twitch travelled across Pandora's nostrils, her eyelids batted very fast, then opened to reveal two stunning eyes. A great smile appeared on her lips. She was ravishing.

"Good morning," she murmured, "when do we set off?"

"Good morning," replied Zeus, rubbing his hands contentedly. "My son Hermes will lead you to earth and to the world of men. You are expected in the house of Epimetheus."

Athena could foretell that Zeus was preparing a nasty trick against men. He was undoubtedly going to use this first woman of the world in order to take revenge on Prometheus. She immediately sent word of warning to Prometheus of what was being prepared. The Titan hurried to his brother Epimetheus: "Swear to me that you will not accept any gift coming from the gods of Olympus!" he cried to him. "Swear this to me, quick!" His brother's authoritative manner always had a profound effect on Epimetheus. He hastily gave his word and Prometheus went back to his own house reassured. Yet Pandora was already on her way to Epimetheus' house, accompanied by Hermes. Would Epimetheus be wise enough to refuse such a gift?

To be continued…

EPISODE 37

IN WHICH WE DISCOVER THE PUNISHMENT OF PROMETHEUS

Previously: Zeus has just created Pandora, the first woman, whom he wishes to offer to Epimetheus. But the wary Prometheus has made Epimetheus promise that he will not accept any gift from the gods.

The way leading from Olympus to the house of Epimetheus appeared really short to Hermes. Pandora was a charming travelling companion. She asked a thousand questions about the world around her and Hermes was glad to have offered her this sense of curiosity. When they arrived at Epimetheus' house, Hermes was sad at the prospect of leaving Pandora. Yet he had a mission to fulfil. He asked her to wait for him a few feet away from the house and he walked towards the front door. Epimetheus came to the doorstep to greet the messenger of Zeus.

"Welcome, Hermes, what brings you to my house?" he said to him.

"I bring you a gift from the gods of Olympus," replied the messenger.

Epimetheus' smile vanished and he lost his head. He stammered: "No, no, thank you, my great lord, but I cannot accept your gift."

"And why ever not?" enquired Hermes.

"Because... because... because I am unworthy of it, that's why!" replied the miserable Epimetheus, who did not know how to keep the promise he had made to his brother without offending the gods of Olympus.

Startled, Hermes then embarked upon a long speech praising the merits of the gift of the gods. "It is a unique gift, most exceptional. Neither god nor any human being has ever possessed anything like it. I envy you! If I could, I would happily keep this gift for myself. You cannot possibly refuse such a gem."

While Hermes had been talking, Epimetheus had continued to say no by shaking his head with his eyes closed, to indicate his refusal. It was then that a soft voice said:

"Would someone perhaps have some cool water to offer me?" It was Pandora, who, urged by her curiosity, had approached Epimetheus' house of her own accord.

Epimetheus was staring at Pandora wide-eyed. He seemed to have succumbed already to her charms. Pandora gave Hermes a conspiratorial wink, while taking a bow before Epimetheus to greet him.

"So, then, what do you think of the gift that the gods have prepared for you?" Hermes asked in a mischievous voice.

"I... I accept it!" stammered Epimetheus, who was hurriedly bidding Pandora to enter and was running to get some fresh water for her. Hermes made a small gesture of farewell to Pandora and then left, his mission accomplished.

During his flight towards Olympus, he wondered why Zeus would have offered such a gift to Epimetheus. It would not be long before he was to find out.

Before that, however, an unpleasant surprise awaited him. He was flying above a long mountain range called Caucasus, when he saw an unfamiliar lump of darkness which seemed to be almost attached to one of the peaks. He made a small detour to see what it was and what he discovered gave him a terrible shock. Prometheus was chained practically naked there upon that mountain! His long hair covered his face. His body, battered by the chains, was exposed to the glacial wind. Zeus had just taken his revenge: Prometheus had disobeyed him twice in a row and he had condemned him to remain for ever chained to the mountain like this. Suddenly a gigantic shadow approached the fettered Titan: it was the royal eagle of Zeus. The ferocious beast perched upon Prometheus and began to devour his liver with his beak! Hermes was so overcome and shattered that he could no longer fly. Tears flowed down his face. The wind swept away Prometheus' hair and Hermes discovered the face of the fettered Titan. He was not weeping. The pain made him wince but his face remained noble and proud. In spite of everything, Zeus had not succeeded in defeating Prometheus. The eagle flew away and Hermes saw that Prometheus' liver instantly grew back. He realized that every day the eagle returned and devoured the liver of the chained Titan. A great sadness invaded his heart. Who would watch over the future of mankind from then on?

To be continued...

€PISODE 38

IN WHICH PANDORA'S CURIOSITY
UNLEASHES A DISASTER

Previously: Pandora has succeeded in seducing Epimetheus and in entering his house; and Hermes has discovered that Zeus has taken cruel revenge on Prometheus, by having him chained to a mountain.

So, then, Epimetheus had accepted the gift of the gods, forgetting every promise he had given to Prometheus. He had hardly set eyes on Pandora before falling in love with her. And very soon he celebrated his marriage to the young woman. Pandora was joyful from morning till night and her husband was thrilled to have accepted this gift from the gods. As soon as she had arrived, the young woman had gone around the house inspecting all the rooms, asking to be shown all the stores of olive oil, wheat and wine. She let out squeals of joy before every new discovery: a pretty fabric covering her bed, a delicate piece of pottery placed on her table... Epimetheus was happy to see his wife's enthusiasm.

When they reached the last room of the house, they found it dark and windowless. A large earthenware jar was placed in one corner and the rest of the room was empty.

"What does this jar contain?" asked Pandora.

"I have no idea," replied Epimetheus gravely, "it belongs to my brother, Prometheus. He asked me to safeguard it here with the greatest care and he made me take an oath never to let anyone open it."

"And you never had the urge to take just a tiny peek inside?" said the ever-curious Pandora in astonishment.

Epimetheus looked horrified: "Most certainly not! Prometheus is very wise. I have given him my word and I keep my promises."

Just as he said this, he remembered that by marrying Pandora he had already betrayed another promise he had made to his brother. But this Pandora did not know. Feeling uneasy, he made Pandora swear that she would never seek to open this jar. The young woman gave her word, swore to it. Epimetheus left the room reassured.

Days and more days went past. Pandora took great pleasure in her home. But she was full of curiosity and she was dying to know what the mysterious jar contained. As soon as her husband went out, she would hurry to the dark room, take a very quick look at the jar and then come out of the room right away. Before long, this jar became an obsession with her. Her curiosity kept her awake at night. She imagined there were all sorts of things inside.

At one point she said to her husband: "And what if this jar contained incredible treasures, jewels, or even gold? Perhaps that is the reason why your brother forbade you to open it? And now that he is in chains on Caucasus, all this wealth will be of no use to him; whereas *we* could put it to good use." Epimetheus, however, got cross and he refused to listen to such talk. Another time she said to him: "Perhaps your brother's jar contains a wine so exquisite that he wanted to save it and drink it all by himself?" Pandora was being quite malicious because she knew that her husband adored wine. Yet even on that occasion Epimetheus did not give in.

One morning, as on all other mornings, she slipped inside the dark room. She always carried with her an oil lamp which shed a flickering light through the half-darkness. She approached the jar one more time and ran her hands over its well-curved sides. Since Athena had had the good inspiration to endow her with intelligence, Pandora always thought ahead before she acted, yet on that particular morning her intelligence proved weaker than the curiosity Hermes had offered her. "I am just going to lift the lid for an instant and then shut it back quickly. Nobody will ever know anything about it," she told herself. Her hand shaking with excitement, she tried to remove the stopper which sealed the jar. She had to try twice. When the lid was finally half lifted, a whirlwind invaded the room, accompanied by the sound of a thunderstorm. Pandora let out a cry.

Hermes, who at that moment had been on an errand near Pandora's house, heard her cry. He hurried over and saw anger, jealousy, envy, wickedness, madness, old age and also death emerge from the house. These were all the ills of mankind. And all these ills spread instantly across the earth. Hermes understood immediately: the prudent Prometheus had locked up everything which might cause misery to mankind, yet Pandora had just set all these afflictions free! Hermes heard great sobs coming from inside the house. He entered and found Pandora collapsed on the floor in the farthest room. The jar was still there. Hermes approached it and saw that Pandora had put the lid back on.

"Is there anything still inside?" asked Hermes.

The tearful young woman replied: "When I managed to replace the lid, there was nothing left at the bottom except one thing: hope."

Hermes instantly felt somewhat reassured. "Fortunately, men have preserved hope, so they will always manage to cope with their misfortunes," he thought. He knelt beside Pandora and tried to console her. A little later, he resumed his way back to Olympus. But his eyes were full of melancholy. Who knew what Prometheus might be thinking, up there on his rock, about the fate of mankind?

To be continued...

EPISODE 39

IN WHICH HERMES IS DISPATCHED
TO PROMETHEUS WITH A MISSION

Previously: Pandora has set free all the ills of mankind by opening the jar where Prometheus had hidden them.

〔〕〔〕〔〕〔〕〔〕〔〕

Zeus was waiting for Hermes in the council hall of the gods. Hermes thought that he would find his father in a triumphant mood. For in fact the ruse of the master of Olympus had now fully succeeded. It was he who had conceived the plan of sending Pandora to earth, and it was he who had asked Hermes to offer his inquisitiveness to this first woman... Yes, Zeus had foreseen everything! This time, his revenge against the rebel Prometheus and against men had been accomplished.

But even so, Hermes discovered that his face was still darkened and tense.

"Is there something wrong?" the young god asked him.

Zeus fiddled nervously with his thunderbolt without replying. Hermes waited. After a long silence, Zeus leapt off his throne:

"Listen to me, Hermes: you must go and see Prometheus on the rock where I keep him captive. And you must get him to talk. He must deliver his secret to me. Otherwise I shall never set him free."

A shudder ran down Hermes' spine. He knew Prometheus far too well to imagine that he would be willing to talk.

"But what secret is this about?" asked the young messenger in a tremulous voice. "What could Prometheus possibly know, that you don't, you, the god of gods?"

With a sigh, Zeus let himself fall back heavily on his throne once more. And, grinding his teeth, he said:

"I too am threatened by one of my children who might want to take my place. Just as I took the place of my father Cronus, who had taken the place of his father, Uranus. One of my sons shall desire my throne. This child has not yet been born. Yet he shall be more powerful than I. Only Prometheus knows the mother's name. I *must* know this. Now go."

Hermes had no choice; he flew away as fast as he could.

When he reached Caucasus' highest peak, the messenger of the gods had a big lump in his throat. He was happy to see Prometheus again and he hoped with all his might that he would be able to secure his liberation. When he found the Titan, the eagle that devoured his liver each day was with him. Hermes watched the horrid bird. Finally it flew away, and Hermes looked at Prometheus chained on his rock. This time, tears flowed down the Titan's face, becoming lost deep down his beard. His lips murmured a few words and Hermes pricked up his ears. "My men, my poor men," Prometheus was murmuring.

"What's to become of them now? Cursed be my brother, and his disobedience! Why did he accept this gift from the gods? My mankind, my poor mankind..."

Hermes was deeply moved. So Prometheus was not crying for his own lot, but for that of the human beings he had created! Hermes approached and said in a voice which he hoped sounded strong:

"Good morning, Prometheus, forgive me for disturbing you, I have a message for you." The Titan lifted up his head. "Zeus has charged me with the task of setting you free on just one condition: you must tell him the name of the mother of the one who will dethrone him. Speak and you shall be free," Hermes said to him.

The Titan replied with the flicker of a smile: "Never. Never shall I deliver that name to him. For I know well that the cruel Zeus will seize on the opportunity to kill that woman right away."

Hermes could not help but admire the tormented Titan's resistance. He insisted: "Prometheus, do reconsider. Men need your protection on earth. And you cannot go on suffering like this, chained to your rock! There will be no end to this if you do not yield!"

Prometheus, however, seemed as unwavering as the rock to which he was tied:

"It is no use, Hermes, I will not speak. I am not afraid of suffering. Zeus thinks that he can command the entire world. He has absolute power. Yet he does not rule over my soul. I am free, in spite of my fetters."

Hermes understood that none of his fine words would succeed in changing the rebel's mind. He was secretly proud of him for this, exceedingly happy that someone dared to defy the master of the universe. Yet he was in despair for having to leave Prometheus to his terrible fate. He bowed his head and for once he could not find any words of farewell that he could speak. So he went away just like that, his throat tied into an even tighter knot than when he had arrived.

Hermes stopped in a nearby valley so he could think. He loved his father but he could not stand this situation. As he was sitting on the banks of a small brook, everything that Roxanne had taught him so he could discover the future came back to his mind. He grabbed some small round pebbles and began right away to throw them into the water, impatient to discover what the future held in store for Prometheus.

To be continued…

EPISODE 40

In which Hermes witnesses the rescue of Prometheus

Previously: Zeus has sent Hermes to Prometheus so that the latter might reveal to him a secret, in exchange for his freedom. The Titan, however, has refused to talk.

itting on the banks of the brook, Hermes was busy throwing his small pebbles in the water. Little by little images of the future appeared. Hermes saw a man approaching the rock, a very big man, and, what is more, a very strong man. He was some kind of athlete with huge muscles, wearing a headband on his forehead and clad in a lion's hide. He was called Heracles and he was travelling across the earth in search of a garden where golden apples grew. He carried a gigantic bow on his back. When Heracles arrived, the eagle was busy devouring the liver of Prometheus. Heracles did not hesitate for an instant. Without even trying to find out who it was that he was dealing with, or why this creature was chained in this manner, he took an arrow from his quiver, bent his bow and shot the arrow at the eagle.

The arrow pierced through the bird's heart and the eagle fell to the ground. Heracles then seized the enormous chains which attached the Titan to the rock and snapped them in two. Hermes was stunned by the strength of this man, who could grind the heavy metal to dust between his fingers. This Heracles seemed quite exceptional. The image was becoming blurred, however. Hermes threw some more small pebbles into the water so that he could see what would happen next.

Prometheus was rubbing his aching wrists and thanking Heracles at the same time, when Zeus appeared, surrounded by flashes of lightning. Was he going to fly into a terrible rage again? Hermes saw instantly from his face that the lord of the gods was in fact rather content. He approached Heracles, dropped his hand lightly on his shoulder and said: "Congratulations, my son! Your arrow has gone straight through the mark. Your strength and your ability fill me with pride. You are a true hero!" Then Zeus turned towards Prometheus. They stared hard at one another for a moment in silence. Finally, Zeus said: "I set you free, Prometheus, since my son has broken your chains. Yet, as a reminder of the punishment that I inflicted on you, you shall always wear a ring around your finger made from the steel of your chains. So you will never forget, I hope, this rightful punishment of your disobedience." Prometheus offered no reply; he did not even lower his eyes. He snatched one of the snapped links of his chains and put it sharply on his finger.

When the image became blurred once more, Hermes felt reassured. He knew that a day would come when Prometheus would be set free and would even be pardoned, and that this would happen without his having to yield. From pure curiosity, he wanted to see a little bit more into the future, so he threw his small pebbles in the water for the third time. In the new image that appeared, he saw a creature half-man, half-horse lying on a bed of straw in the shadow of a cave. It was the Centaur Chiron. He was wounded and he appeared to be in great pain. Heracles was kneeling by his side, holding his head between his hands.

"Cursed be the arrow that has wounded you, my old friend!" exclaimed Heracles.

"Your hand did not desire it, do not cry, Heracles," replied the Centaur. "If only I could die, however, instead of being immortal, my suffering would finally cease!"

At that moment, a shadow approached the cave. It was Prometheus. He too placed his knee upon the ground next to the wretched Centaur and said to him:

"Venerable Chiron, I offer you an exchange: give me your immortality and you shall be able to die in peace."

A twinkle of joy filled the eyes of the wounded Centaur. "But do you think that Zeus will agree to this?" he asked.

"Zeus and I have become reconciled once more," replied Prometheus. "I have asked him already and he agrees to your giving me your immortality, if you so wish it."

Prometheus bent his head low before the Centaur. His long hair swept the ground and Chiron's trembling hand rested on Prometheus' head. A stronger trembling shook him for a moment, as though some invisible fluid were passing through the thin fingers of the Centaur and into the Titan's long hair;

then the hand stopped trembling altogether. It settled down gently like a dead bird in its nest.

In a single breath, Chiron murmured: "Thank you, Prometheus."

Then he smiled and closed his eyes for ever. The darkness of the cave seemed less impenetrable. Heracles did not move, frozen in his posture of despair. Prometheus rose slowly to his feet. He came out of the cave at the very moment that dawn was breaking. The goddess Aurora was travelling across the sky. He was smiling. He had become immortal, like Zeus.

Hermes let this final image of the future become blurred in the water, then he resumed his way. He was glad about Prometheus' future. Yet the farther he walked, the more he was gripped by a new anxiety. Zeus had sent him to the chained Prometheus so that he might obtain the name of the mother of the one who would take his place. And Prometheus had refused to talk. How would Zeus react to the fact that he had failed in his mission?

To be continued...

EPISODE 41

*Previously: Hermes returns home having set his
mind at rest regarding the future of Prometheus,
who is soon to be freed from his rock by Heracles.*

As he reached Olympus, Hermes dreaded his father's anger following the failure of his mission to Prometheus. Yet hardly had he pushed the palace door open than he was told that Zeus needed him, and that he was waiting for him on earth. Without wasting a second, Hermes again left to join the god of gods. He found him not too far from Thebes, sitting alone by the roadside.

"Hermes, help me, something terrible has happened," said Zeus, sounding deeply distraught. "White-armed Hera has succeeded in causing the death of a woman that I loved. This woman Semele was carrying a child, my child. I took the unborn baby from his mother's womb and I have hidden him so that he might escape my cruel wife. I would like to place him

157

in someone's care so he will be looked after. I thought of the Nymphs of Nysa, they are gentle and kind. I would like you to take the baby to them."

Hermes could not leave his father in his distress and he was not at all averse to playing a trick at Hera's expense. Yet he could not help asking himself how it could be that an as yet unborn baby had been saved.

"Let us go and get that baby quickly," he replied. "Where have you hidden it?"

Hermes then saw Zeus get up, bend down towards his thigh... and pull out the baby from it! This was where he had put the child to protect it and so that it might continue to grow.

Hermes was dumbfounded: "A baby born from the thigh of Zeus, who would have thought it..."

It was a little boy with golden locks and laughing eyes. He was plump, podgy even, and seemed to be a very contented baby. Hermes was immediately seduced by this new little brother. Zeus was gazing at him tenderly. He murmured:

"Even though your mother was not a goddess, you shall be a god among us. This is what I have decided. You shall be called Dionysus, he who has been born twice, and you shall be the god of Intoxication, Pleasure and Delight."

Then Zeus placed his latest offspring in the arms of the messenger god, who instantly flew away.

Nysa was the most beautiful valley on earth. No one, however, knew its precise location. And yet Hermes was, with the exception of Zeus, the cleverest of the gods, after all. What is more, he was not the god of travellers for nothing. After having searched a great deal, he eventually found that secret place. He cast a satisfied glance upon the fields of flowers, the flowing streams, the vineyards stuffed with grapes and the trees heavily laden with fruit. The baby was going to grow up free in one of the most beautiful landscapes in the world. With an easy mind, Hermes placed Dionysus in the care of the local nymphs. He kissed him tenderly and murmured to him before leaving him: "You will always be under my protection. Be happy." Then he returned to Olympus.

He found Zeus caught up in one of Hera's bouts of anger and thought it better to hide behind a curtain. The goddess was walking up and down, throwing her arms about violently. She had found out about Dionysus' rescue and her anger was terrible.

"How many children are you still going to beget outside this house?" she was shouting. "First there is that darling daughter of yours, Athena. She is the one you conceived inside your head. Yes, indeed, without the help of any woman! Then there are Apollo, Artemis and Hermes. But at least their mothers come from our own world, they are deities themselves. Now you include among us the son of an earthling! And you have even entrusted him with a mission! When will you ever stop, Zeus?"

The great king of Olympus was trying to make himself as small as a mouse. He said to his wife in the voice of a scolded child:

"I promise you that it's over. The family of Olympus is now complete. Dionysus will be its last-born." At these words Hera seemed to calm down and she went out in silence. Hermes then came out of his hiding place:

"Father, all is well, your son is in the hands of the nymphs of Nysa," he said to him.

Zeus sighed, however: "Even so, he is not safe from Hera!"

Hermes knew well that his father was right. On his way to the palace he had learnt by what means Hera had caused Semele's death. She had gone to the young woman disguised as a simple passer-by. "Are you quite certain that the man sleeping beside you is Zeus? You have never seen him in all his glory, have you now?" she had said to her.

On the following day, Semele had implored Zeus: "Promise me that you will grant me my dearest wish!" Zeus, deeply in love, had promised. And so Semele had said to him: "My dearest wish is to see you in all your glory!" Upon hearing this, Zeus had turned pale. He had recognized immediately Hera's wicked counsel. To appear in all his glory was to show himself with his thunderbolt. And no mortal could see him like this without being struck dead. He had tried to make Semele understand this. Yet nothing could make her change her mind. She wanted proof that her lover was truly Zeus. Zeus had been obliged to keep his promise. He had shown himself to her therefore as the master of Olympus with the lightning bolt of the thunderstorm, and the young woman had instantly fallen thunderstruck. Zeus had just had time to hide in his thigh the unborn baby she had been carrying. This was how Dionysus had been saved. Hermes wondered anxiously how far Hera's jealousy could possibly go.

To be continued...

ΕΡΙSΟDΕ 42

IN WHICH THE YOUNG IO IS
HOUNDED BY HERA'S JEALOUSY

*Previously: Hermes has just helped his father Zeus save
a new child he has fathered, called Dionysus. Yet he
is worried that Hera's jealousy might strike again.*

One morning, not very long after the birth of little Dionysus, Hermes was once again summoned by his father. He found him looking mournful, his voice sounding weary.

"My boy," sighed Zeus, "I find myself once more in a very awkward situation. While I was paying a visit on earth to a young woman called Io, my wife Hera arrived there as well. Knowing her jealousy, I immediately transformed Io into a small cow in order to hide her away from her eyes. But Hera was not hoodwinked: she asked me to offer her the pretty cow that was by my side. I could find no reason to refuse, you understand... I was obliged to say yes. Since then, she has locked up Io and she has put Argus, her faithful guardian, the one with the hundred eyes, to keep watch over her. When he closes some of his eyes to sleep, others remain open, it is impossible to outsmart him!" Having thus taken Hermes in his confidence, Zeus fell silent.

Hermes understood what Zeus wanted from him. He placed his fingers on his father's arm and said: "Let me deal with this, I will take care of everything." Then he flew away immediately.

Hermes located the prisoner and her warder very quickly. The cow was tied by a rope to an olive tree. She was looking forlornly to right and left. A hideous individual sat very close to her. Hermes landed on a rock not far from Argus. He hid his god's clothes and disguised himself as a shepherd, then he took out a reed from his pocket and began to play. The sound of the flute was beautiful and Argus, who was getting awfully bored watching over this cow, beckoned to him to come closer. Skipping his way over, the boy did not need to be asked twice. And he began to chatter on and on... For his plan was to lull this monster to sleep by telling him stories. And as far as stories were concerned, Hermes knew thousands of them! He talked and talked, he played and played so much, that little by little Argus fell asleep. One after the other his eyelids closed shut. When ninety-nine of them had closed, lulled by Hermes' voice and music, Hermes approached the monster gingerly, holding a great stone in his hand. The hundredth eye also closed at last, Hermes pounced, and knocked the monster senseless with his stone. Then he lopped off its head, and set Io free.

When he returned to Olympus, Zeus embraced his son tightly in his arms. Then he said to him, laughing: "Look at you! You have become the god of thieves, my son!" White-armed Hera, when she learnt of the death of her beloved watchman, began to howl with rage everywhere in the palace. In remembrance of Argus, she took the monster's eyes and pinned them on the peacock's tail. And ever since that day, peacocks don mysterious eyes on the feathers of their tails.

Her anger was not placated, however, and so Hera sent a gadfly, a great stinging fly, to chase after poor Io. Io began to run like mad in every direction. She travelled for miles and miles along a rocky shore. In remembrance of her frenzied race, the sea along which she had run took her name and has since been called the Ionian Sea.

Fortunately, her flight came to an end on the banks of a long and majestic river called the Nile. Zeus came there to join her and restored to her once more her human form. Io could now resume her peaceful existence. Having saved first Dionysus and then Io, as it were, Hermes was really hoping to be able to get some rest. It was clear that he did not know his father well!

To be continued...

ƐPISODƐ 43

In which we meet an extraordinary couple of lovers, Philemon and Baucis

Previously: A young woman called Io, with whom Zeus had fallen in love, had suffered Hera's persecution. But Hermes has managed to set the young woman free.

L ying on the grass, not very far from the palace's secret door, Hermes was looking at the sky. He had an appointment with his father and he was very curious to know what new adventure Zeus would take him on this time. A light breeze was blowing and the young god watched with delight the racing clouds. He lay in wait for their ever-changing, soft forms, conjuring up a thousand stories based on one single little cloud. At five, Zeus pushed the door quietly open. This door allowed one to depart from Olympus unseen. When Zeus arrived, he was dressed in rags. Without a word, he handed Hermes clothes as torn and filthy as his own. Then he beckoned to him to follow and they both descended from Olympus. One of Zeus' greatest pleasures was to disguise himself as a simple mortal and to go off wandering across the earth unrecognized. In this way, he could observe men unhindered and assess the way they led their lives. Hermes just loved these trips. "You see, my son," the king of the gods said finally, "today we are going to verify whether men are welcoming towards one another. For there is nothing more important than to be hospitable."

With their filthy, tattered clothes, their dishevelled hair and their bare feet, Zeus and Hermes looked just like real beggars. And it was in this disguise that they went to knock on every door.

"Spare some alms, please," asked Zeus, in the trembling voice of an old man.

"Give us a coin, a morsel of bread, for pity's sake," pleaded Hermes.

Yet no one took any interest in them. Those who met them on their way turned their eyes away, feigning not to see them. Or again they would quicken their step, as though they were all of a sudden in a great hurry. Others again refused to open their doors to them—that is to say, they did so on the rare occasion when they did not set their dogs on them!

The more they advanced, the more the doors shut at their passing. Zeus could sense his anger rising inside him. So this was how men loved one another! This was how they respected their duty to be charitable and hospitable! Not even Hermes' banter could draw a smile from him.

The two wayfarers arrived at long last before a small, dismal-looking house. As soon as they knocked, the door opened and two old people begged them to enter. In that poor hut there was but one room with a floor of beaten earth and two or three pieces of rickety wooden furniture. "We do not have much to offer you," said the old lady, "but all we can give will be given wholeheartedly." She was called Baucis and her husband's name was Philemon. They had lived for more than forty years in that ramshackle house. Zeus looked at the old lady bustling about, rekindling the fire and putting water to boil so she could prepare a soup. Philemon had picked a big cabbage in the garden and he tossed it into the soup. Then he took down their last piece of lard which hung from one of the rafters and added it to the cauldron. Neither had asked a single question. They were making these strangers welcome in their house with natural simplicity. Baucis had slipped a piece of wood under the leg of the wobbly table and had offered blankets to her guests so they could warm themselves up. Philemon was serving them a spicy wine mixed with water.

The fine fragrance of cabbage and lard was spreading across the air. Hermes' mouth was watering. He quite liked the ambrosia accompanied by nectar which was served at the table of the gods, but there was hardly any variety in the menu. And so Zeus and Hermes devoured the modest meal with a hearty appetite. The two little old people watched them eat with great delight, not noticing that although Philemon had never stopped filling their guests' glasses, his amphora of wine still remained full!

In the end, the old people discovered what was happening and they were greatly alarmed. But Zeus got up to reassure them:

"You have nothing to fear, I am Zeus, the god of gods, and this is my son, Hermes. We thank you for your kindness. And you shall be rewarded for it." As he spoke, the dismal hut transformed itself little by little into a magnificent palace. Philemon and Baucis were holding hands, wide-eyed. "All this belongs to you from now on," Zeus announced to them. "Ask me for anything you want, your wish shall be granted." And so Baucis said with a gentle voice:

"Most honoured lord, we are old now and we have never been apart. Our dearest wish is to die together."

Zeus looked fondly at the two old people in love. He agreed to grant their wish without hesitation:

"The rest of mankind shall know soon enough the fruits of my wrath on account of their selfishness. But you, may you be happy."

Later, in the course of his numerous travels, Hermes frequently stopped by to give his greetings to the old couple. One day, as he was passing by to see them, he did not find them in their house. Instead, a strange tree had grown on their threshold: the trunk of an oak and that of a linden tree had intertwined to form a single trunk, while their branches intermingled. Hermes smiled and understood that Zeus had kept his promise: Philemon and Baucis were to remain together in this way for all eternity.

To be continued...

EPISODE 44

IN WHICH HERMES IS INVITED
TO A VERY STRANGE DINNER

*Previously: Zeus has come to realize that
men are not at all hospitable towards one
another. He intends to punish them.*

Zeus' anger against men was increasing day by day. One evening, Hermes confided in his sister Athena:

"I feel quite concerned, sister," the young god said to her as he joined her on one of the terraces of the palace, "men are gradually forgetting all the rules they need in order to live together. Our father will not tolerate this for much longer. I fear for those whom Prometheus took under his protection..."

Upon hearing the name of her friend Prometheus, the goddess of Wisdom let out a faint sigh. Her gaze rested on the earth far down below. She replied:

"It is precisely ever since Prometheus has no longer been there to guide them that men have become barbarians. Human beings are weak and defenceless. I too fear for their sake."

Hermes and Athena stopped talking all of a sudden—there were footsteps approaching. Zeus appeared dressed as a wayfarer and ready to depart.

"My children, I have been looking for you. You are to come with me on a short trip around the earth. I wish to give those accursed men one last chance."

And so it was that they went, all three of them, on a journey to the kingdom of Arcadia. They were dressed as simple wayfarers; however, the trio did not pass unnoticed. Night was falling when they arrived at the court of King Lycaon. He was an exceedingly brutal king, full of arrogance. He was only interested in war. His fifty sons spread terror across the entire kingdom and he did nothing except encourage them further. For a very long time now there were daily murders, thefts, assaults and insults in the kingdom of Arcadia. As the three visitors passed, the inhabitants would break into a murmur. Some of them would begin even to pray, as though recognizing that these were divine beings. Lycaon was informed of the arrival of the three individuals and of his people's attitude towards them—and he was extremely annoyed. Yet he came to greet his guests himself. Lycaon's face was red and scowling, and Hermes instantly found him loathsome. Lycaon first led his guests to their room, so they could rest before participating in a banquet in the great hall of state. The corridors of the palace were covered with litter. This squalor did not seem to bother King Lycaon. "I leave you now," he said to his visitors. "I have orders to give to the cooks." And he went away.

Hermes slipped discreetly behind him. And what he saw in the palace kitchens horrified him. Lycaon had just given orders for a servant to be killed and boiled in a great cauldron so he might be served to the guests! He was slapping his thighs and laughing hard, and he was telling his cook, who had turned ashen pale: "Either these three are real gods, in which case they will realize we are serving them human flesh, or they are simple wayfarers, and in that case, what does it matter if we are making them eat man flesh?" His horrendous laughter resonated throughout the kitchen. Some of his sons laughed with him.

Soon, it was dinner time. Yet Hermes had not had time to warn his father of what was being prepared. Lycaon had noticed Hermes in one of the corridors and had not left his side until the banquet. They proceeded to the table in a silence which had suddenly become heavy. The abhorrent dish was placed in front of Zeus. A wry smile was sketched on the faces of the royal family of Arcadia. Zeus took the dish and threw it brusquely on the floor. He had recognized the horrid food being served to him for what it was. Trembling with fury, he looked at Lycaon and yelled at him: "You are nothing but a savage beast and you shall remain one for the rest of your life from now on!"

The king tried to reply, yet a long howl came out of his mouth instead. He fell on his knees, his arms changed into forepaws, his head became elongated and his nose became a muzzle. And long, dirty grey hair covered his entire body. Lycaon made one more attempt to speak, and from his jaws now came a howling full of doom. Lycaon had been transformed into a savage wolf! His fifty sons became wolves in their turn. Furious, Zeus hurled his thunderbolt and set the palace ablaze. Then he hounded the pack of wolves right into the heart of the deepest forest of the kingdom.

The three gods resumed their way back to Olympus, yet the more they advanced, the more Zeus' anger increased.

"Dogs!" he cried. "Savage beasts, this is what men have become! They no longer respect anything; they don't even have any respect for *us*. Their punishment must be terrible!"

Athena and Hermes did not know what to do. Hermes mustered all his courage and said:

"Father, perhaps they are not all of them as bad... Allow them one last chance." Zeus cut him short:

"Enough! This *was* their last chance!" And this threat made Hermes tremble. What was to become of men?

To be continued...

€PISODE 45

IN THE COURSE OF WHICH A GREAT
FLOOD COVERS THE EARTH

*Previously: Zeus has allowed men one last
chance. Yet he came upon the palace of Lycaon,
a savage king who tried to make him eat human
flesh! He is preparing a terrible revenge.*

A voice is calling in the night. It is the voice of Prometheus, chained upon his rock. He calls, groans, he knows that men, his children, are under threat. He has given them life; he cannot bear to see them disappear. For he has guessed that Zeus intends to eliminate them all from the face of the earth. And this is why the chained Titan cries out for the very first time.

"Deucalion! Deucalion!" He is calling his favourite son. And his voice steals through the night, it reaches the ears of the sleeping Deucalion. "Deucalion, my son, wake up," says the voice. "Build a great wooden crate, pile up in that crate as many provisions as possible, get your wife on board, and sit next to her yourself. Do as I tell you and you shall be saved. But above all, make haste!"

Deucalion peered wide-eyed into the darkness.

"Father? Is that you?"

He had of course recognized Prometheus' voice. Yet Prometheus no longer answered. There was nothing around him except the silence of the night. The words of Prometheus' message were still ringing in Deucalion's head. He got out of bed, woke up his wife Pyrrha and immediately began to obey his father's voice. He cut wood, sawed and hammered nails all night long, while Pyrrha prepared bags of food. At daybreak the crate was finished. Deucalion and Pyrrha climbed inside, then they waited.

As soon as he was back on Mount Olympus, Zeus had summoned his brother Poseidon, the god of the Seas. Since that time they had been closeted together in the council hall of the gods. Hermes wandered around the palace passageways, trying to guess what was being prepared. At last, the two great gods came stern-faced out of the hall. They advanced towards the palace terrace and observed the earth in silence. Zeus then said to Poseidon:

"Come, you go first!"

And so the god of the Seas raised his arms and began to command the tides:

"O sea, oceans and lakes, overflow and spread across the earth! And you rivers and streams, come out of your beds!"

Hermes shuddered as he listened to his uncle's cavernous voice. He craned his neck down towards the earth and he was left aghast by what he saw. A flowing tide was sprawling everywhere. The seaside villages, the hamlets which had been built along a river, all these had already been drowned under great masses of water. Driven mad with fear, human beings were trying to escape the tidal wave. They ran and ran till they were out of breath. Some climbed on trees, others tried to seek refuge on the mountain tops. Terror and dismay reigned on earth.

At that instant, Zeus seized his thunderbolt and made it crack several times in the sky. He cried: "Now, black clouds, burst and empty yourselves upon the earth!" Immediately, a terrible thunderstorm broke out. The sky was streaked with violent flashes of lightning and torrential rain came crashing down on the earth—a continuous rain, which fell brutally and joined the tidal wave already engulfing everything. Before this raging sky, Zeus' face remained immobile. The blinding flashes of lightning did not even make him blink. Hermes watched in turn this unleashing of violence in the sky and his father's impassive face. He admired his father's power. The punishment meted out to mankind was terrible, but their crime had been immense. They had forgotten the laws of the gods, they no longer knew how to welcome strangers. They had no respect for one another, they had become barbarians. Satisfied with the flood they had unleashed, Zeus and Poseidon separated. The rain continued to fall incessantly in this way for nine days and nine nights. By the end of the ninth day, when the water stopped trickling down the sky, it had engulfed the entire earth. There was nothing left except a vast area of water. Hermes looked down with sadness and observed this boundless sea, which by now covered the entire earth. His eyes searched desperately for some sign of the presence of a living creature. Everything seemed dead down below. The messenger of the gods could not believe that this was the end of mankind. He descended from Olympus and flew above the liquid mass, still hoping to find some sign of life. Yet nothing troubled the smooth surface of the water. "Have all men drowned, then?" Hermes asked himself, devastated.

To be continued...

EPISODE 46

IN WHICH DEUCALION AND PYRRHA
ARE RESCUED FROM THE WATERS

*Previously: To avenge himself against men, Zeus, aided
by his brother Poseidon, has sent a vast deluge upon the
earth. Everything has drowned under the waters. Hermes
is afraid that the human race may have totally perished.*

ermes had been flying for hours without being able to locate
the slightest sign of life, when his gaze was suddenly drawn
to an object floating on the water's surface. This object was
whirling round and was being tossed about by the currents. The
messenger of the gods decided to go near it. When he was a few
feet away from the object, Hermes realized that it was a crate.
And inside that crate there was a man and a woman! Hermes
immediately recognized Deucalion, the son of Prometheus, and
Pyrrha, the daughter of Epimetheus and Pandora. The couple
had not yet seen Hermes. They were curled up inside the crate,
nestling in each other's arms.

Hermes was moved to see them like this. But what was to

become of these two human beings floating adrift? He decided to go and persuade Zeus to save them.

When he found Zeus, Hermes discovered with relief that the master of the gods had regained his usual good-natured mien. His anger was visibly gone, washed off by the deluge inflicted upon men.

"Father," said Hermes, drawing very close to Zeus, "men have now been punished enough for their barbarity. But do you remember Deucalion, the son of Prometheus, and his wife Pyrrha?"

Rather startled, Zeus replied: "Yes, my son, I remember them, why?"

"Well, were they guilty too? Did they deserve the same punishment?" asked the canny Hermes.

Zeus sighed: "These two were innocent. They were honest people and just, they respected both men and the gods. It is a great pity that they were not spared, but what could I do?" And he let his hand fall back on his thigh dejectedly.

"Father, you can still save them!" cried Hermes. And he knelt on one knee, the better to beseech Zeus.

"How is that possible?" Zeus asked, astonished. "All men were drowned under my divine wrath."

"They are the only ones left on earth. I beseech you, father, save them. Let there be a new human race. I promise you that they shall be honourable and proud and that they shall not fall back either into wickedness or violence. I promise you that they shall honour the gods!"

Zeus was observing Hermes with astonishment. He was a little vexed to see him put so much passion into his defence of the creatures of Prometheus, yet he loved his son. He loved to please him. And besides, his anger had subsided and he now wondered whether it was in fact quite fair that, through his own fault, the innocent should have died together with the guilty.

Zeus rose from his seat and smiled. Then he said: "All right, then, Hermes, your words have managed to convince me. I grant you their survival." The young god leapt to his feet and, unable to restrain himself, placed a sonorous kiss on his father's cheek before darting out of the room.

Far down below in the flowing vastness, the wooden crate was still drifting afloat. Suddenly, Deucalion caught sight of a hillock of earth, which protruded from the waters. "Look, Pyrrha," he cried, "there is a mountain that the deluge did not enshroud with its waters. It looks like Mount Parnassus, the mountain where the nursemaids of the gods live! The gods must certainly have spared it in order to save the three nurses of their babies!" Aiding himself with a branch, Deucalion steered the crate towards Mount Parnassus. They made landfall and set foot at last on a stretch of firm ground. Deucalion gathered up a handful of earth and, turning towards the sky, he said: "Thank you Zeus, thank you." At that moment the waters slowly began to recede. At Zeus' request, Poseidon had just commanded the rivers and the streams to return to their beds, and ordered the seas to regain their shores. Yet the two human beings found themselves all alone in a deserted world. And Hermes wondered whether they would be able to cope, and what new trials might still be in store for them.

To be continued...

Episode 47

Whereupon a new race of men is born, the men of stone

Previously: Hermes has managed to obtain Zeus' consent to save Deucalion and Pyrrha, the sole survivors of the deluge. Yet they are not out of all danger yet.

Trembling with happiness, Deucalion and Pyrrha looked at the receding waters. Hermes, who had descended from Olympus, was observing his little protégés with tenderness. The young couple held hands and walked slowly onwards, happy to see the devoured landscapes re-emerge. And so they descended from Mount Parnassus. Soon, they came near a temple. It was covered with seaweed and mosses after its long stay underwater. The building was almost falling to ruin. Deucalion and Pyrrha went inside the temple and decided to offer thanks one more time to the gods for having spared their lives.

"It seems to me that the statues of the gods are looking at us benevolently," whispered Pyrrha in Deucalion's ear.

179

"You are right," murmured Deucalion, and walked to the centre of the temple. Then in a loud voice he beseeched the gods: "O gods, who have saved our lives, help us! We are alone in the world; we cannot survive in this solitude. Help us! Protect us!"

Hidden behind a pillar, Hermes was waiting. He was hoping wholeheartedly that the other gods would be listening to this prayer as well. Yet he could never have imagined the odd response that the couple would receive.

It was dark and damp in the temple Deucalion and Pyrrha had just entered. The young woman shivered from the cold. Yet she kept her face turned towards the statues of the gods from whom she hoped to receive help. Deucalion had managed to light a fire and he was looking round the temple. All of a sudden, a voice was heard coming from nowhere. The voice said:

"Hide your faces, leave the temple and throw behind you your mother's bones but do not turn around to look."

"Our mother's bones? I have no idea what this means..." murmured Deucalion, surprised.

Pyrrha had fallen frightened and sobbing on her knees. Deucalion took her in his arms in silence. What *did* the voice mean? Hermes, who was still hiding behind a pillar so he could observe his protégés, wondered what it was that Zeus wanted from them. Had he not convinced his father to save them?

The couple remained interlocked in each other's arms in the shadow of the damp stones. Deucalion was thinking hard. Suddenly, he pulled himself straight and said: "Listen, Pyrrha, our mother, the mother of us all, is the earth, isn't that so? The earth's bones are the stones on the ground. Perhaps this is what the gods mean. Come!" He helped his wife to her feet and they both left the temple, hiding their faces. Then they each collected some large stones. After that they began to walk, throwing them behind their backs one by one. They could hear the sound of each stone hitting the ground, but they could not see what was going on, because they were not allowed to turn around. Hermes, for his part, did not miss a single detail of the scene which unfolded under his eyes: each stone thrown by Deucalion as it struck the ground turned into a man! And each stone thrown by Pyrrha became a woman! When they had finished throwing all the stones they had collected, Deucalion and Pyrrha turned around. Behind them, dozens of men and women had emerged, replacing the stones. They felt so happy to see other human beings that they threw themselves into each other's arms. Equally happy, Hermes watched as this new race of men embraced one another. "Since they have come from stones," he said, "I hope they shall be strong and hard, so they may endure and survive. I hope that they shall know how to stay together." Then he left on the tips of his toes. His work was done.

As he flew towards Olympus, Hermes thought he heard a distant voice cry out: "Thank you, Hermes!" The messenger of the gods recognized the voice of Prometheus and smiled. Hermes did not know, however, that by pleading on behalf of the survival of men, he had also created for himself new enemies among the gods.

To be continued…

EPISODE 48

IN WHICH HERMES
BECOMES A THIEF AGAIN

Previously: By throwing stones over their shoulders,
Deucalion and Pyrrha have given birth to a new race of
men. Hermes is glad to have helped to save humanity.

eaning against the parapet of one of the terraces of Olympus, a god and a goddess looked down angrily at what was happening on earth. The god tugged furiously at his long white beard, muttering threats against Hermes:

"Accursed little messenger! You have contrived to persuade my brother to take the earth out of the water, but just you wait! One day I will find a way to take my revenge."

It was Poseidon, the king of the Seas. When the waters of the deluge had engulfed the earth, he had become its master. Yet when, at Zeus' orders, all the waters had withdrawn back to the seas, the lakes, the rivers and the streams, he had lost everything. The goddess was nervously wringing her beautiful white hands, sighing:

"So that's that! Men are once again inhabiting the earth. And once more Zeus will fall in love with the most beautiful women."

It was Hera, Zeus' wife. She had watched with satisfaction the men and especially the women disappear under the waters. And so when the human race had been saved thanks to Hermes, Hera had been deeply disappointed. "Accursed little messenger!" she said through her teeth, "just you wait, one day I will find a way to take my revenge." Poseidon and Hera were not the best of friends. Yet this time, they decided to join forces and to do everything within their power to take revenge on Hermes. After thinking together for a while, they each went their own way. Poseidon returned to the oceans and Hera mounted her chariot and went for a drive on Mount Olympus.

Hermes did not suspect a thing. He was flying over the earth and felt his heart bounce with joy. The waters had withdrawn everywhere and already rays of sunshine were drying the waterlogged fields. As he was passing above the ocean, his eye was caught by something shiny on a rock. He swooped down towards the luminous object. Imagine his surprise at discovering that it was Poseidon's trident! The three-pronged fork had been placed there on an island lost amidst the waves. Hermes had always admired this magnificent trident. Yet how could Poseidon have dropped it there? Hermes went around the little rocky island. It appeared to be uninhabited. A strange noise could be heard, however. It was a sort of muffled, regular grunting. When he discovered the source of the noise, Hermes bit his lips to stop himself from bursting into laughter: it was the snoring of a sleeper and the snorer was his uncle Poseidon, the god of the Seas! In fact, the powerful god was lying in the shadow of a rock and was taking a nap. Hermes definitely did not want to wake up Poseidon. He was sure to be very cross at having been seen in such an undignified state. Hermes tiptoed away.

He was about to leave the island, when he went past the trident again. The bright glint attracted him to it once more. He placed a trembling hand on it. The metal was vibrating gently. It contained all the power of the king of the Seas. And suddenly, without even thinking, Hermes seized the trident and flew away! He had just stolen from Poseidon the symbol of his power.

Just then, Hermes heard a neighing and found himself face to face with three magnificent horses. One was as white as snow, the other as black as night and the third was sorrel, like fire. They were pulling a gleaming chariot, beautifully decorated with gilt woodwork. Hermes recognized Hera's chariot immediately. He had always admired this superb team of horses and he was thrilled finally to be able to get close to them. But how could Hera have abandoned them like that? Hermes began to inspect his surroundings. Some feet away from a cave, he heard a strange and regular sound. He followed the curious noise and came right up to Hera sleeping! This time it was the white-armed goddess who was napping in the shade of a rock... and who herself also snored! Hermes tiptoed away, convinced that Hera would fly into a passion if she knew that he had surprised her in that state.

The young god was about to leave when his eyes fell on the chariot and its three superb horses. The animals were pawing the ground with their hooves. It was as though they were signalling to him! "Oh, go on, then," Hermes told himself, "it will only be for a short drive... I will be back before Hera is awake and she will never suspect a thing." And he leapt onto the gleaming chariot. At once, the horses shot away at a full gallop. Hermes was radiant with happiness. Yet the gods he had just robbed would be quick to react...

To be continued...

ΕΡΙSΟDΕ 49

IN WHICH HERMES IS PROPERLY PUNISHED

*Previously: By helping to save mankind from the
deluge, Hermes has made himself two enemies without
knowing it: Poseidon and Hera. And now he has just
stolen the trident of Poseidon and Hera's chariot.*

arried away by the great gallop of Hera's horses,
Hermes had lost all sense of the passage of time. He
was drunk with speed. The chariot took him far away from
Olympus and the landscapes through which he travelled
were stunningly beautiful. The people he met along the
way looked at him admiringly for driving such a superb
team. Hermes felt proud. From time to time, he would
let go of the horses' reins and he would place one hand
on Poseidon's magnificent trident by his side. Hermes had
never felt himself so powerful before.

Suddenly, as he turned a corner, someone appeared
unexpectedly in front of his chariot. His horses reared up and
neighed noisily, yet Hermes managed to calm them down. It

was Ares himself who stood in the middle of the road, the son of Zeus and Hera.

"What do you want with me, god of War?" shouted Hermes.

With arms crossed over his chest and a deprecating smirk on his face, Ares replied: "You are nothing but a pathetic little thief, Hermes and our father Zeus sends me to escort you back to Olympus."

Ares' gloating got on Hermes' nerves. Yet he kept his rage inside him and tried to keep calm. He had to obey his father's orders. And Zeus' anger was likely to be terrible.

They were already expecting him in the council hall of the gods by the time Hermes reached Olympus. He entered with his head sunk low, already regretting what he had done. All the gods were gathered around his father and he felt as though he were back on the day of his arrival at the palace. His father's face was stern. No one was smiling at him, not even his beloved sister Artemis. Not even the gentle Hestia, who was looking at him disapprovingly. Hermes bowed his head again. He understood that by stealing from the other gods in this way, he had committed an unpardonable act. And this time he would have to muster all his eloquence to get out of his tight corner.

Zeus said first of all: "Thank you, Ares, for having caught this little thief." At that, Ares went haughtily back to his seat. "And you, miserable son, what have you to say to justify your conduct?" enquired Zeus drily.

"O god of gods, I know that I must appear inexcusable," Hermes began, "and yet I thought I was doing the right thing by acting in this way. Poseidon's trident had been abandoned on a deserted little island when I discovered it. I only took it in order to bring it back to its owner. And the chariot was abandoned too, just left there on a road when I discovered it. I mounted it in order to bring it back to its owner. I never had any intention of *stealing* either of these things."

Hermes watched the effect his words had produced on his father's face. He saw a twinkle of amusement cross his eyes and he thought that once again he would win the round. Hera too, however, had sensed that Zeus was softening. She did not allow the master of Olympus time to speak; she sprang to her feet and said:

"That's enough! You'll do well to keep your fine talk to yourself, Hermes. I have been robbed and humiliated and I demand reparation. I want him banished from Olympus!" She resumed her seat, and Poseidon rose directly:

"I too demand justice. This godling has no place among us!" growled the god of the Seas.

Zeus let out a sigh of exasperation. He had to give due satisfaction to his wife and to his brother, yet he did not wish to be separated for ever from Hermes. Once more, he was trying to displease no one; then, suddenly, he had an idea: "Hermes, my son, you will go and spend three months in the Underworld with your uncle Hades before you may return to the palace." Hermes' smile vanished. Tears welled up in his eyes. He was going to have to stay away from his father's palace for three long months! Hermes looked at Hera and the conniving smiles she was exchanging with Poseidon suddenly made it all clear for him: he had fallen into a trap! The truth was that Hera and Poseidon had prearranged everything in order to separate him from Zeus. They had not been napping when Hermes had come across them, they had only been pretending. And he, poor simpleton that he was, had not been able to resist the temptation to take what did not belong to him. Yet there was no more time for talk. Zeus had risen to his feet. Hermes left the council hall, shuddering at the thought of the kingdom of the Underworld which awaited him.

To be continued…

EPISODE 50

DURING WHICH HERMES MEETS THE MYSTERIOUS CHARON

Previously: Hermes has been punished for having stolen Hera's chariot and Poseidon's trident. He must go and spend three months in the Underworld in his uncle Hades' house and place himself from now on in his service.

It was with a heavy heart that Hermes set out towards the Underworld. He had never yet been in the underground kingdom of his uncle Hades, but the idea of being shut up below the earth, where the sun and the air never entered, frightened him. Furthermore, he did not know Hades all that well, yet his stern aspect intimidated him. He had sometimes met him in the palace and he seemed to be a querulous man, mean even. Like everyone else, Hermes did not like the company of the dead. And that was just it: Hades reigned over the kingdom of the dead.

When he reached the cave which was the entrance to the Underworld, Hermes found himself before a wide, black river overcast by a lingering fog. "I cannot very well swim across it," murmured the young god. "And it is impossible to fly over it in this fog—one cannot even see the opposite bank." He was mulling things over in his mind when he heard a strange lapping sound. It was like the sound of slowly approaching oars. Suddenly, a boat emerged from the mists. It was steered by an old man, whose head was covered by a black hood. The old man pressed with a slow and precise motion on the great oar which he used to move the vessel along. Soon, the boat had reached the shore where Hermes stood.

Just then, a host of shadows began to push and shove in order to get on board the boat. Hermes had not heard them arrive. Where had they come from? Where were they going? Who were they? They seemed exhausted and they pressed on so they might not miss the boarding. The old man scrutinized them one by one. He examined them from head to toe, then he made them turn around. After this check, some were given permission to board the boat while others were firmly thrown back onto the shore. Those who had been refused passage beseeched the old man, hanging themselves from his sleeves, weeping. But nothing seemed capable of changing his mind. Hermes looked at these shadows as they wept and his heart sank, without knowing the reason why. He could understand nothing of the scene unfolding before his eyes, yet it unsettled him in a strange way.

He remembered that his mission was to gain entrance to the Underworld. So he tried in his turn to climb on board the small boat.

"My name is Hermes," he said to the old man, and he stretched out his hand in greeting.

"And I am Charon, and this black river is the Styx," muttered the other, who did not take Hermes' extended hand. "No living person, however, can cross this river. You cannot board now. Wait until you are dead." And he pushed Hermes away roughly back onto the shore.

"But I am immortal!" Hermes exclaimed. "I am Hades' nephew and I have a message for him from his brother Zeus."

It was too late. Charon had picked up his oar once more and the boat was already disappearing into the fog, ferrying the shades of the dead, who sat huddled close to one another.

Hermes sat on the ground to think. Around him, the shadows bewailed their lot.

"We don't have any luck," said one, "if only we had been decently buried, according to the rites, Charon would not have refused us entry to the kingdom of the dead."

"The road to this place has been long and difficult to find, I am so tired," sighed another. "And I shall have to remain on earth for another hundred years before I may board that boat..."

"A hundred years, during which we shall never be able to find rest," wept another still, "since the only place of rest for us is the kingdom of Hades. And we don't have the right to enter it!"

So these shadows were the souls of the dead. Hermes understood everything now. He knew that it was the duty of human beings to bury their dead with dignity. Failing that, the souls were condemned to roam on earth for a hundred years. Hermes felt great pity for these forsaken souls. He saw them drift slowly apart as each mournfully took their own way.

Yet he still needed to find a means to cross to the other side of this river. Hermes gathered together some pieces of driftwood which lay scattered on the shore, tied them securely together with a piece of thin rope and in that way fashioned a raft for himself. His clever trick had restored his good humour back to him. The wood floated very well and he was going to be able to cross the black and icy waters of the Styx. But what would he find on the other side?

To be continued…

Episode 51

In which Hermes finds himself face to face with Cerberus

Previously: Hermes is trying to cross the river which leads to the Underworld on a raft.

The raft of Hermes made slow progress on the black waters of the Styx. The young god was using as an oar his caduceus, the rod on which two serpents were intertwined. The fog lingering about him became thicker and thicker. Soon, he could no longer see the riverbank he had just left. He shuddered. The daylight diminished unrelentingly and an unnerving silence filled the surrounding space. In an effort to reassure himself, Hermes shouted in a loud voice: "Hello! Is there anyone there?" But only the echo of his own voice came back to him.

Suddenly the fog was torn asunder and Hermes saw the opposite bank. When his raft touched the riverfront, Hermes was not at all displeased to be able to jump ashore. But the darkness made it impossible for him to make out what surrounded him. Hermes decided to equip himself with a proper light in order to proceed with his exploring. He knelt on the ground, took out of his bag some dry wood and some stones and began to make a fire, just as he had done on the day he was born. When a small flame leapt up, he fashioned himself a torch and stood up again. He carried the torch in circles around him and was horrified by what he discovered. An enormous dog towered before him, a dog almost as big as he was. And this dog had three heads, three gaping mouths, each revealing a row of dagger-sharp teeth capable of tearing anyone to pieces in an instant! Hermes no longer dared to make a single movement. The monstrous beast took a step towards him. And as it did so, Hermes noticed the enormous dragon's tail which completed its body. It struck the soil at every step and the noise of the tail crashing on the ground reverberated against the cave walls with a deafening rumble.

The dog began to bark. Its horrible muzzles were but a hair's breadth away from Hermes. Suddenly the young god brandished his torch in the direction of the beast and forced it to stop. His position, however, remained delicate. Behind him, the icy waters of the Styx blocked his retreat. And in front of him, the monster threatened to gobble him up in a single mouthful as soon as his torch was extinguished. Hermes tried to talk to the dog. In a shaky voice, he said to it:

"Good morning, my name is Hermes, and I have come to pay a visit to my uncle Hades, the god of the Underworld." Yet the dog was barking so loudly that his words were lost in the pandemonium.

Suddenly, a deep voice rang out close by:

"Who are you, you foolhardy young man, to dare attack Cerberus, the guardian of the Underworld? And how dare you disturb Hades in his own home?"

An old man had appeared abruptly by his side. He had a long, grey beard and his eyes with their drooping eyelids gave him an air of infinite sorrow. He held a helmet in his hand. Hermes let out a sigh of relief as he recognized Hades and he regained the use of his glib tongue once more:

"Good morning, uncle, I am Hermes, your nephew, don't you recognize me? I am so very glad to see you at last. Zeus and Hera send me with their greetings... and also so that I may place myself in your service." Hades silenced his dog by a clicking of his tongue. "You have arrived just in time, uncle," Hermes said to him, "I was just about to become your dog's snack! Brrr... It is not very warm in your palace."

The young man's naturalness and spontaneity put Hades off his guard, used as he was to others trembling before him. Yet this unforeseen visit vexed him a little as well. Why couldn't Zeus mind his own business, instead of sending him his son like this?

The horrid Cerberus had calmed down. Its three repulsive muzzles now sniffed Hermes from head to toe. Hermes did not budge at all. At last he said:

"He... he seems rather sweet, that dog of yours, uncle..."

A glint of astonishment, then of amusement crossed Hades' stern gaze.

"Well, come along, then. I will show you round my kingdom," he said.

Old Hades seemed a little tamer already. Hermes trembled with curiosity. He was going to discover the Underworld.

To be continued...

ϵPISODϵ 52

In which Hermes makes his entrance
into the kingdom of the dead

Previously: When he reached the Underworld,
Hermes managed to escape Cerberus,
the monstrous three-headed dog.

A long, dark corridor, then another, then another still... Hermes was following his uncle Hades in silence. The more they advanced, the more they plunged deep down below the earth. Hermes kept wondering how he would ever be able to come out of these depths. In any case, he felt quite unable to find his way back on his own. Their steps resonated against the stone walls. It got warmer and warmer. The passageway became so narrow that Hermes felt he would suffocate. At that instant, an underground river appeared. Hermes, who was dying of thirst, hastened to drink. Yet Hades pushed him back sharply. "Never drink of this water, you fool, this is the river Lethe, the river which makes you forget everything! If you swallow the merest drop of this liquid, you will lose all memory of your life for ever!" Hermes drew back immediately. He did not want to have his memories erased.

They resumed their way. Soon, the passage widened and they reached the junction of three roads. "This is where my kingdom begins. And here are my faithful servants, the judges," said Hades. He was pointing with his finger at three figures sitting there and blocking the way. Before them waited a long line of shades. Each shade passed in turn before each of the three judges. And the judges questioned it about its past life. Then they discussed in low voices among themselves and afterwards they indicated to the shade one of the three roads behind them.

Hermes was trying to understand what was taking place there, yet Hades did not give him the chance. "Come on!" he ordered. They took the first road, on which most of the shades were sent, and they reached a great flat and monotonous site. There was nothing at all to catch one's eye. The place was plunged in half-darkness. Shades crossed paths gloomily. They did not speak to one another, nor did they look at each other. They glided from one point of the meadow to another incessantly. Some greeted Hades and Hermes with a slight wave of their hand. Hermes raised his winged hat politely to them. Yet Hades did not respond to the greeting.

"All these dead are far too numerous, I cannot spend my day saying good morning to them," he grumbled.

They had hardly been there a few minutes and Hermes was already feeling mortally bored.

"Where are we?" he asked.

"We are in the Asphodel meadows, this is the first of my regions," replied Hades. "All those who have never done anything truly good or truly bad ever in their lives are sent here; and that means most men."

Hermes was in a hurry to move away from this sad place where nothing ever happened. They returned to the junction of the three roads. They took the second path, on which very few of the shades were sent, and they reached an immense space full of greenery. It was a vast meadow, as pale green as the grass can be in the spring. Countless flowers were strewn everywhere on this carpet. Their perfumes embraced Hermes instantly. He went enchanted from a rose bush to a grove of budding cherry trees, slipped under the protective foliage of a weeping willow, listened to the warbling of the birds in the branches. He would never have guessed that he would find below the earth such eternal springtime! The most astonishing thing of all was the light which flooded this part of the Underworld, a light as bright as daylight. "And yet we are still under the earth!" Hermes said in astonishment. He noticed then shades lying on the grass. Yet these shades were no longer suffering or sad, not at all, these were laughing gaily. Some were whispering secrets to one another, others were listening to a poet's shade reciting verses, and others still let themselves be transported by a sweet and melodious music. Their faces were serene. Everything here was in perfect harmony.

"Where are we?" asked the young god, mesmerized.

"We are in the fields of Elysium," replied Hades, his voice full of pride. "Only the dead who have accomplished great exploits during their lifetime have the right to stay here. Entry is forbidden to those who have lacked either courage or kindness."

Hermes could not get enough of watching these shadows which seemed so happy. Yet Hades was already calling him:

"Come, we still need to visit the third of my regions."

Along this road the shades were few in number. Yet those who had been sent this way by the three judges were shedding heavy tears.

"Prepare yourself for what you are about to see," Hades told him.

Hermes was trembling, yet he could no longer turn back.

To be continued...

ΕΡΙSΟΔΕ 53

In which Hermes discovers the depths of Tartarus

Previously: Hades is showing Hermes around the kingdom of the dead. He is now taking him to Tartarus, the most horrifying part of the Underworld.

Hermes gasped at the stifling heat which seized him by the throat. The place he had just come to was full of screams and moans. "The shadows who are sent here have committed crimes during their lifetimes. Their punishment is to end up in the depths of Tartarus," explained Hades. They entered a first cave, dark and humid, where it was terribly hot. There, the shadows of about fifty young girls were busy in front of an enormous barrel. They carried great pitchers on their shoulders. They would first go to a well, lower their pitcher into the water, fill it up and then carry it, heavy as it was, to the barrel. There they emptied the water into the barrel and left straight away to go once more to the well. The female shadows never paused. "These are the shadows of the Danaids," said Hades. "These young women killed their husbands. They have been condemned to fill this barrel and they may not stop until it is full!" At these words, Hades dissolved into laughter. Hermes, who was observing the shadows of the Danaids, understood why his uncle laughed so cruelly: the barrel was pierced with many holes and the water leaked to the ground. This barrel could never be full, and the shadows would never be able to rest.

Hades led Hermes to a second cave. It was as humid and dark as the cave of the Danaids, yet it was even hotter there and the ceiling was much higher. At first, it was too dark and Hermes could not see a thing. Then his eyes became accustomed to the blackness and he could just make out a shadow, that of an almost naked man. This shadow was pushing a rock much bigger than itself towards the top of a mountain. A grimace twisted the man's face, but he kept toiling with all his strength. Little by little, the rock moved up the slope. Suddenly, Hades jibed: "So, then, Sisyphus, have you almost reached the top?" and he again broke into laughter. Hermes understood what made his uncle laugh: the instant Sisyphus arrived at the summit, his enormous rock hurtled down the slope on the other side of the mountain and was down at the bottom again. Sisyphus ran behind it with a look of total despair on his face. Too late! He was obliged to begin the entire process from the start. So he turned around and again began to push with all his might against the rock to bring it back to the top of the mountain. "Don't lose heart, Sisyphus!" mocked Hades.

Astonished, Hermes asked: "But why is he so determined to push this block of stone all the way to the top of this mountain?"

The face of the god of the Underworld became stern: "Zeus has condemned him to push against this rock for all eternity."

"But what crime did he commit to receive such a horrific sentence?" asked Hermes.

"He is an informer," answered Hades. "One day, he saw Zeus leave with one of his sweethearts. The father of this young girl was looking for her everywhere. No one would answer his questions, because everyone was shielding the lovers' escape. When he asked Sisyphus, well, Sisyphus went right ahead and reported what he had seen, thus betraying Zeus! To punish him for informing on him Zeus has condemned him to this sentence for ever."

Hermes remained silent. Hades, who seemed thrilled to have shown him round his kingdom, began to speak again. "But you haven't seen everything yet, nephew! Follow me, there are other men who believed themselves to be stronger than the gods, and who are now condemned to terrible torments."

This time they entered into a cave which was bright and peaceful. A stream flowed there softly. There were trees full of ripe fruit. Yet Hermes discovered a man's shadow attached to one of the tree branches, and suspended above the stream.

"I am thirsty! I am hungry!" it cried when it saw Hades.

"Tantalus, you ought to have thought of this before you tried to deceive the gods," replied Hades. Attached to his branch, Tantalus squirmed in every direction in order to reach the water of the stream or even one of the fragrant fruits. Yet neither his mouth nor his hand could ever get close to the water or the fruit.

Hermes left this third cave thinking about the power of his father, the god of gods.

To be continued...

€PISOD€ 54

IN WHICH HERMES AGREES TO
UNDERTAKE A NEW MISSION

*Previously: Hermes has visited the Underworld
with his uncle Hades. He has discovered
Tartarus, the most dreadful region of all, the
one where serious criminals are sent.*

To complete their visit of the Underworld, Hades led Hermes to a high-walled cave which was illuminated by torches. It was the centre of the earth, the heart of the Underworld. Hades had set up his palace there, a cold and grey residence with countless doors, all locked by key. He took Hermes to the throne room and made him sit beside him. "Now, tell me the news from up there," he asked. Hermes needed no coaxing. He told him everything, about Zeus' escapades and Hera's anger, about Athena's studies; about the grace of Apollo, the coquettishness of Aphrodite and the savagery of Ares; about the talent of Hephaestus, the prodigious birth of Dionysus and the hunts of Artemis... Hermes was a marvellous storyteller. He did not leave out a single detail or the littlest joke. Soon enough, a smile appeared on Hades' face. "Dear child, I have not felt so light-hearted in a very long time," he said. "Your words feel like honey pouring down my throat. My brother was right in sending you here." And this is how Hermes came to stay in Hades' palace. "I am the richest brother among the three of us," said Hades proudly. "My kingdom has by far more subjects than those of Zeus and Poseidon." It was true: the dead were much more numerous than the creatures living on earth or in the seas.

Hermes learnt quickly how to find his way around the different parts of this immense underground network. Sometimes his uncle would lend him his helmet of invisibility to play with. Hermes would put it on his head and disappear from sight right away. This game amused him greatly at first. He loved taking his uncle's servants by surprise or even the shades of the dead, by appearing abruptly exactly when they least expected it. The only one who would never let himself be fooled was the dog Cerberus. He stood watch before his bronze door in order to prevent the dead from going out again. One of his three muzzles always managed to sniff out Hermes before he was able to pull his dragon's tail. And when that happened, Hermes had good reason to run away as fast as he might...

The one Hermes loved making jump with fright the most was old Charon, the ferryman of the shades of the dead. Charon would almost make his boat capsize every time. But Hermes only teased him in this manner when his boat was empty. He respected the shadows of the dead far too much to take the risk of making them fall in the water. Each time that new shadows arrived, Hermes was deeply moved. They had searched for so long to find the way to the Underworld, that they arrived there exhausted. Hermes rather began to like the shadows.

Yet the more the days passed, the more Hermes lost his cheerfulness. He dreamt of seeing again the open air and the sun. Life below the earth was beginning to bore him. He had nothing to occupy himself with and he missed being able to make himself useful. Seeing the young god become a little less talkative each day, Hades understood what the matter was. One morning, he summoned Hermes to the throne room: "My dear nephew, I like listening to your words and to your jingling laughter. Yet you will soon have nothing more to tell me about," he sighed. "Go to the earth and fill up your bag of stories." And, so that he could be certain that his nephew would soon come back to see him again, the powerful Hades entrusted him with a mission: "I have noticed well that you like the subjects of my kingdom, the shadows of the dead. I would like you to accompany them on their way here. They often have great difficulty finding their way. You, on the other hand, would know how to point them in the right direction. I am counting on you to speak to them, to make them laugh, and to lead them gently here to my kingdom. And don't forget to come and give me a hug when you have brought a shadow over."

Hermes agreed to this with great joy. He was thrilled to regain the outdoors once more. He felt happy to be able to help the shadows of the dead. Yet above all he was proud of Hades' confidence in him. From now on, he had a role to perform in the Underworld. And the young man now returned to Olympus charged with this important mission. When Hera saw him arrive, she furiously pursed her lips, but she said nothing. Because Zeus was far too happy to have his son back once more.

To be continued...

€PISODE 55

In which Zeus hangs
stars up in the sky

*Previously: Hermes has left the kingdom of the
Underworld. From now on, each time he meets the shadow
of a person who has died, he will have to help it find the
way to the Underworld. He is glad to be back at Olympus.*

That morning, Zeus was descending Mount Olympus at a
brisk pace. He would stop at times, turn around sighing
and wait so that Hermes, who idled far behind, could catch
up. Hermes was so happy to rediscover the light of day that he
could not stop gambolling about even more than usual. His long
underground stay had given him an even greater yearning to
make the most of life. Zeus pretended to be annoyed, but deep
down he understood well his son's happiness.

"If only you knew to whom we are going to pay a visit this
time, you would hurry a bit more," said Zeus.

Now it was Hermes who walked ahead of his father, saying:
"Come on, come on, then, faster!"

This is how they soon reached the foot of a mountain that was well familiar to Hermes: it was the mountain where he had been born. "Mummy!" he cried, overjoyed. And without waiting any longer he flew all the way to the cave where his mother Maia lived.

Even before entering the coolness of the cave, he recognized his mother's smell. She was sitting on her heels with her back turned and did not see him enter. Hermes was about to hasten to her when she got up and turned around. Hermes stopped hard on his tracks, startled: Maia was looking smilingly at a child she was holding in her arms. Who *was* this baby? *Where* did it come from? And *why* was his mother smiling tenderly at it? Hermes was overcome by a surge of jealousy. Maia lifted up her eyes and saw Zeus and Hermes both at the same time. She passed by Hermes' side, stroked his cheek softly and said: "Good morning, darling," then she came close to Zeus. She held the baby out to him and murmured:

"Your son Arcas is doing well. But don't wake him, he has only just fallen asleep. He cannot easily go back to sleep away from his mother." Zeus leant towards the little boy and took it clumsily in his arms.

Hermes felt another violent pang of jealousy. His father and mother busied themselves over this baby as though he, Hermes, no longer existed. He cleared his throat to attract their attention, but they did not even turn their heads around.

"Thank you, Maia," said Zeus in a grave voice. "I knew when I trusted you with the safekeeping of this child that you would know how to look after him."

"Do you have any news of his mother?" asked Maia softly.

"Alas," sighed Zeus, "it is as I had feared. My wife, white-armed Hera, discovered the existence of this baby that I had fathered with the nymph Callisto. Furious, she immediately transformed Callisto into a great bear that has since been living in the woods, like a wild beast."

Hermes had heard everything. His jealousy towards this baby disappeared instantly. He was filled with pity for him and looked at him with tenderness. Zeus turned towards him:

"Hermes, as my older son, would you accept to look after this youngster?"

Hermes promised that he would. So as not to attract Hera's attention, Zeus and Hermes had to take their leave of Maia and the baby quickly. Yet from that day on, Hermes would often go and pay a visit to little Arcas.

As he grew up, the boy became a handsome young man. Hunting was his passion. He ran in the woods and looked for game for hours on end. Yet there was an inward sadness about him, the sadness of children who have been separated from their mothers. Neither Maia nor Hermes had told him what had happened to his mother. Then, one day, he found himself face to face with a great bear. He pointed his bow and arrow in the animal's direction, yet he hesitated for a few moments. The bear did not try to escape and was looking at him. Something in the bear's affectionate gaze troubled him. It was his own mother, but Arcas did not know that. Fortunately for him, Hermes was not far away. He rushed to Zeus, shouting: "Father! Father! Come quick! Arcas is about to kill his mother without

211

knowing it!" The young hunter had just drawn his arrow when Zeus appeared. He barely had enough time to divert the arrow from its course. The great bear approached and dropped her paw lightly on Arcas' head. The young man's heart softened and he fell upon his knees. And, so that mother and son would never again be separated, Zeus transformed the young man into a bear and affixed both son and mother for ever in the sky as constellations of stars. Since that time, one has been called the Great Bear and the other the Little Bear. And each time that Hermes would fly in the night sky, he never failed to wave to the mother and son, reunited at last.

Faithful to his new mission, Hermes no longer contents himself only with delivering the messages of the gods. He travels across the earth seeking the shadows of the dead. Once he has seen one of them, he will approach gently; he will indicate with a slight gesture that it should follow him. He takes by the hand the more tired shadows, those who have already been looking for the way to the Underworld for a long time. And he leads them in this manner to the banks of the river of the Underworld. Hermes' reward is the smile on their faces once they have arrived at long last at the kingdom of the dead. His task ends there. Sometimes he crosses the river with them in order to go and say hello to his uncle Hades. More often than not, however, he goes away again immediately.

To be continued…

ϵPISODϵ 56

IN WHICH A YOUNG GODDESS DISAPPEARS

Previously: Hermes has resumed his travels with Zeus.
In this way he has been able to protect little Arcas,
whose mother had been transformed into a bear.

There was, in the palace of Olympus, a goddess whom Hermes almost never saw, and that was his aunt Demeter. The reason was that she spent little time in the company of the other gods. Her duties brought her most often down to earth. She was the goddess of the Harvest. It was she who made the wheat grow in the fields and all the good things that men could cultivate and eat. This generous goddess had had a daughter with Zeus, called Persephone. Demeter was besotted with her: to put it simply, she lived only for her daughter's sake. Whenever Demeter left to go down to the earth so she could take care of the harvests, she would return as soon as possible so she might be reunited with Persephone.

Persephone too adored her mother. Yet she would have liked to be allowed a little more freedom.

"Mummy," she would implore, "let me go out a little without you. What could possibly happen to me? I am tired of waiting for you to come back so I can go to the earth for a walk."

Yet Demeter always refused: "You are far too pretty, my flower of love, something awful might happen to you, and I could never bear it." And she would press Persephone tight against her heart.

A day came when, as a result of her relentless insisting, Persephone finally got permission to go down to the earth for a walk without her mother. It was a beautiful spring morning and Demeter had to help men sow. Accompanied by fifty or so nymphs, Persephone headed for a great flowering meadow nearby. The young goddess looked ravishing. The fields burst with colourful flowers. The beautiful Persephone began to pick great bunches of them. There were roses, irises, bluebells and crocuses, everything one needed to make the most sumptuous flower arrangement. Suddenly, her gaze was caught by an absolutely extraordinary flower, a flower she had never seen before. This flower was red and silver and it was called narcissus—and neither god nor man had ever come across such a wonder. Persephone approached and bent down to pick the flower, when suddenly an enormous pit opened in front of her and she vanished inside it. As she fell, the young goddess let out a scream. At the other end of the earth, her mother Demeter heard her daughter's cry. Mad with worry, she came running. "What has happened? Where is Persephone?" shouted the poor mother. But her daughter's companions did not know what to reply. They could only shake their heads and weep: they had seen nothing except a strange flower and then a great pit which had gobbled up the young goddess. At that, Demeter also let out a rending scream and threw herself onto the ground weeping. But where had Persephone disappeared to?

To be continued…

EPISODE 57

IN WHICH WE WITNESS A
MOTHER'S DESPAIR

*Previously: Persephone, the beloved daughter of
Demeter, the goddess of the Harvest, has disappeared.*

Demeter's lament rang out across the entire universe. Night had fallen by the time she stood up again. The goddess lit a torch and set out into the world to look for her daughter. She walked on and on and on, without allowing herself a moment's rest. She did not stop to drink, eat or sleep. Only the scream let out by her daughter repeated itself endlessly in her mind. In a voice full of anguish, she asked each person she met along her way: "You haven't seen my daughter Persephone, by any chance?" But no one had. It was as though Persephone had vanished from the face of the earth.

Hermes was very unhappy about what was happening. As soon as he had learnt of the disappearance of the young goddess, he too had sought to discover what had happened to his cousin. As he was ferreting for clues in the palace corridors, he caught sight of his uncle Hades. Well, that *was* surprising... The god of the Underworld must surely have some matter of great importance to settle if he had come here himself. His curiosity aroused, Hermes approached on tiptoe and glued his ear against the door of the council hall where Zeus and Hades were talking in private.

"You *cannot* refuse me this!" growled Hades. "I have been madly in love with Persephone since the day I saw her. I want to marry her."

With great embarrassment in his voice, Zeus replied to him:

"My dear brother, I would very much like to make you happy, but Demeter would never forgive me if I let you take Persephone to live with you in the Underworld far away from her."

"Be careful, Zeus, I am the god of the Underworld, and I too am very powerful," threatened Hades' voice.

Hermes gave a little jump. He wondered how his father would be able to get out of this.

Zeus replied: "I do not underestimate your power, Hades, quite on the contrary, as I will prove to you: you are, in fact, so powerful that you can do without Zeus in order to take care of this sort of business..."

Silence ensued. Hades had understood the message: he was free to do as he pleased and Zeus would turn a blind eye to his conduct. Behind the door, Hermes shuddered. He saw Hades leave the palace discreetly. The conversation he had overheard identified the culprit of the abduction. Yet he could not speak about it without betraying the fact that he had listened behind closed doors! He could do no more than follow Demeter's course, hoping that she would pick up a trail in the end.

After nine days and nine nights of walking like a madwoman, Demeter was hardly recognizable. She had lost weight, her plump cheeks had become hollow, her rosy complexion had turned extremely sallow, her hair had grown white like that of a very old woman and her clothes, now rent and covered with dust, made her look like a beggar. On the morning of the tenth day, Demeter presented herself at the door of the palace of Helios. The servants of the sun god refused to allow her to enter, filthy and miserable as they saw her. Yet rosy-fingered Aurora was returning to the palace just then. She recognized Demeter immediately and was filled with pity. At that instant, Helios, the sun god, was taking out his chariot to begin the day's race. Aurora seized the horses by their harness and stopped Helios:

"Helios, look at this mother's despair! Look at her anguish and her suffering! You cannot remain indifferent. Just looking at her makes the tears well up in my eyes. You are the sun, you always see everything that takes place on earth and *you know* what has happened to her daughter. I beseech you, you must tell her!"

Helios' head was bowed. He did not dare look Demeter in the face. Yes, of course he knew. Demeter looked at him, her hands clasped together, waiting for him to decide to speak. Aurora was holding back the horses, which were beginning to get impatient. The day had to rise now without fail and with no further delay. Helios turned at last towards Demeter and said to her:

"It is Hades who has abducted your daughter to make her his wife. She has been living in the Underworld. And Zeus, who is fully aware of this, has let him go ahead with it." After saying these words, he tore the reins away from Aurora's hands and stormed away in his chariot at a full gallop.

Demeter did not have the presence of mind to thank him or the rosy-fingered Aurora, for that matter. As soon as she learnt the appalling news, she buried her head in her hands. Her daughter, condemned to live below the earth for ever! Her daughter, whom she would never see again! Shattered, she walked away from the palace of Helios without a word. A violent anger was surging up inside her. So, Zeus had been cowardly enough to allow his own daughter to be taken to the Underworld! Well, since this was the way things were, Demeter decided never to return to Olympus. "I am no longer a member of this family of hypocritical and lying gods," she murmured. "I will no longer take care of anything whatsoever on earth, neither the sowings nor the harvests, until my daughter has been restored to me."

Hermes looked at her as she grew distant on the road ahead, her body bent like an old woman's, and his heart became heavy. If the generous Demeter were to forsake her place among the gods, who was going to look after the earth? Who would make the grains and the plants grow? Was the earth going to turn into a desert?

To be continued...

ΣPISODΣ 58

IN WHICH DEMETER SOWS SADNESS

*Previously: Demeter, the goddess of the Harvest,
has discovered that her beloved daughter has been
abducted by Hades, the god of the Underworld.
She has also learnt that Zeus has not protected his
daughter. Mad with grief, she refuses to return to
Olympus and decides to tend no longer to anything on
earth until her daughter has been restored to her.*

It had been days and days since anything had grown on earth. The plants had lost their leaves, the flowers had withered and the fruit had dried up on the trees. Soon there was nothing left except dry and yellowed grass instead of wheat. The animals, who could no longer find anything to eat, died one after the other. And men, who became hungrier and hungrier, began to die as well. They wept and beseeched the good goddess Demeter to resume her place among the gods. They called her name and hoped that she would return to tend the harvests. But the goddess had disappeared.

Looking at the devastation on earth, Hermes was despairing as well. He had always liked men, the protégés of Prometheus, and their misfortune made him miserable. When he flew above the earth, all these desolate landscapes filled him with sorrow. He searched for Demeter so he could convince her to come back. But no one could recognize the goddess any more, who walked barefoot in the dust like an old beggar woman and knocked on doors so she might be offered a glass of water or a chunk of bread.

While Hermes had been looking for her, Demeter had reached the doors of a palace, the palace of King Keleos. The king's maidservants had let this tired old woman into the kitchen. Exhausted by her long march, Demeter had sat down in the inglenook of the fireplace. She was very thirsty. So when one of the servants offered her a bowl of mint-scented water, she drank it quickly. Aah! How sweet that fragrant water felt in her throat! She drank so quickly that she spilt a little on the side. She had not noticed that a small child called Abas had come into the kitchen and was watching her drink. "Oh, how messily you drink!" the child said to her.

Demeter turned her head round sharply on Abas, she looked at him intensely and the child was instantly changed into a lizard! The lizard fled in zigzags out of the kitchen. The maidservants, who had seen nothing, came into the kitchen shouting: "Abas! Abas! Where are you hiding?"

They asked the old beggar woman, who was resting by the fire, whether she might not have seen the eldest son of King Keleos, a little boy called Abas. Yet she shook her head to say no, and the maidservants left to search for the little boy farther away. Demeter already regretted having changed the king's eldest son into a lizard. Yet she could do nothing for him now.

That evening, the entire palace bewailed the sudden disappearance of little Abas. Seeing the king and the queen weep, Demeter decided to do something for their second son. That child was a baby a mere few days old. Demeter chose to make him immortal. She slipped inside the child's room; the nursemaid who looked after him had fallen asleep at the foot of his crib. Demeter took the baby delicately in her arms and went back to the kitchen on the tips of her toes. "How cute you are, little one," Demeter murmured to him. "You remind me of my beloved daughter Persephone when she was born." Once in the kitchen, Demeter told him: "Do not be afraid, I shall give you eternal life. When I am done, you will be beyond the reach of death." She then took out of her pocket a flask containing ambrosia and nectar with which she rubbed the baby's entire body. Then she placed the baby over the flames in the fireplace and began to pronounce spells of immortality. The child was encircled by the fire, but it did not burn. The magic was almost ready to work, when the child's nursemaid entered abruptly into the kitchen. She had woken up with a start and, discovering the crib empty, had searched for the baby everywhere. She saw the old beggar woman holding the baby in the midst of the flames and she let out a sharp yell. The scream startled Demeter, and the goddess stopped her magic incantations. But as the child was not yet immortal, it instantly caught fire. Furious, Demeter set the baby down on the ground. She looked at it with tenderness and said to him: "I am truly sorry, baby. Don't worry, your burns

222

will heal soon, but you will never be immortal. You too shall grow and become a man, then an old man. And one day you too shall die, like all men. I wish you a good and happy life. Good bye!" The baby was now wailing; the goddess placed a kiss on his brow and then she fled into the night.

The day rose. Hermes, who was still looking for his aunt, could see nothing but the hard and cracked earth, the blackened trunks of the shrivelled olive trees and the yellowed undergrowth. With tears in his eyes, he decided to try to persuade Zeus to intervene.

Would Hermes be able to get his father to listen to him? Would he be able to save the earth?

To be continued...

EPISODE 59

In which Hermes is assigned
a very delicate mission

*Previously: Ever since the goddess Demeter has
been refusing to tend to it, the earth has gone dry.
Hermes has decided to persuade Zeus to intervene.*

When he reached Mount Olympus, Hermes saw a throng
of gods and goddesses assembled on one of the palace
terraces. He landed in their midst and he realized that they
were all talking about how catastrophic the situation was for
the earth and for mankind.

"This cannot go on any longer!" said someone.

"Demeter must resume her work!" said another.

"She is so irresponsible! She thinks only of herself!" cried
the high-pitched voice of white-armed Hera.

"No, it is Hades who is irresponsible," Athena replied drily
to her, "he should not have abducted her daughter."

The gods were all arguing in this manner while looking at
the earth, where nothing grew any more. At that moment, Zeus

made his appearance. There was instant silence. His worries had dug two furrows on his forehead. Hermes swallowed hard; it was not going to be easy to ask him for anything today…

"Where is Hermes?" asked Zeus all of a sudden. "Someone fetch Hermes immediately!" The crowd drew back to let the messenger god get past, who said in a very small voice:

"I am here, daddy…"

"My son," said Zeus, placing both hands on Hermes' shoulders, "you are well acquainted with the Underworld, my brother Hades' kingdom. You will go there without delay and you will try to bring Persephone back in our midst. Tell my brother that unless he gives Persephone back to her mother, the earth and mankind will perish. Come, off you go, and make sure you succeed!"

His father's hands pressed hard on Hermes' shoulders. This new mission was certainly one of the most difficult ones in his life. The messenger of the gods flew as swiftly as he could to the Underworld. He waited for old Charon to arrive with his boat in order to cross the River Styx.

"You've come all alone today," grumbled Charon. "You haven't accompanied anyone dead here."

Hermes boarded the boat without replying. Then he asked: "So what news from the Underworld?"

"Oh, don't even ask," replied Charon with his trailing voice. "Hades is in love. But his sweetheart will not stop crying. She wants to see the light of day again. She wants to see her mother again. Hades does not know what to do any more to stop her from crying! It's all too depressing…"

When he arrived at Hades' palace, Hermes discovered Persephone, pale, streaming with tears, sitting on the throne next to Hades' own. She was clutching her handkerchief tight against her body with an air of utter despair. Down on his knees, Hades was squeezing her hand telling her sweet words of love. Yet the young goddess could only reply:

"I have nothing against you, sire, but I cannot bear to live without the sun and without my mother."

Hades drew such a long sigh that Hermes was touched. He gave a slight cough to indicate his presence. Hades sprang up, a little embarrassed to have been caught kneeling at his wife's feet.

"Good morning, nephew, to what do I owe your visit?"

"Good morning, dear uncle, king of the Underworld, and good morning to you too, my beautiful cousin Persephone," replied Hermes after bowing deeply before them. "It is Zeus who has sent me. You see, we are in a very, very awkward situation. Since you abducted and married Persephone, her mother is so distraught that she no longer does her job. The earth and the men on it are dying." And the skilled wordsmith began to describe in great detail the catastrophic situation on earth. Hades listened without saying anything, while Persephone wept even more heartily... Hermes concluded his speech with the following words: "Zeus beseeches you to restore Persephone back to her mother." A long silence ensued, interrupted only by the hiccups and snifflings of Persephone. Hades then turned towards her and said:

"My fair friend, know that if you had been happy with me, I would never have listened to a word of Zeus' request. But I love you too much to be able to bear your grief any longer. Go back to your mother, since this is what you must do." He placed a kiss on her hand and left the room.

"He truly loves you!" said Hermes to his cousin. "Lovers like that don't come often..." Persephone had stopped crying. The idea of seeing the light of day again filled her with happiness. And she, who had not eaten anything for ten days, suddenly felt famished. She took out of her pocket a pomegranate that the god of the Underworld had offered her and bit into it. "Spit that out!" cried Hermes. "Spit it out quickly!" And he snatched the fruit from her and threw it far away. Panic-stricken, Persephone spat out what she had just bitten off. "Have you swallowed any of it?" asked Hermes, trembling.

"No... well, yes, just three little seeds, that's all..." stammered the goddess. "Is it serious?"

It was far more serious than she could possibly imagine...

To be continued...

ΣPISODΣ 60

IN WHICH A MOTHER AND DAUGHTER ARE REUNITED AT LAST

Previously: Hermes has gone to fetch Persephone from the Underworld. Hades has agreed to let her go away again, but she has just swallowed three pomegranate seeds which put her at risk...

Why had Hermes been trembling in this manner ever since his cousin Persephone had swallowed these three seeds of pomegranate? Hermes had grasped her hand at once and had begun to run towards the exit of the cavern. The sun which greeted them as they came out was dazzling. Persephone forgot the matter of the seeds immediately and let her joy explode. She stretched out her arms and began to twirl around in the light air. And she laughed and laughed. Her long hair floated in a crown all around her. As he looked at her, Hermes thought of Hades' love, a love so great that the god of the Underworld had agreed to lose the young girl so she might regain her smile. He led Persephone away with him. "Come, we still have a long distance to cover."

As soon as she saw the state the earth was in, this parched earth where nothing grew any longer, Persephone understood how much her mother must have suffered by her absence to abandon her work in this way. Night was falling when Hermes and Persephone came near a great high-columned building of stone. It was the temple of Eleusis. The setting sun cast a splendid red flush on it. Suddenly, a woman appeared on the threshold. She had a thin, wrinkled face and grey hair which fell all over it; she wore filthy and torn clothes. And the red sunlight which lit up her face gave it a troubling aspect. Persephone hesitated for an instant: she did not recognize her own mother, once so beautiful, in this old woman. But Demeter recognized her daughter immediately and rushed into her arms. Hermes moved discreetly a little farther away, to let mother and daughter reunite.

After several long moments, Demeter turned towards Hermes to thank him for having returned her daughter to her. But there was something quite difficult that Hermes still had to do.

"Dear aunt Demeter," began the little messenger, "Zeus sent me to fetch your daughter from the Underworld and Hades agreed, because of his love for her, to let her go. There is just one thing, though: according to the laws of the Underworld, anyone who has tasted the food of that realm is condemned to remain there for ever." Persephone gave out a faint groan: she realized now that her misfortunes were perhaps not over yet. "The fact is that Persephone ate three seeds from a fruit that grew in the Underworld..."

When she heard these words, Demeter turned very pale. "I shall *never* let her go back down there," she shouted.

"Wait! Don't lose your temper! All along the way here, I have been thinking the matter over, and I believe that I have come up with an idea: your daughter only swallowed three seeds, so I propose that she spend three months of the year with Hades in the Underworld and the rest of the time with you. What do you think?"

The goddess Demeter did not have time to reply, because Zeus appeared just then. "Well done, Hermes. Not only have you succeeded in your mission, but the suggestion you have just made seems to me ideal. It shall be so." Then he turned towards Persephone and said in her ear: "You'll see; you will be quite happy to be able to get away from your mother now and then. And after all, Hades has been a very attentive lover towards you..." Persephone smiled and accepted.

Demeter was furious at the idea of having to be separated from her daughter once more, but this time she would have to yield. So she shouted at Zeus: "Well, then, during the three months that my beloved daughter will be taken away from me, I too will take myself away from the world, and I will cease to work while I wait for her return."

This is how, from that day onwards, and during three months of each year, when winter sets in, nothing grows any longer on earth. While Demeter bewails her daughter, who joins Hades in the Underworld, the plants fall asleep, the trees no longer have leaves and the flowers and the fruit disappear. Afterwards, as soon as the goddess finds her daughter once more, it is spring: everything blossoms anew and everything grows on earth. The goddess works and works, summer arrives with its fruit and ripe grain. Then Demeter begins to dread once more her daughter's departure. Autumn comes, the leaves turn yellow. And it is time for Persephone's sojourn in the Underworld. Demeter locks herself up during the three long winter months and weeps. The soil waits. It waits for the return of the beautiful Persephone in the springtime. Hermes went back to Olympus very pleased for having managed to bring prosperity back on earth. While he was flying towards the palace, he thought about the mysteries of love. "People in love are capable of absolutely incredible things. I would very much like to know where love comes from."

To be continued...

EPISODE 61

Previously: Persephone has been reunited with her mother Demeter but she returns every year to rejoin Hades in the Underworld during the three winter months.

Hermes had been invited to the wedding of young Orpheus. He had a particular fondness for this handsome young man. Orpheus was the first baby that Hermes had seen being born. He still remembered that magical night when he had accompanied his sister Artemis to the home of the nymph Calliope, who was giving birth to her child. On that night, Hermes had discovered the mysteries of birth. Furthermore, Orpheus became the most extraordinary musician in the world when he grew up. He played every instrument so gracefully that all men and all beasts were entranced by his music.

The celebration took place in a beautiful clearing. The tables had been set in the middle of the meadow. There were flowers everywhere. There was even a small brook flowing past. Hermes was awestruck when he met the young woman whom Orpheus was going to marry. She was called Eurydice and her eyes were as black as her hair. She had stuck white and purple flowers in her long plaits and a golden headband secured the blue veil which hung loose upon her head. The graceful Eurydice did not take her eyes off Orpheus. And Orpheus never stopped singing glorious tunes to her, accompanying the singing with his lyre. Watching the two young people in love, Hermes thought that being loved made one beautiful. Yet the more he looked at them, the less he understood from where this love was born. Why did these two love one another? That was a mystery...

Eurydice had wandered a few paces away from her husband. Orpheus was singing and playing his lyre. In order to be able to dance better, Eurydice had untied the laces of her sandals. Her naked feet stepped lightly onto the grass as she twirled around. All of a sudden, she stepped onto a snake hiding in the grass. In a flash, the snake bit her on the ankle. Eurydice let out a faint scream and fell on the ground. Orpheus hurried to his beloved, took her in his arms, yet life was fleeing away from her already. Eurydice's lips turned pale and the snake's venom reached her heart. The young woman died. Orpheus' grief burst out violently. Weeping, he clutched his wife against his body. And all the guests wept with him.

As he did with all the dead, Hermes accompanied Eurydice's shade to the Underworld. When he returned from the realm of Hades, he discovered that Orpheus' distress had not ceased to increase. Orpheus cried day after day, inconsolable for having lost his love.

"You, who guide the dead to Hades' realm," Orpheus said to him, "help me bring back my beloved to the world of the living. I cannot go on living without her."

But Hermes did not have the right to bring a living person to the realm of the dead. He replied: "Zeus alone can grant you leave to go to the Underworld."

Orpheus immediately made up his mind to go and persuade Zeus. He went to the palace of Olympus and brought his lyre with him. When he was in the presence of the gods, he began to play and to sing. His song had a sad beauty unlike any other. His music moved all the gods and goddesses.

"Are you aware that the journey to the Underworld is dangerous?" Zeus asked him.

"Yes, I am," answered Orpheus. "But to live without Eurydice is even more dangerous."

Zeus smiled. He knew well that being in love sometimes allowed one to overcome every obstacle. "So be it, then. Hermes, take Orpheus to Hades," he said.

The journey to the Underworld seemed short to Hermes, because all along the way Orpheus sang of his love for the beautiful Eurydice. When they arrived before old Charon, young Orpheus did not tremble. He continued to play. And Charon, who had at first refused to let this living man board the boat of the dead, fell, little by little, under the music's spell. He agreed to carry Orpheus to the opposite bank of the Styx. Hermes was left speechless before Orpheus' courage. But he thought that, before Cerberus, the terrible dog of the Underworld, Orpheus would be frightened and give up. Would the force of this love be enough to bring Eurydice back to life?

To be continued...

EPISODE 62

IN WHICH WE SEE THAT THE LACK
OF FAITH CAN COST DEARLY

*Previously: Eurydice was bitten by a snake on her wedding
day and she is now dead. Her husband, Orpheus, is
inconsolable. He goes to fetch her from the Underworld.*

H ermes dreaded the meeting between Orpheus and Cerberus, the terrible dog of the Underworld. Orpheus himself, however, was not afraid. He knew that no human being had ever gone as far as this, yet his love seemed to protect him from everything. He descended from Charon's boat untrembling. And when Cerberus, the monstrous dog, pointed his three gaping mouths towards him, he did not flinch. No, he continued to sing of his love for his beautiful vanished wife. The dog stopped, listened, and then slowly it stepped back. Orpheus' music had succeeded in what no one else had ever succeeded in doing: softening the beast's heart. Cerberus lay down; with his heads resting on his paws and with drooping eyelids, he listened to the sweet melody.

When Hermes and Orpheus arrived at Hades' palace, Orpheus' face still showed no fear. One thing alone occupied his mind: to find his wife again. He looked at all the shadows that surrounded him, seeking Eurydice among them. Hermes, who had prepared a long speech to beguile Hades and Persephone, was not allowed time to talk. As soon as the god of the Underworld and his wife entered, Orpheus began to sing. And there too the music touched Persephone and Hades in the deepest recesses of their hearts. Tears flowed down Persephone's face and Hades broke into a slight cough to conceal his emotion. Little by little, the music spread everywhere in the Underworld. When they heard the song of Orpheus, the Danaids stopped filling up their barrel, Sisyphus stopped pushing his heavy stone and Tantalus was no longer either thirsty or hungry. The music reached even the remotest parts of Tartarus, where the Cyclopes and the hundred-handed Giants were imprisoned. These monsters let their forge grow cold, the better to listen to the song.

The shadows of the dead had all drawn near. And suddenly, one of them took a step forward. It was Eurydice. Orpheus recognized her immediately and his song was transformed. The sweet and doleful music became lively and joyful. Orpheus sang for a long while of love, and then he fell silent. Persephone murmured a few words in her husband's ear. Hades rose to his feet and said: "Orpheus, your courage, your love and your art have conquered us. I will grant you leave to do what no human being has ever had the right to do before: you shall take Eurydice with you back to the light. But only on one sole condition: do not turn around before you have departed from the Underworld.

Do not look at her before you are returned to the light, or you shall lose her for ever." A murmur rose from the throng of assembled shades. A murmur of surprise, but also of hope: if Eurydice could return to life, why not they also? "Leave now; Eurydice will follow you," said Hades.

Mad with joy, Orpheus stammered his thanks and set off hastily on the journey back. Hermes accompanied him. Orpheus could hardly believe his happiness.

"How is it possible? So have I really succeeded?" he would cry to Hermes.

"But of course, of course, calm down now," Hermes would reply.

Orpheus was burning with impatience, he wanted to turn round and take his wife in his arms. "Hermes, you are quite sure that she is following us? Tell me, Hermes, can you see her?" Orpheus would say, losing patience.

And this is how it went for the entire journey. They climbed into Charon's boat, who was astounded to see one of the dead going out again. Once they had reached the other side, Orpheus leapt out of the boat, while Hermes stayed a little behind to talk with Charon. Only a few paces remained before their exit from the Underworld. They could already make out the light of day.

Yet Orpheus was in doubt. What if Hades had tricked him? What if it wasn't Eurydice who had followed him? He reached the light and, unable to restrain himself any longer, he turned round to look at his wife. Alas! Eurydice had not completed the journey; she was still under the shadow of the dead. Orpheus had looked at her... He just had time enough to see her whole, as she stretched out her arms towards him in a gesture of despair, and then she disappeared in the Underworld for all eternity.

A few moments later, Hermes came out in his turn. He discovered Orpheus sprawled on the grass, weeping. He immediately understood what had just happened and a great anger seethed up inside him. No! This was far too unfair! Hermes needed to understand. Love had been stronger, it had vanquished every obstacle. Who was it who determined life and death in this manner? He made up his mind to return to Pausania and penetrate the mysteries of men's fate.

To be continued...

ϵPISODϵ 63

IN WHICH HERMES DISCOVERS THE EXISTENCE OF THE MOIRAE

Previously: Thanks to the power of his love, Orpheus has succeeded in getting permission to bring Eurydice back to life. But he looked at her too soon, before she had come out of the Underworld. And now he has just lost her for ever. Hermes wishes to understand who determines the fate of men and he goes back to see Pausania.

"Look at you, how you've grown!" said old Pausania when she saw Hermes appear at the end of the road. "So this is why you don't come to see me any more... You already have the answers to all your questions."

"Oh, no, good nurse," sighed Hermes, "I always have questions which keep turning and turning in my head. The more things I see, the more I understand, and the more questions I have."

Pausania smiled: "The day when you shall no longer have questions in your head will be a very sad day for you."

The messenger of the gods looked at Pausania's wrinkled face and a profound serenity settled in him. *She* was wisdom itself and she was going to help him see.

"Dear Pausania," he asked her, "why are there men and women who die just as their lives have barely begun? Please, I would like to know who decides the life and the death of human beings."

Pausania raised her hand to draw the head of the young god onto her lap, as she was wont to do to lull him to sleep, and she said: "Come, we will pay a visit to the three Moirae. You will understand."

When Hermes reopened his eyes, he did not know where he was. This place was neither house nor cave, and yet he could not see the sky.

"Where are we?" he whispered in Pausania's ear.

"No one knows that, my child. It is a mystery..." answered the old nurse gently. "Look!"

Very close nearby, three women were sitting with their backs turned to them. They all three wore long white dresses made out of a soft and light fabric, similar to a spider's web. Their long, loose white hair almost touched the ground. They did not speak to one another, yet Hermes could guess that their hands never stopped fiddling about. From time to time, one of them would rise, always the same one. She would approach an immense wall on which signs had been engraved. She would indicate one of the signs with a pointed stick which she held in her hand and she would return to her seat. At that, the hands of the three old women seemed to grow restless once more. Hermes observed this strange scene for a long moment. He could understand nothing as yet, but everything about the attitude of these three women fascinated him.

"Let us approach," murmured Pausania. When he discovered the faces of the three old women, Hermes' surprise was immense: all three had wide-open white eyes—for they were blind. The one who stood up regularly seemed to be the youngest of the three. "She is called Clotho," Pausania told him. "Look, the long, pointed stick that she is holding is a spindle, a spindle similar to the ones that you have seen on earth in the hands of shepherdesses spinning wool. This spindle too can serve to make yarn, but the yarn that Clotho fabricates is the thread of each man's life." Clotho had risen and was pointing with her spindle at a sign engraved on the great wall. Seeing Hermes' interrogating gaze, Pausania continued with her explanations. "Here is the list of the names of every human being. Once a man comes into the world, his name is engraved on this great wall. And after that Clotho fabricates the thread of his life. She then passes the thread to her sister Lachesis. Look, Lachesis is taking the thread and measuring it with her ruler. She is the one who determines the length of each life. You see, there are some very long threads and also some which are very short." Hermes did not take his eyes off the thin white fingers of the two sisters. He saw with great emotion the thread of a life being born, he saw it being stretched and stretched until it reached the length chosen by Lachesis. It was then that the third old woman intervened. She was the smallest of the three and yet appeared to be the eldest. Her stern face, her open eyes with their blank stare frightened Hermes. He would have preferred not to look at her any more and yet he could not stop himself from doing so, as though it were impossible to escape the eldest of the three Moirae. "This one is Atropos," whispered Pausania in his ear. She did not have to explain what Atropos did; Hermes had just understood. Once Clotho had finished spinning a life's thread, Lachesis measured its length and passed it afterwards to Atropos, who took her long scissors and snipped it. Each time that the cruel scissors of Atropos cut a thread too short, Hermes felt a pinch in his heart.

The air was glacially cold and Hermes shivered. He stayed there for a very long time looking at the three Moirae spinning the destiny of each man. This was where Atropos had severed with a clean snip of her scissors the so very short thread of Eurydice's life, a thread too short for her life to continue beyond that accursed day when the snake had bitten her. Hermes would have wanted to go near the wall where all the names of mankind were engraved, but Pausania held him back. "No, don't go! No one must know the name of a man before the time of his birth! It is time to go back now." Before leaving, Hermes could not keep himself from reading one name in passing, that of the man whose life-thread Clotho was spinning. He was called Perseus.

To be continued...

EPISODE 64

*Previously: Hermes has discovered the three Moirae,
those who determine the lives of men. They are
three sisters: one spins the thread of life, the other
measures it and the third cuts it. The last man whose
thread they have fabricated is called Perseus.*

After leaving Pausania, Hermes set off once more for Olympus. He had already been journeying for some time and was flying above the sea when he detected a crate floating on the surface of the waves. Night was falling, and the crate was hardly visible, tossed about as it was by the currents. Hermes was drawn by a strange noise coming from it. It sounded like a child's laughter. Intrigued, Hermes approached the crate. Imagine his surprise when he heard not one but two human voices coming out of it!

The first, that of a woman, scolded gently: "You oughtn't to laugh like this, my son, your grandfather had us thrown into the sea so we would drown!"

The other voice, that of a child, replied, laughing: "Then, mother, the fish will teach us how to swim! And what is more, didn't you tell me that Zeus, the god of gods, was my father? He will surely come to our aid." And the boy dissolved again into laughter.

Hermes gave a little jump when he heard this. Why didn't Zeus intervene to save his son in danger? Hermes could well remember that Zeus had promised his wife Hera not to increase the family of the gods any more, yet this was no reason to let this youngster and his mother die.

Winds ever stronger and more violent agitated the sea. Each wave threatened to sink the crate in which the child and his mother were locked up. Hermes had to act fast. He decided to warn his uncle Poseidon about this. Poseidon agreed to intervene right away, and two of his servants, two Tritons, half-men, half-fish, emerged from the ocean depths and pulled the crate away from the storm. While the Tritons were towing the crate towards the shore, Hermes listened to what the mother and the child were saying to each other. From the depths of the crate, a lullaby rose softly. Hermes was touched to hear the mother sing like this to put her child to sleep. He thought of his own mother, Maia, and tears came to his eyes. "Sleep well, my little Perseus," murmured the mother. Perseus? So this, then, was Perseus! Hermes smiled into the night.

Rosy-fingered Aurora came at last and chased away the night. The Tritons deposited the wooden crate on a beach and disappeared. Hermes went to knock at the door of a fisherman's house not too far away from this beach. A good man called Dictys lived there with his wife, both left childless. Awakened by the noise, Dictys and his wife were astonished to find no one at their doorstep. Yet they immediately saw the crate and they went quickly to open it. Dictys broke it with his axe and watched with surprise as a young woman and her child emerged from it.

"I am called Danae, and this is Perseus," she said in a trembling voice.

"Welcome to our house," said the fisherman's wife. "Come and revive yourselves and stay for as long as you like." The child sprang to his feet and burst into laughter.

"How the deuce did you come to find yourselves imprisoned in that crate?" asked the old fisherman, once the young woman and her son had warmed themselves up again.

Danae gave a faint smile: "It's quite hard to believe this," she murmured, "but it is my own father, Acrisius, who is to blame for this. The oracles had predicted to him that I would have a son who would one day kill him. So he locked me up in a tower of bronze, without either doors or windows. But this tower also had no roof, so that I might have some air and light. And one day, seeing my sadness and my misery, Zeus paid me a visit under the guise of a rain of gold. This is how my son was conceived, a real joy to me, such a merry, happy child, Oh, if only you knew! At first, my father did not notice anything. Then one day he heard Perseus' laughter echo against the bronze and he discovered his grandson's existence. Seething with rage, he had us locked up in this wooden crate and thrown in the open sea, as far as possible from every shore."

Hermes had heard it all. He could feel his anger rising against Acrisius. "Another old king who clings to his crown no matter what it takes," he thought. In the poor fisherman's house there were peals of laughter. It was Perseus, who was having fun playing with the cat.

Hermes went away telling himself that the boy should be left to grow in peace. Yet he promised himself to take Perseus under his protection. Because he could already foresee that a life of exceptional adventures lay in store for him.

To be continued...

ΕPISODE 65

IN WHICH PERSEUS PUTS HIMSELF
IN A PERILOUS POSITION

*Previously: Hermes saved young Perseus and
his mother from the waters when they had
been locked up in a wooden crate and thrown
into the sea by Perseus' own grandfather. Both
the mother and the child have been received
into the home of a fisherman and his wife.*

he years have passed, Perseus has grown. He has become
a handsome young man, strong and brave. On this island,
however, where he had been so warmly welcomed, an enemy is
lying in wait for him. The king of the island has fallen in love
with his mother, the beautiful Danae. This king is a brute and
Danae does not want to be his wife. She refuses to marry him,
claiming that she must stay with her son to look after him.
King Polydectes, however, has no intention of giving up on this
marriage. So he decides to get rid of Perseus. He invites him to
dine at the palace, planning to set a trap for him.

That evening, Perseus is among the first guests to arrive at the palace. All the young men on the island had been invited and they rejoiced in advance at the idea of having a really good time. Perseus' good looks did not pass unnoticed. The maidservants whispered with admiration as he passed and the young man noted this with pleasure. Because he really liked to please and to be noticed. The more the evening progressed, the more Perseus talked and laughed loud. The wine flowed in currents and he never ceased to drink, and to drink even more. Presiding at the banquet, at the centre of the table, the king did not take his eyes off Perseus. Soon, the king rose and asked for everyone's silence. "Dear friends," he began, "it is with great pleasure that I welcome each of you in my house. Amuse yourselves well! I would like to thank all those of you who have brought me gifts. You, Lycos, for this magnificent black horse which is pawing the ground outside my door. You, Nepumenus, for this splendid grey mare. And you, Aristos, for this golden-eyed colt, which shall be the pride of my stables." The king addressed himself in turn to all the guests present around the table. Most of them, knowing his passion for horses, had offered him a new one.

The others had brought him gems or precious objects. As he heard the list of gifts, Perseus began to blush. He was too poor; he had come empty-handed. His turn was about to come and he felt crushed by shame. So as not to lose face, the proud young man leapt into the middle of the room before his name had even been pronounced. Wine and the thrill of the moment were making his head spin.

He shouted: "I, Perseus, the son of Danae, shall bring you the most extraordinary gift of all. I shall offer you the head of Medusa, the terrible Gorgon."

A murmur ran through the assembled guests. The Gorgons were three monstrous creatures who spread the reign of terror. These three repugnant sisters had, instead of hair, a multitude of serpents swarming on their heads. Above all, however, they transformed into stone any man who dared to look at them, even if it were only for an instant.

The king was delighted: his trap had worked. He had had strong hopes that Perseus, exasperated, would do something foolish. He said, smiling:

"Very well, my dear Perseus. Leave then at once and fetch me that Gorgon's head."

Perseus had made himself the centre of everyone's attention. Yet he had also just thrown himself into an adventure fraught with danger, for no one had ever come out alive from an encounter with the Gorgon.

Perseus went outside. The cold night wind lashed his face. Little by little he regained his spirits. His pride had made him throw himself right into the wolf's mouth. Without some help from the gods, he would never be able to pull through this one. He had been walking along the beach with his head bowed for quite some time, when someone laid a hand on his shoulder. It was Hermes, who had come to offer his assistance to his young protégé.

"I am Hermes, your half-brother," the god said to him.

"I could tell," replied Perseus, "there is no one else but you who wears a winged helmet and sandals."

They both sat on a rock. "I heard everything. Do you know where the Gorgons live?" asked Hermes.

Perseus shook his head mournfully: "Not even that!" he sighed.

"Well, in that case, you must first meet the Graeae. They are their sisters. They, and they alone, know where the Gorgons live. But be very careful, for they are as formidable themselves." As he leant over Perseus, Hermes really looked like an older brother advising the younger one. The moon was shedding a white light on them.

"You... will you come with me?" stammered Perseus, his voice hesitant all of a sudden. Nothing remained any more of the young braggart who had been boasting a few hours earlier in the king's palace.

Hermes smiled. He had not forgotten the laughter of the child shut up in the crate. "Yes," he replied, "I will accompany you."

They both decided to wait for dawn before setting out. They lay on the sand, huddling close to each other, and tried to get some rest.

To be continued...

€PISODE 66

IN WHICH PERSEUS MEETS
THREE HORRID OLD WOMEN

*Previously: Perseus has promised a king that he would
bring back to him the head of the Gorgon Medusa,
a terrible monster with a head bristling with snakes.
Hermes has come to join him and offer him his help.*

Perseus' meeting with Hermes had bolstered up his spirits, and he came to the mountain where the three Graeae lived feeling confident. The air was scalding hot and a cloud of dust rose at each step he took. The closer he approached, the more the landscape turned grey. The rays of the sun did not reach into this sinister region. The journey was long and painful. Yet each time he hesitated about which path to follow, Hermes would point him in the right direction. When he arrived at the cave of the three old women, he hid himself not too far from the entrance and waited. Soon he saw them appear. One could just barely make out their forms in the flickering light of a candle that one of them was carrying. They were horrible to look at. Their skin was yellow and wrinkled, like old crumpled paper. Their white hair fell in disarray over their shoulders, like skeins of string. And a foul smell exuded from their bodies, a smell of withered flowers and mustiness which stung one's throat.

"It is my turn to look! Pass me the eye!" said one of them in a harsh, metallic voice.

"No! It's my turn!" replied the other old woman, in an equally rasping tone.

"I am hungry, so give me the tooth!" cried the third sister.

Perseus then saw the one who had spoken first take out her solitary tooth and hand it to her sister. In the meantime, the second removed her solitary eye and passed it to the third sister. The three sisters shared a single eye and a single tooth among them. Perseus observed the three old women playing this game of pass the parcel; then he did as Hermes advised. As one of them was removing her eye to give it to one of the other two, he leapt forward and snatched the eye. The three Graeae could no longer see a thing! They began to shout and argue among themselves to find out which had taken the eye, but Perseus interrupted them and said in a strong voice: "It is I, Perseus, who holds your eye. If you wish me to give it back to you, show me the way that will lead me to your sisters the Gorgons." After a moment of bewilderment, the Graeae gave him all the directions he needed to reach the den where their horrible sisters were hiding. Perseus hesitated as to whether he ought to give them back the eye. Yet he had promised and he had to keep his word. He returned the eye to them and departed immediately.

Hermes had left him a little earlier and Perseus was now travelling alone.

"Well done, Perseus, continue like this, I am proud of you and I will help you too."

Who was speaking like this in Perseus' ear? Where did this congratulatory voice come from? Surprised, the young man stopped walking. He said rather nervously:

"But... But who are you? Show yourself!"

He heard a little laughter. Then a woman appeared on his path. She bore a helmet and a spear and she stood proudly erect in her armour. Perseus recognized immediately the goddess Athena.

"You are a brave young man," she said. "I know that my brother Hermes protects you but I would like to help you as well. After all, we all have the same father, don't we?" Intimidated by the great goddess, Perseus gave no answer. She approached him and held her shield out to him. "You know this already: any person who meets Medusa's gaze is transformed into stone. Take my shield. When you are in the presence of Medusa, turn the shield towards you, and use it as a mirror. You will be able to see her reflection on it. In this way, you can fight her without ever looking at her straight in the face."

Perseus took Athena's shield. It shone like the sun. When he lifted up his dazzled head to thank the goddess, she had already vanished...

To be continued...

EPISODE 67

IN WHICH PERSEUS FACES THE GORGONS

*Previously: Perseus has used his cunning and has
succeeded in finding out where the Gorgons are hiding.
Athena has offered him her shield so that he may confront
Medusa without looking at her straight in the face.*

Perseus was walking sure-footed towards the den of the three
monsters, but Hermes did not feel so easy in his mind. That's
why he had gone away: to seek help. Soon enough, he rejoined
Perseus along the way, carrying a huge sack on his shoulder.

Hermes asked him: "Are you quite sure that you have
everything you need in order to win?"

With the insouciance of his youth, Perseus answered: "Oh,
well, we'll see when we get there!"

Hermes shook his head unhappily and sat on a rock. All of
a sudden he, the spirited and impulsive young god, was feeling
much more sensible than Perseus. "Perhaps as a result of learning
more things and of discovering the world," he mulled, "I am
becoming a little wiser?" He took the sack he had been carrying

on his shoulder and threw it over to the young man. "Catch this bag, you might need it. You will find inside the helmet which makes one invisible, the one belonging to my uncle Hades, the king of the Underworld. I borrowed it from him. There is also a long and mighty sword, a sword so sturdy that even the Gorgons' thick, hard skin will not be able to withstand it. As for the sack itself, it is magical: it takes the form of whatever you slip inside it." Then he slowly took off his shoes and held out the winged sandals to Perseus. "I will lend these to you as well. You can return everything to me later."

This time, Perseus was properly armed to wage battle against the Gorgons. Happy as a child in front of new toys, he put on the winged sandals, drew the long sword out of its scabbard, grabbed hold of Athena's shield and put on the helmet of Hades. He instantly became invisible and flew away towards the Gorgons' den. "Do not forget," Hermes cried after him, "you can only kill Medusa. She is the only one of the three Gorgons who can die, the other two are immortal, do not attack them!" Perseus, however, was already far away. Hermes' words were lost in the wind. The messenger god decided to follow the young man in order to keep an eye on him.

The Gorgons lived on an icy island battered by raging winds. Perseus flew first of all across the ocean, until he noticed an island with beautiful cold and deserted beaches. There he discovered an absolutely incredible landscape and he knew that he was approaching the Gorgons' lair. There were animals of every kind and some men as well. But as he approached, he realized that these were statues of stone. Each had met the gaze of one of the

Gorgons and had been immediately transformed into a statue! Perseus landed and began to walk amidst the statues of stone. He was touched by the fate of all these wretched creatures and his anger rose up inside him. When he reached the cave where the Gorgons lived, they were all three asleep. Perseus observed them on Athena's shield, which served him as a mirror. They were even more appalling than anything Perseus had been able to imagine. Their heads were aswarm with snakes writhing in every direction and their necks were covered with dragon scales. They had enormous golden wings and their hands bore talons of bronze. He flew above the sleeping Gorgons, yet his hand was reluctant to strike. If he missed his target, what would happen once the monstrous sisters were awake? And, what is more, which of the three was Medusa? Hermes again came to his aid. He indicated Medusa to him with a motion of his hand. Perseus then brandished his heavy sword while keeping a keen eye on Medusa on the mirror-shield.

And Athena, who was also watching discreetly from the heights of Olympus, guided his hand. His magic sword came crashing down and lopped off Medusa's head with one clean blow. He came down immediately, grabbed the head, catching hold of it by its vile snake-hair, and slipped it inside his sack without looking at it. He had thus escaped the terrible gaze which turned people into stone.

Instantly, an incredible winged horse emerged from Medusa's body, by the name of Pegasus. For a moment Perseus stood there dazzled, his breath taken away by the winged horse's beauty. He stretched out his hand towards the animal to catch it, but the horse immediately flew away towards Olympus and disappeared from Perseus' sight.

In the meantime, the other two Gorgons had woken up and were getting ready to go after Medusa's murderer. Would Perseus manage to escape his pursuers?

To be continued...

ΣPISODE 68

IN WHICH PERSEUS SETS FREE A
BEAUTIFUL YOUNG WOMAN

Previously: Well armed by Hermes and Athena,
Perseus has succeeded in cutting off Medusa's head
without ever looking at her. But he must now flee as
swiftly as possible, pursued by Medusa's two sisters...

The winged sandals that Hermes had lent to Perseus were extraordinarily swift. And so he took flight. Behind him, the two Gorgons tore howling along. They screamed, spat, yelled with rage, threatened Perseus with a thousand cruel sufferings. But where had he gone? Perseus had just put back on the helmet that made him invisible. And soon enough they had to abandon their chase, for they couldn't see him anywhere. Perseus was wild with joy to have succeeded in such an exploit.

The day rose. Perseus came in sight of a black, rocky coast bounded by crystalline blue water. Suddenly a sun ray revealed to him an extraordinary sight. A naked young woman was chained to an enormous rock right by the sea. She was so beautiful, with her dark skin and its shimmering reflections, and her hair floating in the wind, that Perseus fell instantly in love with her. He drew nearer. She remained motionless and stared hard at the sea while silent tears ran down her cheeks.

"What are you doing here chained like this?" asked Perseus.

The young woman gave a little jump when she saw him appear. "I am called Andromeda and I am the only daughter of the king of Ethiopia," she murmured. "And I am waiting for the sea monster who is supposed to come and devour me."

Perseus could not believe his ears. "But what have you done to deserve such a horrid fate?" he exclaimed.

"I? Nothing!" Andromeda sighed. "But my mother is so proud of me that she declared everywhere that I was the most beautiful of all. She even dared say that I was more beautiful than the sea nymphs. The nymphs became vexed and asked Poseidon, the god of the Seas, to avenge them." Andromeda stopped speaking. She was staring hard at the horizon and Perseus followed her gaze. He saw something writhing on the sea surface. And this something was coming closer and closer. He felt the young girl shake like a leaf. "This is it! This is it!" she cried. "This horrid sea monster ravages everything in its passage. It makes my father's people suffer, devours the fishermen and their boats. And I must be sacrificed to it to placate its anger..."

The monster was just a few feet away from Andromeda. You could see its gaping mouth and its scaly skin. Its pointed tail thrashed the waves, splattering the sky with spume. Its enormous torso cut through the water like a ship sailing at full speed. Perseus unsheathed his magic sword and, with a kick of his winged sandals, landed on the monster's spine. Then he thrust his sword into the monster's shoulder. Surprised, the monster bucked. Yet Perseus did not lose his balance. Three times his sword came crashing down, and three times the sharp blade gashed the monster's neck. A torrent of blood was flowing out now, dyeing the sea red. The monster lowed; then, after having squirmed in every direction, it gave up the fight and let itself sink to the bottom of the sea. Perseus barely had time to withdraw his sword and fly away again. On the shore, a symphony of applause burst out. The country's inhabitants were arriving in all haste to hail the hero who had defeated the monster and rescued their princess. Among those enthusiastic spectators was also Hermes. He had watched his protégé with keen attention, ready to intervene if things went awry. But he was proud of Perseus: he had known how to manage on his own.

Perseus paid no attention to his public. He had hurried to Andromeda and with a stroke of his magic sword had severed the chains which held her prisoner. Andromeda's parents rushed forward and took her in their arms. But Andromeda pulled herself free and turned smiling towards Perseus. She opened her arms and the young man held her fast against his heart. The marriage of the two young people in love was decided immediately. Hermes looked smilingly at Perseus as he was led in triumph to the palace of Andromeda's father, then he decided to return to Olympus. Yet he heard behind him something which troubled him. A voice in the crowd had just said: "I'll kill that Perseus!" Hermes jerked round sharply but there were too many people around him. He could not discover who had uttered that threat. He therefore decided to follow the crowd to the palace in order to try to find out who could possibly wish to harm Perseus.

To be continued…

EPISODE 69

IN WHICH PERSEUS ESCAPES DEATH
AND PUNISHES HIS ENEMIES

*Previously: After having killed the Gorgon Medusa,
Perseus met Andromeda, a beautiful young girl
condemned to be devoured by a sea monster. He has killed
the monster and is getting ready to marry Andromeda.*

The palace of the king of Ethiopia was of great splendour, yet Perseus paid no attention to it. He was dazzled by a single beauty, that of Andromeda. A sumptuous banquet was being given to celebrate their wedding, but Perseus did not look either at the succulent dishes filing past, or at the great crowd of guests. He tasted neither the wine nor the music. He only had eyes for Andromeda. And this is how he did not come to notice a man arriving at the banqueting hall accompanied by a squadron of armed men. This man was a cousin of the king to whom Andromeda had been promised in marriage. He was called Phineas. He drew his sword abruptly from its scabbard and began to taunt Perseus. Addressing himself to the guests, he shouted:

"*Who* is this stranger who comes to steal the most beautiful women of our country?" Then, turning towards the young groom, he yelled: "Perseus, you are not from these parts, you are not worthy of Andromeda! Go back where you came from!"

Hermes, who had slipped in among the guests, heard murmurs: "He is right!" someone said. "This foreigner should leave our princess alone!" added another.

Perseus' position was shaky. Yet he answered sarcastically: "You love her well now, your princess, but when I found her, chained to a rock, there was no one by her side! You, the great swaggerer, who now come to claim her, did *you* have the courage to rescue her from the monster's claws?"

By way of an answer, Phineas hurled his spear at Perseus. The spear planted itself right at the feet of the young man, who immediately drew his sword. A battle ensued. The clangour of arms replaced the wedding music. The soldiers of the king defended Perseus and Andromeda, but the friends of Phineas were numerous. Soon blood began to flow instead of wine. So Perseus shouted: "Those who are my friends, turn your eyes away now!" And he took out of his sack Medusa's horrid head. Instantly, the company of Phineas and those guests who had rallied to his side were transformed into statues of stone. They stood there, frozen in the position they were in. Reassured, Hermes then returned to Olympus to get some rest, for his young protégé had adventures which were quite exhausting even for a god!

Perseus was happy living with his wife, yet he was dying to return home. He was worried about his mother Danae, whom he had left behind while that appalling king of the island wished to make her his wife. And what if the king had succeeded in forcing her to marry him? He had a ship built and he decided to take Andromeda home with him.

When he arrived on the island, the young couple went to the house of Dictys, the fisherman who had rescued Perseus and his mother. But alas, he found Dictys and his wife plunged in deep sorrow. The two old people welcomed him with tears, happy to find him alive, but despairing about Danae's fate.

"What has happened to mummy? Speak! Is she dead?" cried Perseus.

"No, thanks be to the gods, but the king pursued her so persistently that in order to escape him she had to seek refuge in the temple of Athena. Since then, she cannot come out unless she agrees to marry him."

Boiling with rage, Perseus hurried to the king's palace. He entered the throne room like a whirlwind. Seeing him burst in like this, the king gave a sneering laugh:

"Well, well, here is Perseus, the great Perseus, Perseus the valiant! We believed you dead, my little one, after all this time," he scoffed. "So, then, have you brought me back the head of the Gorgon Medusa, as promised?"

At these words the entire company broke into an enormous laughter. But Perseus, white with rage, replied:

"Now you mention it, here it is!" And he took Medusa's head out from his sack. The king did not even have time to let out a cry—he was turned into stone. A scowl of surprise and fear was branded on his sculptured face. He had been punished.

All those who were in a circle around him were petrified at the same moment.

Once rid of this cruel tyrant, Perseus ran to the temple of Athena. "Mother!" he cried. Danae turned around. Perseus clasped her tight in his arms. Then he placed the sack containing the Gorgon's head at the feet of the statue of Athena, together with the shield. From that day on, Athena would always bear on her shield the image of that head swarming with snakes. Perseus put his arms around his mother's shoulders and led her gently out into the light of day. It was over! He would never let anyone make her suffer again.

To be continued...

EPISODE 70

IN WHICH PERSEUS' DESTINY IS FULFILLED

*Previously: Perseus has returned to the island
of Seriphos, where he has turned into stone the
king who was tyrannizing his mother.*

Calm had returned to the island. Perseus had no desire
to become king. He had installed upon the throne the
old fisherman Dictys and his wife. They were good and wise
people, and they would bring prosperity to the inhabitants.
Each morning, Perseus left the arms of his wife Andromeda and
went to the beach where he had met Hermes. And he waited.
He waited patiently for an hour, two hours, and then he went
away again. At last, one day, as he watched the horizon keenly,
he saw the messenger god appear.

"You have been waiting for me?" Hermes asked, astonished.

Without replying, Perseus smiled and held out to him his
winged sandals.

"You had only lent them to me," he said. He also returned
to Hermes the magic sword and the helmet of invisibility. "I

no longer need these now. I can handle things on my own. But don't abandon me altogether. I still have one thing I need to accomplish. I wish to meet my grandfather Acrisius. I know that he threw us into the sea, mummy and me, because someone had predicted that one day I would kill him. But I have no intention of doing so. I don't bear any grudge against him. I just want to meet him. What do you think?"

Hermes took the helmet, the sword and the sandals and sat on the sand. He then spoke the words that Pausania had said to him one day and which he had never forgotten:

"In order to understand who you are, you must first know where you come from."

Hermes' words rang inside Perseus' head as he returned to his house absorbed in thought. His mind was made up, he would go and meet his grandfather Acrisius. Perseus took to the sea once more and set course towards his grandfather's kingdom. When he arrived full of joy at the doors of Acrisius' palace, news of his arrival had preceded him. Panic had seized Acrisius when he was told that his grandson was alive; convinced that he was now coming to see him in order to seek revenge, he had taken flight. Perseus was about to enter the palace portal when he saw a chariot drawn by three powerful horses leaving in all haste.

"Make way for the king! Make way for the king!" shouted the guards.

"Hey! Wait for me!" shouted Perseus. "I am Perseus, your grandson!"

Upon hearing these words, Acrisius urged on his horses even harder. Perseus barely had time to see his face as the chariot disappeared far away in the distance, enveloped in a cloud of dust. Perseus ran to buy a horse and followed his grandfather's trail.

This is how he arrived a few days later in a city. It was very difficult for him to find the old king, for the streets were flooded by great throngs of people.

"What is happening here?" Perseus asked.

"Don't you know, stranger?" they answered him. "Our king is organizing great athletic games. Come see our heroes in the stadium."

For all that he had grown, Perseus still remained the young man who loved to have fun and above all to shine and to be admired. He decided that the search for his grandfather could wait and he put his name down for the games. No one knew Perseus, but he quickly emerged as the best of all the contestants. First of all he won the foot race. Then he carried away the victory at wrestling. The spectators cried: "Perseus! Perseus! Long Live Perseus!" The young man radiated with pleasure. In the crowd, an old man lowered his head so as not to be recognized. It was Acrisius, who hoped to pass unnoticed in the midst of all these people. Perseus, ecstatic with joy, could see that he was going to be crowned champion of the games. There was only the discus event left for him to win. He threw the heavy discus with skill and precision. Soon there were only two contestants. Perseus threw his discus one more time. All of a sudden, a brisk and violent gust of wind turned the discus away from its target and made it land among the crowd. One spectator received the heavy projectile full on the head and died on the spot. Perseus hurried to him. The victim was Acrisius, his own grandfather.

At that instant, someone came out of the crowd and put his arms around the shoulders of the devastated young man. He helped him stand up again, dried his tears and tried to console him. "You were not responsible, Perseus. It was an accident. It was also your destiny." That someone was none other than Hermes. He had followed him unseen. He accompanied him back to his homeland and returned him to the arms of Andromeda. He did not worry about the prospects of his young protégé. By questioning the pebbles which allowed him to foretell the future, Hermes had seen him found a great city which would be very powerful one day, a city called Mycenae.

And he knew that Perseus and Andromeda would end their lives welcomed by the gods, who would place them as stars in the sky.

Hermes had learnt much by accompanying Perseus on all his adventures. Yet one question remained unanswered in his mind: what had become of the magnificent winged horse Pegasus, born of the Gorgon's blood?

To be continued...

EPISODE 71

IN WHICH HERMES MEETS UP AGAIN WITH PEGASUS, THE WINGED HORSE

Previously: Perseus has accidentally killed his grandfather. Hermes has decided to take him back to his homeland and then their paths separate. He wonders what could have become of Pegasus.

Hermes was flying languidly, letting himself be carried by the air currents. He had for once no errand to carry out, no letter to deliver, no dead person to accompany to the Underworld, and he was offering himself a well-deserved break of daydreaming. As he lay on a cloud, eyes staring blankly into the distance, he suddenly saw a small white dot descending from Olympus and heading towards the earth. The white dot grew bigger and Hermes could soon make out two immense white wings. He thought that he had seen Pegasus, the winged horse occupying his thoughts. But soon the white dot and the two wings were hidden away by a cloud. Undoubtedly, it had been but a dream... But in order to make sure, Hermes got up from his cloud and flew towards where the white dot had disappeared. He landed on earth, just below the cloud. There was a fountain there. Fine lush green grass grew in front of it. Hermes' heart gave a leap: there, in the middle of this grassy patch, was Pegasus, grazing serenely. The magnificent horse with the white wings had descended from the sky to eat this exquisite grass and to drink this pure water.

Hermes was still admiring the animal when he discovered the presence of another admirer, hidden away in the shadows. It was a young boy, barely fifteen years old. The boy's hair bristled. He held a golden bridle in his hand. "How about that!" murmured Hermes. "This is the bridle of Athena's horse! Why did my sister give her bridle to this child?" He did not have the time to ask himself more questions, for the boy had just come out of the shadows. The horse reared up its head sharply. It shook its mane and neighed violently. Its every muscle was tense, it was about to bolt, when the boy held the golden bridle out to him.

"Pegasus, do not go! I am called Bellerophon. I am the son of the king of Corinth. I have dreamt of you so much, day and night, for such a long time, that Athena took pity on me on account of my passion, and she gave me this bridle of gold, the only harness that you could ever tolerate. Do not go away!" The horse neighed one more time and now it sounded like a neigh of delight. Hermes saw something incredible happen: Pegasus let the child pass the bridle around its neck and it even went down on its knees to allow the boy to climb on its back! A quarter of an hour later, the whole world could see the proud Bellerophon astride Pegasus, turning mad somersaults in the sky. Hermes, a trifle jealous, returned to Olympus without wasting more time.

But Bellerophon, who had succeeded in taming the untameable Pegasus, was drunk with pride. He decided to set himself a new challenge: he was going to kill the Chimera. This was a monster with the body of a goat, a serpent's tail and a lion's head. She belched forth flames and everywhere the Chimera went, people died, the flocks disappeared, the fields and the houses burned down. On the back of his winged horse, Bellerophon felt king of the world. He thought himself invincible. He therefore set off immediately.

From the heights of Olympus, leaning against the parapet of the palace terrace, Zeus was observing the earth. By his side, Hermes grumbled:

"I don't understand why my sister Athena has offered this boy the privilege of being the only one to ride on Pegasus' back!"

Zeus flashed a smile: "You wouldn't be jealous now, Hermes? You already have wings on your feet, what need do you have of those of a horse? Stay here with me; we are going to watch from above how Bellerophon will pull through this. You don't like him? He amuses me. I like men who are audacious. Look, here he is, already approaching the Chimera..."

To be continued...

EPISODE 72

*Previously: The young Bellerophon has succeeded in
taming Pegasus, the winged horse. But today he has
set his mind on killing the monstrous Chimera.*

The Chimera was drawing closer to Bellerophon, its mouth
agape, its tail swishing; slowly the hair on the young man's
head stood up on end. He had just seen her swallow in the
fraction of a second an entire herd of well-fattened cows. He
had just seen her belch a long burst of flames and set an entire
little wood afire. Bellerophon stroked the winged horse's neck
to give himself courage; then he took his spear and made a
sign to Pegasus to take off. The monster was utterly surprised
to see Pegasus and his rider appear from the sky above. When
it received the first spear blow from Bellerophon, it let out a
scream of pain, turned towards them a head livid with rage
and spewed out fire. With a mighty flapping of his wings,
however, Pegasus was already far away in the heavens. The

horse nosedived down several times to attack the monster. Bellerophon would plunge his weapon and then he would immediately get himself out of range. The Chimera's blood flowed liberally, yet she fought relentlessly. That was when the fire disgorged by the monster touched the tip of Bellerophon's spear, which was covered with lead. This heavy metal melted under the effect of the heat, detached itself from the lance and fell on the Chimera's head. The piece of lead killed the Chimera clean on the spot. Pegasus turned a joyful somersault in the sky and Bellerophon let out a triumphant yell which rang all the way to Olympus: "*I am the stroooooongest!*" Zeus placed his hands over his ears and said to Hermes, who was still leaning on his elbows against the parapet next to him: "He does not lack either pluck or courage, but he is beginning to get on my nerves with his presumptuousness."

Hermes did not reply; he was not even listening to him. His gaze had been drawn to a completely different part of the earth. Instead of following the combat between Bellerophon and the Chimera, Hermes could not take his eyes off a ravishing young girl bathing under a waterfall. The water was streaming down her body and the droplets remained attached to her curly hair like so many pearls. She was humming a tune and the notes rose high in the warm breath of summer, exquisite and pure. Hermes had never felt such an emotion before. He was overwhelmed by it. Astonished by his son's uncustomary silence, Zeus had turned his head and he was contemplating the sight as well.

"You have good taste, my son," he said. "She is ravishing."

Hermes started as though he had been caught red-handed. He stammered: "And... and what... what has happened to Bellerophon?"

Zeus repressed a smile under his beard before answering: "Like many men, alas, he's lost his good sense. His triumph has gone to his head. Look, he is trying to convince Pegasus to bring him here."

For the first time, Pegasus was refusing to obey Bellerophon. "Take me to Olympus, my good steed," he implored. "I have well earned the right to know the house of the gods. You saw how strong I am, didn't you? I am every bit as good as a god, no?" But Pegasus refused to obey. So Bellerophon ceased to beg and he now commanded: "That's enough! I demand that you take me to Zeus. I am sufficiently superior to all other men to be the equal of a god. I am entitled to it. I have the golden reins of Athena, you must obey me." Pegasus cast a very long glance at the young man, a sad, reproachful glance. But he had no choice. He had to obey the reins of Athena. Slowly, the sublime horse ascended into the heaven above. Bellerophon laughed, drunk with joy.

He was still laughing when they reached Olympus. Zeus was watching from high up on the terrace. He let out a sigh and murmured: "What a pity, I had rather taken a liking to him..." Then he shouted with a thunderous voice: "Here is what you get, little man, for daring to compare yourself to the gods!" And the master of Olympus sent his thunderbolt towards the winged horse. The animal jolted aside to avoid the lightning bolt. Bellerophon lost his balance, slipped and went crashing all the way down to the earth. Pegasus let out a long neigh of woe and returned to Zeus' stables. "Well, the little braggart has now been punished, my son," said Zeus, turning towards Hermes. But where had Hermes gone? Zeus was all of a sudden alone on the terrace.

Down there, all the way down on earth, Hermes was experiencing his first romance, with the beautiful Antianeira.

To be continued...

EPISODE 73

IN WHICH HERMES LIVES HIS FIRST LOVE

Previously: Bellerophon was so conceited that he thought himself equal to the gods and had demanded that Pegasus take him to Olympus. In order to punish him for his overweening pride, Zeus struck him with his thunderbolt. In the meantime, Hermes has fallen in love for the first time...

Antianeira's hair attracted Hermes irresistibly. It was like soft, silky moss and Hermes longed to plunge his fingers into it. He had left Olympus in order to get closer to the young girl and since then, hiding behind a tree, he had not stopped observing her. She had finished shaking herself under the waterfall, had wrung her hair dry and had thrown herself down on the tall grass. She was letting herself dry in the sun, sighing with happiness. Hermes was gazing at the little drops shining on her skin like so many sparks of precious stones and he wished this moment might never end.

Yet the chariot of the sun was already completing its course. Evening was falling, Antianeira was shivering. She sprang to her feet. Suddenly Hermes was afraid that she would disappear and the very idea seemed unbearable to him. Without a second thought, he came out of his hiding place. The young girl let out a faint scream of surprise and snatched her tunic smartly to cover her body. "Do not be afraid," murmured Hermes. And after that he did not know what to say. He, the great talker, was at a loss for words! Antianeira opened her dark eyes wide but did not say anything either. They both stood there looking at each other. They instantly captured one another's hearts.

Once their words finally came back to them, neither could tell what they said to each other. Lovers' words are secret, meant for them alone. No one can share them. No one must hear them.

Night had fallen. Antianeira had rested her head on Hermes' shoulder and they were gazing at the stars together. Hermes discovered that all the happy experiences he had known so far were nothing compared to this warmth which burned his body, this tenderness which made his temples vibrate, this desire for her which inhabited him. He could sense Antianeira's face beside him and it was as though this face had always existed. So this was what they called love. At that moment, Hermes thought of the beautiful Maia, his mother, and of Zeus, his father. And he smiled in the darkness.

The following day, when he returned to Olympus, Hermes found it very difficult to think of anything else besides Antianeira. He got several of the messages that his father had asked him to deliver mixed up. He listened with such a distracted ear to his aunt Hestia that she stopped in the middle of a sentence without him noticing it... He even almost guided to the Underworld the soul of a man who was dying but was not yet dead! His mind was turned wholly towards his beloved. Would she love him for ever? Would he show himself worthy of her love? He discovered a new fear, an unknown one, that of losing this newborn love. For her part, Antianeira too was wholly taken by the thought of Hermes. When she decided to sit down and weave, as she did every day, she broke so many threads that her mother, exasperated, in the end sent her outside. Even the laughter and the games of her companions irritated her. Only the poems which some of them were reciting interested her, because they spoke of the emotions which unsettled the depths of her heart. Antianeira was counting the hours separating her from Hermes.

When, at the end of the day, finally free of their tasks, they rejoined one another, there was the same sense of enchantment. The two lovers never tired of speaking, of telling all about themselves to one another. And this happened each night anew. Little by little, Hermes began to look at the world differently, as though he were seeing it through her eyes. And he found the world even more beautiful. Little by little Antianeira began to look at the world through his eyes. And she found the world even greater.

This is how in the course of time they began to love one another. And this is how they felt the desire to beget a child.

One evening, Antianeira and Hermes had met up again on a beach. The young woman suddenly felt a strange wave rising inside her, a vibration, like someone's call. Surprised, she caught Hermes' hand and placed it on her belly.

"But what is the matter?" asked Hermes, bewildered.

"Shhh!" murmured Antianeira without letting go of his hand.

Long moments went by. All of a sudden, something quivered under Hermes' fingers. A life was signalling to him. Inside Antianeira's belly a child was moving. Hermes remained petrified. Antianeira on the other hand smiled, happy and confident. Yet he was trembling all over. Inside him a small voice was going mad: "Hermes, Hermes, what is happening here? *A dad?* Are you going to be a dad?"

To be continued...

EPISODE 74

IN WHICH HERMES BECOMES A DAD

Previously: Hermes has fallen in love for the first time and is having a beautiful romance with young Antianeira. They both desire a child, but Hermes wonders nervously whether he will know how to be a dad.

That morning, Hermes could not stay still. He pushed now one door, now another, entered the palace kitchen, came out again after having pinched a little nectar, bent down over a fountain and drank long gulps of ambrosia. Finally, he went to join his father in the great council hall. He gave a short, embarrassed cough, then asked:

"Hmm, Zeus, you who know everything, could you tell me what it is like to be a dad?" Startled, Zeus looked at his son. He had not noticed him grow up and he was astonished to find now by his side this handsome young man. "Well, *well?*" said Hermes, growing impatient.

But Zeus did not quite know what to answer... "A dad is, hmm, authority, a great deal of authority," he said to him. Vexed not to have found the right words, he sent Hermes away: "I have work to do, you know, I don't have time to chatter, go for a walk!"

Feeling rather snubbed, Hermes came across gentle Hestia in the corridor, the house mistress of the palace. "Hestia, sweet aunt, can you explain to me what it's like to be a dad?"

But Hestia was swamped. She had a pile of laundry in her arms and merely replied: "A dad? Hmm, it's a great deal of affection, nothing but affection!"

Hermes, getting more and more disconcerted, ran then into Aphrodite and dared to ask her his question. But the goddess of Beauty broke into a mocking laughter: "Oh look at the great clumsy ninny! I thought you were just having a nice love affair with Antianeira. You ought to know the answer... A dad is just love, nothing but love." And she left him alone and distraught in the corridor.

"Authority, affection, love," he muttered, "I will never know..."

At that moment the nymphs who accompanied Artemis, the goddess of Birth, came running. Hermes followed them as fast as he could. When he reached the earth, Antianeira was lying there on a bed of moss and fern. Her hair spread in a crown around her head, and the pallor of her face, the blackness of her eyes and the bright red of her lips moved Hermes deeply once more. By her side, with her back turned, stood Artemis. She turned round, holding in her hands two tiny children. She held them out to Hermes, saying: "Here are your sons!" Hermes gave a little jump: *two* babies! Antianeira had just brought into the world two babies! Artemis smiled and said to him: "Well, yes, they are twins, like Apollo and me!" Trembling, Hermes took the babies in his arms. The eyes of the child he was holding in his right arm sought his gaze. They found it. "He shall be called Echion," said Artemis. Hermes then turned his gaze towards the baby placed in his left arm. The child's eyes sought his gaze. They found it. "This one will be called Eurytus," said Artemis. Hermes turned from one child to the other and a great lump of emotion rose in his throat. So he, Zeus' little troublemaker, had become a father in his turn.

The two babies began all of a sudden to cry. Yet, and this was the incredible thing, their wailing was not ear-splitting, like the wailing of newborns—no, they were crying as though they were telling a story. They were crying as though they were already singing their story. Hermes knelt beside Antianeira. He delicately placed the twins in the cavity of her arms, accompanied his gesture with a kiss on her forehead and then he went away.

He needed to regain his inner calm. He needed to think. "I am a dad, I am a dad," he kept repeating to himself as he walked. "Am I the same person? Am I someone else?" Suddenly he was seized by a great anxiety. "But from now on I am responsible for them! What life will my children have? Oh, that nothing bad may ever happen to them!" With questions rioting in his head, Hermes came before a fountain. He bent down, picked up some pebbles and threw them into the water, just as the nurse had taught him to do, in order to read what would happen in Echion's and Eurytus' future.

Hermes stayed for a long time bent over the fountain. When he lifted his head up again, a smile had burgeoned on his lips. He had just learnt that Echion and Eurytus would take part in one of the greatest adventures of their time, the quest undertaken by a certain Jason for the Golden Fleece. He was proud to have discovered that such a future awaited his little ones. But already he was feeling anxious for them because of the dangers they would have to face. He had truly become a dad. And who was this Jason, that adventurer whom his sons were soon going to follow? And why did he wish to seize this Golden Fleece? Hermes promised himself that he would find out.

To be continued...

EPISODE 75

IN WHICH HERMES MAKES
ENQUIRIES ABOUT JASON

*Previously: Hermes has just become the father of
two boys, Echion and Eurytus. He discovers that
his sons will participate in Jason's expedition
to conquer the Golden Fleece and he decides
to find out a bit more about this Jason.*

Hermes set off on his quest for Jason and it wasn't long before
he picked up his trail. There was someone called Chiron
who lived up on a mountain. He had a body half-man, half-horse,
because he was a Centaur. What is more, he was the oldest and
the wisest of the Centaurs. He was so knowledgeable that the
most prestigious kings had chosen him as tutor for their sons.
He was a person of great renown. Not only did Chiron teach
his students music, poetry and all the arts, but he also taught
them how to be just men, good and brave. He made them into
great future kings. There was among his pupils a young man
who seemed to manifest exceptional talents; and that was Jason.

As he approached the cave where Chiron lived, Hermes discovered an astonishing scene. Five young boys were training in wrestling. They were scantily dressed, for all that the mountain was covered in snow. They rolled themselves in the snow as if they had been fighting on grass. Now and then Chiron would interpose in a loud voice: "Do not take advantage of your adversary's weakness, let him get up before resuming the fighting," he said to one. "No foul play, respect the rules of the game," he would tell another. Hermes observed them for a long moment, fascinated by the teacher's methods. He taught his students to respect one another, as well as to have confidence in themselves.

At last, Hermes approached and greeted Chiron with great deference. He said:

"Good morning, venerable teacher, I have just come to pay you my respects, for your renown has reached even my ears."

The old Centaur ran his fingers through his long white beard, and smiled:

"Your words do me honour, messenger god, I am but a modest tutor. Come along, and I will introduce you to my pupils." This is how Hermes found himself face to face with Jason. "This one was entrusted to me when he was four months old," explained Chiron. "Soon, he will be eighteen years old. He will be able to leave and go into the world. I have complete faith in him."

Hermes instantly liked the honesty in Jason's eyes. One could sense in that face a yearning for life and the world.

"If you ever have need of me one day," he said to Jason, "do not hesitate to send for me." Hermes spent the evening with the old teacher and then he returned to Olympus reassured.

He could feel proud that his sons would be accompanying this courageous young man.

That night, Hermes had hardly left the Centaur's cave when old Chiron approached Jason. The young man was whittling part of a reed to a point with his knife. He was fashioning a long, sharp tip to use as a spear. Chiron sat by his side.

"Jason, you are now old enough to know the whole truth about your story. You are a king's son. Your father was king of Iolcus. But your uncle Pelias took his kingdom. And so that you might never reclaim it from him, he sought to kill you. Your parents entrusted you to me to save you from this horrid Pelias."

When he heard these words, Jason stopped his whittling. He stood up, threw his point to the ground, and said simply:

"Well, then, it is about time I went and put things right. Pelias must return my kingdom back to me. And believe me, Chiron, he *shall* give it back to me!"

Old Chiron smiled under his beard. He had expected no lesser reaction from this pupil whom he loved so much.

"I will leave tomorrow," Jason said to him, gazing far into the distance.

"I do not need to wish you to be brave when you face your enemies," Chiron replied, "for you do not lack courage. But never forget that a king's son must always come to the aid of others. Be brotherly, my child, and you shall overcome every danger."

Would the advice of the old Centaur suffice to make Jason victorious?

To be continued…

€PISODE 76

IN WHICH JASON BUILDS THE
SHIP OF THE ARGONAUTS

*Previously: Hermes went to meet young Jason, who had
been raised by the old Centaur Chiron. Jason has just
been told that his uncle had stolen his kingdom and he
decides to go away without delay and reclaim it from him.*

J ason had never left old Chiron's side. On that particular
morning, the sun had barely risen when he set off on his
journey. His long, curly hair floated loose on his shoulders. He
was clad in a leopard's skin, a parting gift from his old teacher.
And in each hand he carried a spear he had carved himself.
Chiron looked at him go. His gait was proud and light. The
world awaited him.

Soon Jason came to the banks of a bubbling torrent. The
waters had overflown and were cutting off the road. A very old
woman was sitting on a stone by the roadside. She was dressed
in old, bedraggled clothes and she trembled like a leaf. When he
saw her, Jason took pity on her. He said to her: "Hey, old woman,

would you like me to help you cross the torrent? Climb on my back and hold on tight." The old woman accepted and knotted her arms around the young man's neck. Jason entered the icy waters. The old woman, for all that she had been trembling a moment ago, was clutching Jason's throat with astonishing strength. The current was strong, but Jason was even stronger. Suddenly his foot sank in the mud, and so that he would not fall into the stream, he tugged sharply at his leg. His sandal was torn from his foot and remained in the torrent, but he managed to cross and set the old woman down on the opposite bank. She was no longer trembling. Her glittering eyes were staring hard at the young man. She thanked him and left. Jason was unaware that he had just carried on his back the goddess Hera, the wife of Zeus. She had wished to put his generosity to the test. His behaviour had won her over: from that moment on Jason would be under her protection.

After he had walked for a long time, Jason arrived at Iolcus. No one knew him there and yet everyone turned around as he passed. And what is more, everyone smiled at him, to Jason's great astonishment. An oracle had predicted to the cruel king Pelias that he would be overthrown by a stranger who would arrive wearing only one sandal on his feet. The inhabitants of Iolcus detested King Pelias, and they hailed Jason with his solitary sandal as the one who would rid them of Pelias.

When Jason arrived at the palace, Pelias received him trembling. He could not take his eyes off the feet of the young man. Jason revealed his identity right away:

"Good morning, uncle, I am Jason, your brother's son. I have not come to seek a quarrel with you. You may keep your riches, you only have to return to me my throne and my kingdom."

Pelias had no desire at all to oppose Jason. Yet he was even less willing to return the throne to him. He therefore proposed the following:

"Nephew, in order to be king, you must prove your mettle. I shall return to you your throne if you can prove to me that you are worthy of it. Bring me back the Golden Fleece, and I shall cede my place to you."

This Golden Fleece was very far away, in a country called Colchis. And, what is more, it was guarded by a ferocious dragon. Pelias was certain to be rid of Jason in this manner for all eternity. Yet he obviously did not know his nephew very well. Jason replied in a clear voice:

"Have no fear, Pelias, I shall return, *with* the Golden Fleece!" Then he left the palace, to prepare his departure.

The news spread very quickly across the entire land. Many a brave youth yearning for adventures volunteered to accompany Jason. During the months which followed, Jason assembled around him a company of fifty young men, ready to follow him to life or death. At the same time, he had been building an enormous ship, the biggest and the most beautiful of all the vessels that had ever sailed the seas. Jason decided to go and seek for the prow of the ship an old oak tree which had spent its life near Chiron. He hoped that he would take with him in this manner a little of his old teacher's wisdom. And in fact, once the huge tree trunk was in place at the front of the ship, every time Jason huddled beside it at night the tree would begin to speak and counsel him. Thus was this ship built, which was given the name *Argo*. And the company of Jason's men were called the Argonauts.

The ship was ready to depart. The last cases of food were being loaded when two young boys presented themselves. They were two brothers. They were quite young and frail, and Jason frowned.

"In what way could you be useful to me?" he asked.

"You need someone to sing and tell of the adventures you shall experience," replied the first.

"You need someone to carry all your messages," added the other.

Jason smiled; and he accepted. He had just received on board with him Echion and Eurytus, the two sons of Hermes. As the worthy sons of their father, they had grown up in no time at all. Some hours after his birth, Hermes had already been walking. Some months after their own, Echion and Eurytus were young adolescents.

"We are now ready," cried Jason, "cast off the mooring ropes, and let us set out on the quest for the Golden Fleece!"

To be continued...

Episode 77

In which the Argonauts reach the island of women

Previously: Jason has come to reclaim his kingdom from his uncle Pelias. He in turn has asked him to bring back to him the Golden Fleece. Jason has therefore organized a great expedition. He has had an enormous ship built, the Argo, and has taken fifty-two companions on board.

The shore was full of people when the *Argo* took to the sea. Hermes had slipped amidst the crowd to witness the great departure. He had recognized his sons among the Argonauts sitting at the oars and he was very proud of them. Soon, a melodious music could be heard. It was one of the Argonauts playing the lyre. Hermes drew nearer and to his joy he recognized Orpheus. Right then, one might have said that it was Orpheus' music which was gently pushing the enormous ship towards the open sea. Everyone applauded and Hermes was among the first to rejoice at this spectacle.

Jason and his friends rowed with great zeal. The *Argo* was making fast progress. After some weeks, food began to grow scarce. Jason decided to bring the ship into berth at an island. Warriors in full armour began to appear on the shore where the Argonauts were going to disembark. Jason had no desire to fight, but they needed to restock with provisions. Little Echion was then seen sidling through to the front line; he leapt onto the ground and approached the warriors: "Noble inhabitants of this island, we have not come here as foes, we are the Argonauts. And if it so pleases you, I shall go ahead and tell you our story…" Startled, the warriors lowered their spears and their shields. Their faces remained concealed behind the visors of their helmets, but they appeared to be listening to the frail young man. Echion then told them the story of Jason, whose kingdom had been usurped by Pelias; then about the way in which the *Argo* had been built. He did not omit a single detail and he spoke for a long, long time. "Fifty-two of us left from Iolcus, and our leader is called Jason. He is noble and valiant and we must go and conquer the Golden Fleece, which is guarded by a dragon." When Echion had finished telling his whole story, the warriors no longer had any desire to fight. They threw their weapons on the ground and removed their helmets. And what did the Argonauts discover then? That the warriors were women! All of them women! On that island, men had cruelly mistreated their wives. So one day the women had killed all the men, and they had lived since only among themselves, wearing their husbands' armour to defend themselves.

"Is there no woman among the Argonauts?" asked the queen, surprised.

"Yes, there is, me!" replied a female voice. The Argonauts stepped aside, letting a young beauty get through who was dressed like a man. "My name is Atalanta," she said.

Atalanta was a redhead, clear-skinned and with green eyes. She was a champion at hunting and at the foot race. No one had ever succeeded in defeating her, not even a man. She was fearless and as sturdy as a rock. She had pleaded so hard with Jason that in the end he had agreed to take her on board. The queen of Lemnos appreciated the fact that Jason had taken a woman with him in his company. "Welcome to all of you," she said. Now everyone on that shore was laughing. The women of Lemnos led the Argonauts to their homes. They ate and they drank and they slept as much as they wanted. The women were not in a hurry to see them leave, and time went by in this manner.

One man alone had stayed on board the ship, and that was Orpheus. He was always thinking of Eurydice, his lost love, and he did not wish to be received by any other woman. Every evening, he played the lyre. After some long nights spent in this way, Orpheus began to feel anxious. And what if this island were a trap? What if the Argonauts never left the arms of the women of Lemnos? He decided therefore to play a more fiery music, an impatient and restless music. A music which told of the sea and of the great horizon. He played the whole night through. Jason heard the song of Orpheus and a shiver ran through him, that of adventure. He stood up and went to knock on the doors of the houses where his companions slept. "Come on, we are leaving again, the Golden Fleece awaits us!" Despite the tears and the supplications of the women, the Argonauts took to the sea once more.

Jason was happy to be sailing again. On the following night, he went to speak to the great oak. "We almost allowed ourselves to be seduced by the sweetness of life," Jason said to it. "I had not foreseen that sort of danger! Do you see any other peril lying in wait for us?"

In a soft murmur the old tree replied: "Beware of the black shadows..."

To be continued...

€PISODE 78

IN WHICH HERACLES CLASHES
WITH THE GIANT SHADOWS

*Previously: The ship of the Argonauts arrived
at Lemnos, the island of women, and it almost
did not leave again! Yet now it is sailing once
more towards the land of the Golden Fleece.*

The journey was progressing well. The rowers were joyful, the air was pure and the sky very blue. Jason was happy to be the leader of this band of jovial and brave companions. The sea did not scare them. This is how the *Argo* arrived at the country of the Doliones. A long strip of land protruded into the sea and a harbour had been built there. The king of the country came to greet them himself. He was richly dressed, for this was his wedding day. "Be welcome, and come with me to enjoy yourselves!" he said to Jason and his friends, leading them all the way to his wedding banquet. Only Heracles remained on board to keep watch on the ship. All along the way to the king's palace, Jason could not stop looking at an imposing black mountain which towered above them not too far away. He remembered the words of the old oak: "Beware of the black shadows." "You seem somewhat preoccupied," said the king, astonished. "This black mountain will not harm you in the least, for no harm will come to you in my house." Jason threw back his long hair, took a deep breath and chased away his dark thoughts. The wedding celebrations were magnificent.

Night had fallen on the small harbour. Heracles had dozed off on the ship's deck. He did not see the enormous shadows, which now crept in the town's streets, approach. It was as though these Giants had emerged from the belly of the black mountain. They were walking slowly towards the ship. The whole town was revelling at the palace, the streets were deserted. Only one young Argonaut, called Hylas, sneaked out of the palace just then. He was Heracles' equerry and the affection they had for one another was so great that the young boy had decided to leave the banquet to go and keep Heracles company. He was bringing him an amphora of wine to drink. When he saw these enormous creeping masses passing in front of him, Hylas barely had enough time to shrink back so as not to get squashed. The hair on his head stood on end! These Giants had six arms each. They were horrid to look at, and they were walking towards the harbour. In spite of his fear, Hylas pressed against the walls and hurried to reach the ship before the Giants did. Fortunately for him, it was a moonless night. He jumped on the ship's deck just as the first Giant arrived. Quickly, he woke up Heracles: "Pick up your club! We are being attacked by an army of Giants!" he yelled. Heracles woke up with a start, sprang to his feet and without a moment's thought began to swirl his club in front of him. It smashed the skull of the first Giant, who was getting ready to clamber aboard the ship. Heracles knocked out the Giants one by one, without even giving them the time to move their horrid arms. Soon the ship's deck was covered with Giants. Hylas, horrified, ran to the palace to warn Jason. But by the time the Argonauts arrived, Heracles had already won the combat. Piles of Giants were lying on the ground.

Before everyone's stupefied eyes, Heracles simply said: "I am feeling a little peckish now, to be honest; you wouldn't happen to have something for me to eat?"

The king and his subjects burst out with joy: the Giants of the black mountain had been vanquished for the first time.

"Why didn't you warn us of the existence of these monsters?" asked Jason, bewildered.

"Please do not hold it against me," the king apologized, "but we like receiving guests so very much! And no one ever dares to pay us a visit because of these Giants, who attack all strangers. I was afraid that you would have left in a hurry... The Giants caused us no harm, but they have prevented us from receiving passing guests for a great many centuries now."

After many days of feasting with the Doliones, the *Argo* took to the sea once more.

To be continued...

€PISODє 7⊖

In which great misfortunes
befall the Argonauts

*Previously: While the king of the Doliones was
receiving the Argonauts in his palace, an army of
gigantic shadows with six arms attacked the ship. But
Heracles has succeeded in putting them all to flight.*

Since the beginning of their journey, the Argonauts had
encountered a very friendly sea. But after their departure
from the land of the Doliones, everything changed. Was Poseidon
vexed with this company of young men who seemed to fear
nothing? He caused a violent storm to rise. The sea became
turbulent and the waves heaved up the *Argo* on every side. The
ship would plunge into the waters and come out again valiantly,
yet no one could steer it any longer. Jason, besieged by dark
thoughts, decided to question the talking oak in order to learn
their future. Yet the oak only replied: "You shall lose several of
your companions at your next stop." In the days that followed
the storm died down somewhat, but Jason's face remained

preoccupied. Poseidon was satisfied to see these young men stop laughing and jesting at last.

It was in this sad state of mind that they brought the ship to berth close to a forest to spend the night. Heracles decided to take advantage of this opportunity to go and fetch wood in order to carve himself a new oar, for his own had been broken during the tempest. He took with him Hylas, his young equerry. "In that case, take this pitcher with you," shouted one of the Argonauts to the youngster, "and bring us back some fresh water!" While Heracles was felling trees, looking for the best wood for his oar, Hylas went into the undergrowth to look for a spring. He wandered a little farther away from the clearing where Heracles was cutting his wood, and he very quickly found a beautiful spring of cool water. Thrilled with his discovery, Hylas plunged his pitcher into the water. But he did not know that several nymphs lived in that spring. They saw the handsome youth bending down above them, and they thought that his beauty was so very tender, so perfect, that they immediately decided to lure him towards them. They quickly seized him by the neck and dragged him to the bottom of their spring. Hylas only had time to let out a scream and he disappeared deep into the waters. This scream reached the ears of Heracles, who sprang to his feet and began to run through the forest in every direction searching for his equerry. "Hylas! Hylas!" Heracles cried. Only the birds of the forest replied to his calls, however. Filled with despair, he ran like a madman right and left, rummaging inside every tuft of grass, wandering farther and farther away from the ship and from the Argonauts.

On the *Argo*, everything had been made ready for the ship's departure for quite some time now. Some were getting irritated on account of Heracles' and Hylas' absence and were suggesting that they leave without them. Others pleaded that they should wait because Heracles' exceptional force was a formidable protection for them. The hours passed. Then the days. Heracles did not come back. One night, Jason once more consulted the talking oak at the ship's prow.

"What must I do?" he murmured.

And the oak replied: "Other adventures await the mighty Heracles. You must leave him here, for he does not belong among those who will bring back the Golden Fleece."

To be continued...

ΕΡΙΣΟΔΕ 80

IN WHICH A BOXING CHAMPION
CHALLENGES THE ARGONAUTS

*Previously: The Argonauts have just had a
cruel experience: they have been obliged to
abandon Heracles at their last port of call.*

Jason took to the sea again, setting course for the land of the
Golden Fleece. But they soon began to run out of water and
food once more. The ship was approaching an island and they
decided to stop there to replenish their stocks. On the shore where
the Argonauts had just arrived, a crowd of people had assembled
around one man. This man was Amycus, the king of the island.
Jason set foot on land, followed close behind by Echion, and he
approached the king in order to present him his greetings. The
king was still a young man, of massive stature. He was wearing
garments which enhanced his powerful muscles. His attitude
was very arrogant and Jason formed an instant dislike of him.

"Good morning, O king," said Jason, "we are heading towards
Colchis and we need water and provisions."

"It is our custom to invite passing strangers to a boxing match. If they win, they obtain fresh provisions. Otherwise…"

Amycus did not finish his sentence, although a smile appeared on his face. Nothing of this scene escaped Echion. He had understood that a trap was closing up on them. Heracles, the strongest of the Argonauts, was no longer on board and the island appeared to have a fearsome champion. With the smile still on his lips, Amycus said:

"You see that high cliff over there, which plummets straight down into the sea? Look at it well, stranger, for those who refuse to fight our champion are immediately pushed off the top of that cliff!"

Echion could not prevent himself from trembling. He looked in the direction indicated by the king, and the height of the cliff took his breath away. Down below the sea bubbled angrily. Anyone falling in there would inevitably be torn to pieces by the rocks. He closed his eyes for a moment and thought with all his might of his father Hermes. Oh, if only he too had wings on his feet… He reopened his eyes. Unfortunately, he was still surrounded by menacing guards. The nightmare continued.

"In that case," said Jason, "we will send our champion. Who is yours?"

King Amycus puffed out his chest and answered: "It is I, of course. I am the son of Poseidon, the god of the Seas, and I am stronger than any man." He threw a pair of gloves on the ground for the fight, and before he went away he shouted: "We meet this evening in that flowering dale just behind this beach."

Jason went back on board, lost in deep thought. Which of the Argonauts could possibly face this brute with some chance of winning? "Why did I take all these valorous Greeks with me on this adventure?" Jason wondered to himself. But he was not left in doubt for too long. Echion had already told the whole story to the Argonauts. One of them, Polydeuces, came forward:

"I was a boxing champion at the last games at Olympia. I feel ready to fight Amycus. He may be stronger and younger than I am, but even in boxing you also need to use your head."

The evening came. The meeting place was a breathtakingly beautiful dale, carpeted with flowers. Orpheus, who had come with his lyre, could not prevent himself from singing of the beauty of this landscape, to the great astonishment of the inhabitants, who had never taken any notice of it. But once King Amycus arrived at the appointed place of the match, both beauty and music were driven brutally away. He was quite impressive, with his bull's neck and his enormous muscles. Polydeuces, slender, almost thin, was half his weight and twice his age; he risked being wiped out within minutes, especially since he had simple leather gloves, while those of Amycus were embellished with studs of bronze. The match clearly seemed unequal.

The fighting began. Amycus charged dead ahead. Polydeuces contented himself with avoiding the attacks. He observed him, sought to guess his points of weakness. The other roared, exhausted his strength in attacking his opponent, but in vain. Amycus became more and more exasperated. It was as if Polydeuces were not fighting at all since he did not return a single blow. Amycus attacked even more furiously. The fearsome studs of his gloves missed their target each time, but only barely. The combat lasted for several hours. Night was about to fall when Polydeuces, who had been observing Amycus for a long time, at last discovered his flaw. Amycus kept his hands too far apart. Polydeuces took advantage of this to thrust his fist right between them and crush his nose. Taken by surprise, Amycus wavered. Polydeuces then launched a series of blows against which Amycus was unable to defend himself. His great mass of muscles was useless against Polydeuces' precision. He reeled. At that instant, Polydeuces dealt him a huge blow on the temple which left him dead on the ground. There was an eruption of joy from the Argonauts. As the ship sailed away full of provisions, Echion, who was looking at the coastline receding into the distance, murmured in Jason's ear:

"We have just defeated a son of Poseidon."

"I know," replied the leader of the Argonauts softly.

What would be the reaction of the god of the Seas?

To be continued...

ΕΡΙSΟΔΕ 81

IN WHICH THE ARGONAUTS
FIGHT AGAINST THE HARPIES

Previously: Thanks to Polydeuces, one of the Argonauts
who had been an Olympic boxing champion, the fearsome
King Amycus has been defeated. The ship has been able
to sail away again well stocked with water and food.

The ship had been sailing for a day at the most when the
Argonauts heard heart-rending wailings. These came from a
small island past which they were sailing. A man was weeping
somewhere nearby. The Argonauts were all quite overcome by
what they were hearing. Oblivious to all danger, Jason decided
to make landfall. They set off into the night to look for the
sobbing man. They lit torches and about a dozen of them went
ashore. Echion was one of the members of that company, and
so was his brother Eurytus. The wailings were so loud that it
did not take them long to locate their source. They came from
a cave. An offensive smell emanated from it. Despite their
repugnance, Jason and his comrades went inside and found

the most wretched creature one could possibly imagine. Lying on the bare, rocky ground, an old man of incredible thinness was groaning loudly. He was nothing but skin and bones. Upon hearing the Argonauts enter, he turned towards them with gleaming, feverish eyes, and he gestured to them that he was thirsty and hungry. Moved by pity, the young men hurried to him. They lifted him up gently to his feet, helped him sit by the cave's entrance and then they took out food from their bags. The old man was stretching out a trembling hand when a horrible thing happened. Two winged monsters appeared and swooped down on the food. "The Harpies! The Harpies!" howled the old man. They were some kind of great vulture with a woman's head, a crooked beak and sharp talons. These monsters were in the service of Zeus. He sent them from time to time to avenge himself against humans who had disobeyed him. In an instant, the two Harpies had eaten most of the food. They relieved themselves on anything that they had left uneaten, fouled the water too, then they went away again, leaving behind them a dreadful smell. The Argonauts were horrified.

"Who are you and what on earth did you do, for Zeus to punish you in this manner?" asked Jason.

"My name is Phineas," replied the man in a trembling voice. "My only fault is to possess a gift: I am able to predict the future without ever being wrong. Zeus cannot abide the fact that I can unveil all his mysteries. This is why he sends me his Harpies. And I am dying of hunger and thirst in the midst of this vile stench..." Exhausted, King Phineas stopped talking. A tear ran down his cheek.

The Argonauts were appalled. Two among them, Zetes and Calaïs, approached Jason and said to him: "We are the sons of Boreas, the god of the Wind. We are so swift that we can chase after the Harpies. Give us leave to try." Jason did not hesitate for an instant. Phineas' suffering was too unjust.

The Argonauts took out more food to feed the old man. Instantly, the stinking Harpies reappeared. But Zetes and Calaïs were waiting for them, sure-footed, swords drawn. The Harpies approached; the two youths pursued them. The monsters fled but the two sons of the Wind were as fast as they were. They were about to fall crashing upon them when Hermes appeared in the sky by their sides and averted their swords. "Zeus has sent me to stop you from killing his Harpies," he told them. "But in recompense for your bravery, I have convinced Zeus to tell them to leave old Phineas in peace." The Harpies disappeared far into the distance.

The sons of the Wind lowered their weapons and returned to their comrades, accompanied by Hermes. The joy of Echion and Eurytus at seeing their father again was great. Deeply moved, Hermes held them both tight against his heart. He was always amazed by this surge of tenderness, this effervescence inside him each time he held his children in his arms. It was enough for him simply to think of them to be filled with profound happiness. On board the ship the evening was gentle and joyful.

When, early at dawn, Hermes left his sons again, he told them: "I am proud of your courage, my children. But arm yourselves with patience, for the way is still long and full of adventures..."

To be continued...

ΕPΙSΟDΕ 82

IN WHICH THE ARGONAUTS FIND
THEMSELVES BEFORE THE BLUE ROCKS

*Previously: Thanks to two Argonauts, who were the sons
of the god of the Wind, the monstrous Harpies who were
pestering poor King Phineas have been vanquished.*

The following day, Jason and his comrades watched old King
Phineas as he devoured everything that was brought to him.
The old man was already regaining some of his strength.

"I do not know how to thank you for saving my life," he
said to them.

The Argonauts stood around him, proud and content. The
one with the readiest tongue among them, Eurytus, dared to ask:

"King Phineas, since you know so well how to foretell the
future, couldn't you reveal to us all that will happen to us?"

But Phineas replied: "Men should not know everything about
their destiny. If you knew your story before living it, you would
not be free to write it as you wish it to be. The only thing that I
may reveal to you concerns your next adventure. You shall soon

arrive before the fearsome blue rocks. In order to know whether you will succeed in crossing them before they close upon you, release a dove. If the dove succeeds in getting through, you shall pass. If she fails, make an about-turn and abandon this journey. Know that no one has ever succeeded in crossing them. If you can achieve this, they shall remain fixed for all eternity and a pathway will have been opened for every ship."

All the Argonauts thanked the old man for his counsel and left him. But Phineas had one last word of advice for Jason, and for him alone: "If you reach Colchis, in order to take away the Golden Fleece you shall have to place your trust in Aphrodite, the goddess of Love." Jason nodded his head in assent and left.

The atmosphere was very jovial aboard the ship. The oarsmen pushed briskly on their oars, accompanied by the joyful songs of Orpheus. Echion was already composing the narrative of their adventures and it caused great peals of laughter. All of a sudden, a blue-tinted mist descended upon them and enveloped the *Argo*. Nothing could be seen on the sea and they had to lift up their oars. Jason, standing post at the ship's bow, stared hard all around trying to make something out. "The blue rocks!" shouted Eurytus, who discovered them first. Silence fell. Nothing could be heard now except the lapping of the waves. Jason took the dove that they had brought with them and released her. The bird flew away. Through the mist, they could make out the rocks separating and coming together in a frightening manner. The ship was following the dove gently. She avoided the rocks, which were trying to close up on her, and pressed valiantly on. The ship tried to follow her. It now advanced through the blue rocks. They came clashing together, separated again, threatening each time to grind them to dust. But the dove progressed, and so did the ship. Soon the trap was going to be left behind them. All of a sudden, a dull slamming sound was heard: two rocks had just clashed together, plucking two feathers from the dove's tail. And at that very moment a shock was felt abaft: the rocks, as they clashed together, had just pinched off a small section of the *Argo*'s stern. It was nothing serious, however; the ship could continue its course. This is how it reached the other side of the blue rocks. A gigantic shout of joy was heard. They had succeeded! Looking at the dove flying away to freedom, Jason felt tears of joy well up inside him.

During the days that followed, the *Argo* went past the Caucasus mountain range. On one of the mountains, a long-haired Giant was chained to a rock. An eagle would swoop down on him and devour his liver. The Argonauts understood that they had just seen Prometheus. The ones most deeply moved were Echion and Eurytus.

"We cannot abandon him!" cried the one.

"He is the one who created us, he is the father of men!" cried the other.

"You are talking nonsense," scolded Jason, "we cannot go against the will of Zeus, it is he who is master of the world." And he refused to go to Prometheus' aid.

The sons of Hermes were furious with Jason for the first time. Hermes, who was never too far away from the Argonauts, felt a great fondness for his sons. He too had great affection for Prometheus. On the following night, while everyone was asleep, Hermes approached his sons and whispered in their ears: "Don't worry, Heracles will come soon. It is he who shall deliver Prometheus from his chains... You, the Argonauts, must bring back the Golden Fleece. And you haven't won that gamble yet."

To be continued...

EPISODE 83

*Previously: By following the dove, the Argonauts have
successfully forced their way through the perilous blue rocks.
The way to the land of the Golden Fleece is now open.*

Since the start of Jason's expedition, Hermes had been
following them discreetly so he could offer his protection
to his two beloved sons. And so, once the *Argo* was only a few
hours away from Colchis, he decided to give them a little boost.
He knew that white-armed Hera had also decided to protect the
Argonauts, ever since Jason helped her cross a torrent when she
was disguised as an old woman. When he became a dad himself,
Hermes had stopped detesting his stepmother Hera, but he still
mistrusted her. That morning he decided nonetheless to ask
her for her help. And Hera had some good advice to offer. She
whispered her plan in his ear.

"Bravo!" he said admiringly. "But Aphrodite will have to be
persuaded... Not an easy task!"

"I will take care of it," replied Hera.

When Aphrodite, the goddess of Love, saw Hera enter her rooms, she was very surprised. Her sister-in-law never came to her apartments. When she understood that the great goddess had a secret plan and that in order to bring this plan to fruition she needed her help, Aphrodite was filled with enormous pride. She agreed to join the conspiracy. She went in turn to the house of her son Cupid. Cupid was an adorable child whose only pastime was his bow and arrows. Each time he sent one of his arrows into the heart of a man or a woman, he or she fell in love for ever.

"Look, darling," said Aphrodite, holding out to him a pretty golden ball with blue streaks, "this toy belonged to Zeus, your grandfather, when he was a little boy. Look, if you throw the ball in the air, it leaves behind a golden trace, like that of a shooting star."

Cupid's eyes grew big with wonder and he let go for once of his bow and arrows to run after the ball. "Mummy, mummy, I really want this magic ball for myself, please mummy!" said the child.

Aphrodite smiled inwardly: Hera's plan was working to perfection. "All right sweetie, but on one condition: could you first go and shoot at someone with one of your love arrows?"

Cupid accepted, and Aphrodite whispered that person's name in his ear.

In the meantime, the Argonauts had arrived at Colchis. The jovial company of Jason's men had presented themselves at the doors of the king's palace. He received them well, and suggested that before he talked to them they should first be given what they needed to wash themselves with and things to eat. Dirty and tired from their voyage, the young men accepted with pleasure. They were led to one of the palace wings, where preparations had been made for their bath. There were maidservants busying themselves with heating up great basins of water, others who were preparing a banquet. The Argonauts were laughing, singing. A merry bustle reigned everywhere, which could be heard in every corner of the palace. Drawn by the commotion, Princess Medea, the king's daughter, approached. The tubs of water were steaming and vapours filled the room. Medea, hidden behind a pillar, observed the scene. Her gaze suddenly discovered Jason as he was letting the lukewarm water trickle down his tired body. Someone else was also hiding behind a pillar in the room, and that was Cupid. He was only waiting for that gaze before he could act. He took aim and his love arrow landed exactly at the centre of Medea's heart. The young girl felt a pinch in her heart. She flushed red, turned pale, she could not take her eyes off Jason any more. Medea had just fallen in love. High up on Olympus, Hermes and Hera were rubbing their hands: their plan was working as intended. Hermes looked at his two sons showering themselves with one tub of water after the other, screaming with pleasure, and his heart softened: "They are only children. I hope that no harm will come to them," he murmured. He knew that Princess Medea was an enchantress; and there is always something disturbing about magic.

To be continued…

EPISODE 84

*Previously: The Argonauts have been received
into the palace of the king of Colchis. As soon as
she set eyes on Jason, Princess Medea fell in love
with him. Thus have decided the gods who protect
the Argonauts, for Medea is an enchantress.*

回回回回回回

The king of Colchis waited for his guests in the great reception hall surrounded by his court. Now that he had washed and fed them, he could question them. Jason and his companions made a noisy entrance, laughing and talking all together. A little surprised, Aeetes asked:

"Who are you and what has brought you to my kingdom?"

Jason replied: "We are young Greeks, all of us the sons of kings or gods. We have crossed the seas, braved countless dangers, to come and ask you to give us the Golden Fleece."

A blast of anger overcame the king. Who did this pretentious youngster think he was? Who was he to dare lay claim on what

317

was his country's glory and renown? His face hardened and he replied in a cutting voice:

"I would only be able to give our precious Golden Fleece to the man who would demonstrate as much bravery as I have."

"But I am brave! My companions are all brave! Tell me what we must do to prove it to you!" Jason interrupted him in a loud voice.

King Aeetes was now in the grip of rage: so, then, they took themselves for heroes! So, they liked taking risks, did they! In that case, they would get what they asked for.

"First of all you will have to tame two powerful bulls. They were created by the god Hephaestus himself, the god of Blacksmiths. Their hooves are of bronze and they belch out flames. After that you will yoke them to a plough and you shall till the field which I will indicate to you. Then you will sow these dragon's teeth that I give you here in the same field. From each tooth, an armed warrior shall be born, whom you will have to vanquish. All this I have myself accomplished. If you succeed, then I shall give you the Golden Fleece which you have come to claim."

Hearing this list of trials, the entire assembly shuddered. A faint scream escaped from the mouth of a young girl sitting behind the king. It was Princess Medea. She knew that her father was sending Jason to his death. The young man hesitated for a few moments, but he had no choice. He accepted the trials. Then he retired with his comrades. He had not yet looked once at Princess Medea.

That evening every man on the ship beseeched Jason to let him pass the trials in his stead. This one boasted about his strength, the other about his speed, the third about his agility. But the young man was unyielding. King Aeetes had challenged him personally; he had to take up the challenge himself. He left his companions in a great state of anxiety, and he went peacefully to rest. The truth was that he was very worried himself, but he would not have shown it for anything in the world. He counted on the goddess Aphrodite, of whom old Phineas had spoken, to sort things out for him. But the night progressed, and he could not find sleep.

That night in the king's palace someone else could not sleep either. Princess Medea turned and tossed in her bed. Her black, loose hair became tangled on her pillow. Her face had become extremely pale. She burned with love for this young Greek. Horrid images kept coming back before her eyes: she imagined that fine body that she had seen in the baths being torn to pieces by the metal hooves of the two monstrous bulls. She imagined the fire belched up by the beasts setting Jason's long hair on fire and transforming him into a living torch. She imagined the army of warriors piercing his body with a thousand arrows. It was an unbearable vision for this heart in love. At the same time, she thought of her father, the king, who was so proud of his Golden Fleece. Helping Jason meant betraying her father. Yet she, Medea the enchantress, thanks to her magic powers, could save the man she loved. She knew that. She even knew that she was Jason's only chance. Which would she choose, loyalty to her father or her passion for Jason?

To be continued…

EPISODE 85

IN WHICH JASON MEETS MEDEA

*Previously: In order to obtain the Golden Fleece,
Jason must succeed in a series of terrifying
trials. Only Princess Medea can save him.*

It was a truly strange night, a night without end. Medea had slipped outside the palace. She had reached the woods and under the solitary gleam of the moon had sought the herbs and roots that she needed. She was looking for one plant in particular, which had grown at the exact spot where the first drop of Prometheus' blood had fallen. When she found it, tears ran down her cheeks. And she no longer knew whether they were tears of joy or of sorrow. Of joy, because with this unique plant she would be able to render a man invincible for an entire day, and therefore save the stranger with whom she had just fallen in love. Of sorrow, for in this way she would be betraying her father for ever. She returned to her room and prepared an ointment which made one insensitive to fire and to the sword.

Jason could not find rest either. Now that all the Argonauts were asleep, he had got up noiselessly and was staring hard into the darkness. All of a sudden, he saw a shadow move on the beach. The shadow was approaching the ship. Jason held his breath and waited. The shadow was wearing a long hooded cloak which concealed its form completely. Soon, it was only a few paces away, and it climbed agilely on board. Jason was crouching low. He bounced brusquely, seized hold of the stranger from behind and restrained him in a headlock.

"Who are you and why have you come here?" he asked gruffly.

He could feel the stranger tremble and he loosened his grip a little. He snatched a lit torch and brought it sharply closer to the face of the mysterious visitor. Imagine his surprise when he discovered the face of a young woman! She let her hood slip back, and a torrent of black hair flowed on her shoulders. Jason remained speechless.

"I am Medea, King Aeetes' daughter," she said. Her voice was grave, almost gritty, yet the tone was vivid and rapid. "Are you afraid of death?"

Confused, Jason answered: "If I were afraid of death, I would not have come here."

The young woman was throwing quick glances around her, to be sure that she would not be caught by surprise.

"You are brave, this is good, but bravery alone will not suffice. Without me you will be lost. The sun will be rising soon, we must make haste. I have prepared for you an ointment which will render you invincible for a day. Wash yourself and anoint your body with this salve. Do not forget to rub your weapons thoroughly with it as well. In this way no one will be able to defeat you."

And she held out to him a small flask. Jason took it with one hand and with the other caught the wrist of the young girl. He feared this could be a ruse by King Aeetes.

"Why do you do this? Why are you betraying your father? What do you wish in return?" he asked.

Medea answered in a single breath: "Because I love you. In return I want you to promise to take me with you far away from here and marry me."

Jason suddenly remembered the prophecy of old Phineas: "Have faith in Aphrodite, the goddess of Love!" and his mistrust vanished.

He answered: "I promise," then he placed a kiss on the hand he was holding and let it go. The enchantress put her hood back on to hide her face. Before leaving the ship, she gave him one final counsel:

"When the army of warriors is born of the dragon's teeth, throw this stone in their midst and they will kill one another instead of attacking you." Then she disappeared into the night. Jason looked at her go and a shiver ran through him.

When rosy-fingered Aurora appeared, the Argonauts woke up one by one and found Jason washing himself in the sea. He was joyful and confident and he asked them to help him coat his shield, his helmet and all his weapons with a strange balm. Then he pretended to practise. "Comrades, strike my shield with all the strength you can put into your swords," he told them. The first to try brandished his weapon, which fell crashing upon Jason.

Jason did not even flinch. A second struck at him with greater force. Jason did not budge this time either. A third attacked him with even greater might. Still nothing happened. Cries of joy burst out. Jason was invincible! Jason was going to win.

Jason came to the meeting place appointed by King Aeetes accompanied by an astonishing procession. Orpheus was playing wonderful songs which were then taken up by the other youths at the top of their voices. Echion was telling the passers-by episodes of their adventures. Each seemed as joyful as if they had been going to a celebration! "Poor young men, they have lost their senses," sighed the people they came across on their way. "They do not know that they are marching to their deaths."

To be continued...

ΕΡΙSΟDΕ 86

During which Jason
undergoes his trials

*Previously: Medea has come in secret to offer
Jason her help. She has prepared for him a magic
salve which should render him invincible.*

T he field which King Aeetes had set as their meeting place
was a fairly ordinary field. An enormous plough for tilling
the earth was set on the ground. "You only need to attach the
two bulls of Hephaestus to it and then you can dig the furrows!"
sneered Aeetes. The public now waited. Jason was standing in
the middle of the field. Suddenly, the two bulls emerged and a
murmur of terror swept across the assembled crowd. Their metal
hooves raised clouds of dust from the ground, they belched
out flames and a thick smoke enveloped them. The two bulls
charged dead straight at Jason, who did not budge. Soon a haze
enveloped them, preventing the spectators from seeing what
was happening. Was he being trampled on? Was he being burnt?
The smoke, which made their eyes sting, dispersed little by little.

Everyone then saw Jason, who had seized one of the bulls by the horns and was restraining him against his shoulder; and the other bull, which he had forced to the ground, was kept down under his knee. A stupefied murmur spread across the gathered crowd. Jason caught hold of the plough and yoked the bulls to it. He dug furrows in the field to thundering applause. Even the inhabitants of Colchis could not prevent themselves from applauding. Princess Medea, sitting beside her father, had not ceased to mutter protective spells. She was trying not to smile because her father was in a furious mood. He stood up and threw to Jason a helmet full of dragon's teeth. "We'll see whether you still think you are so very clever once you are faced with an army of warriors," he mumbled.

Jason took the dragon's teeth and began to sow them in the furrows. He sowed them all and afterwards he covered the field once more with soil. Everyone then saw the entire field heave up and down in waves, quake and then lift up. Yet from these seeds grew neither flowers nor fruit—no, what emerged instead were spear points and helmets, then, little by little, warriors in full armour. An army of fearsome warriors had just been born. Most of the spectators fled screaming away, panic-stricken. But Jason retained his calm. He threw a glance towards where King Aeetes and his daughter Medea were sitting, saluted them with a deep bow, and then took out of his pocket a large stone. It was the one that Medea had given him as a gift. The ferocious warriors got into ranks, then they marched straight against Jason. They were so numerous that their marching steps made the ground tremble. When they came right up to him, only then did Jason throw the stone in their midst. Everyone instantly saw the warriors halt their advance. They turned towards one another, as though this pebble had been launched by one of them, and they began to fight among themselves. They were not a dragon's offspring for nothing: their ferociousness knew no bounds. They killed one another to the last! The field was red with their blood, but Jason had not spilt a single drop of his own. The victorious hero then walked towards King Aeetes to claim the prize of his victory, the Golden Fleece. But Aeetes, livid with rage, answered him viciously: "Tomorrow, we shall see to this tomorrow," and he returned to his palace. The Argonauts were so happy for their leader's triumph that they did not worry about this at all.

They organized a great feast on the beach. And throughout the entire night there were only songs and dances. The wine flowed in great streams. Echion told time after time of Jason's extraordinary victory, till he lost his voice. In their insouciance, the Argonauts were unaware that Aeetes was preparing a nasty surprise for them...

To be continued...

ΕΡΙΣΟDΕ 87

IN WHICH WE SEE THAT KINGS DO
NOT ALWAYS KEEP THEIR WORD

*Previously: Thanks to Medea's witchcraft, Jason has
succeeded in all the trials. King Aeetes ought now to
offer him the Golden Fleece, the prize of his victory.*

The fires of joy lit by the Argonauts illuminated the beach
with their red reflections. The songs and laughter of their
celebrating could be heard far in the distance. They reached
even as far as the palace of King Aeetes, whose wrath had not
ceased to grow.

"Ah, so these scoundrels are amusing themselves! They are
rejoicing, those louts! If they think they have won, they are
far mistaken!" he howled. "Never, never shall I give them the
Golden Fleece!"

The ministers and counsellors of the king trembled with
fear, yet someone did have the courage to say: "But your Majesty,
Jason has succeeded in his trials and you have promised—"

"And so? What of it?" cried Aeetes. "I am the king, am I

not? I can do as I like." And he ordered that his entire army be quietly marshalled together, to go and attack the Argonauts on the beach. "We shall take them by surprise before sunrise," he laughed unpleasantly, "and we shall burn their accursed ship." The ministers and counsellors looked at one another, shocked to see that their king was not keeping his promise, but they obeyed. Hiding behind a curtain, Medea had heard everything. There was not a moment to lose. She left the palace running, taking her half-brother with her.

At that time of night, there were no watchmen around the *Argo*. Medea came easily to where Jason was. She was out of breath and the words stumbled out of her mouth:

"Quick, quick, Jason, my father has betrayed you. He is getting ready to take you by surprise and to massacre you this very night. Follow me and I shall lead you to the Golden Fleece. Afterwards, we shall have to flee."

The Argonauts, who had formed a circle around her, were suspicious.

"This woman is a sorceress, it is unwise to follow her," said someone.

"It may be a trap," fretted another.

But Jason knew that he could trust her. "Prepare the ship for our departure," he commanded, "I will be back." And he disappeared behind Medea into the night.

The Golden Fleece was hanging from a sacred tree which was a few miles away. Jason knew they were getting near it when he saw a strange phosphorescent light in the darkness. It was a light unlike any that he had ever encountered. Even the moonbeams seemed pale by comparison. Jason approached, fascinated. He then discovered simultaneously the most beautiful thing he had ever seen in his life, and the most atrocious. The Golden Fleece, hanging from a branch, was even more dazzling than it had been in his dreams. But there was a dragon of hideous ugliness coiled around the tree trunk. He was as big as the ship of the Argonauts and his shimmering scales seemed to be made of metal. His mouth spat out fire and venom, his long claws tore to pieces anything that came within their reach. A shiver of horror ran through Jason. How was he going to defeat this monster?

"He is immortal," whispered Medea, "force is no good against him, let me deal with him." And the young girl advanced bravely towards the dragon. He raised his huge mouth in her direction, but the enchantress began to sing and the dragon stood still. Medea's song was solemn, repetitive, spellbinding. While she sang, she pronounced words of magic. Soon the dragon, instead of attacking, began to sway his head gently from right to left, to the rhythm of the music. Without stopping her strange song, Medea picked some branches from a juniper bush which grew at the dragon's feet. Then she shook the branches before the monster's eyes, and the dragon fell asleep. She made a sign to Jason to approach. Jason straddled over the sleeping dragon, climbed on the tree and unhung the Golden Fleece with a trembling hand. They both fled, running. A circle of light enveloped them in the night. This light was so bright that they risked being detected by the king's army.

To be continued...

ΕΡΙSODΕ 88

IN WHICH MEDEA SAVES THE ARGONAUTS

*Previously: Medea has warned Jason that her
father the king was going to attack them. She has
succeeded in casting a spell on the dragon guarding
the Golden Fleece, so that Jason can take it away.*

It was a frenzied race through the night. Jason clutched the
Golden Fleece tight against his body and did not let go of
Medea's hand. Everywhere the soldiers of King Aeetes were
assembling and making their way to the beach. But Medea knew
the region like the back of her hand. She managed to bypass
every band of soldiers and brought Jason back to his ship by
secret paths. Echion, who was standing watch, was the first to
spot them. "Here they are!" he shouted joyfully, forgetting all
need for caution. Rosy-fingered Aurora was finishing her work
and the sun was rising. Jason and Medea climbed aboard the
Argo and the ship left the shore just as the king's army launched
its attack. Livid with rage, King Aeetes recognized his daughter
Medea at the ship's stern, standing tall, her hair flowing in the

wind. She was holding the Golden Fleece in her outstretched arms and she was showing it to him. Then she burst into a mocking laughter, a challenging laughter, and she shouted:

"You shall learn, father, that a true king worthy of his name always keeps his word!"

At that instant, Medea's half-brother Apsyrtus appeared by her side: "Father! Father!" he yelled. "I don't want to go away with her!"

King Aeetes let out a howl. Not only was Medea fleeing with these strangers, but she was taking with her everything that was most precious to him: the Golden Fleece and his beloved son. He instantly ordered that they set out in pursuit of the Argonauts.

Medea did not take her eyes off the coast, which moved away in the distance. She knew that she was seeing her country for the last time and she felt a pinch in her heart. Everything had happened so fast since Jason's arrival that the young girl hadn't had the time to think about her destiny. When she had fallen in love, she had found it difficult to choose between Jason and her father. But when her father had gone back on his word, he had helped her make her choice. Tears ran down the cheeks of the enchantress, but she had not noticed them. Jason had approached noiselessly. He laid his hand on her shoulder.

"Thank you," Jason told her simply.

"Long live Medea!" shouted Echion all of a sudden, who never missed anything of what was happening on board.

"Long live Medea!" shouted the Argonauts in unison. And they rowed with even greater energy.

But King Aeetes had taken out his most powerful ship. It was much smaller than that of the Argonauts, but it was much faster. Other ships full of soldiers followed his. There were so very many that the sea seemed covered by a flock of black beasts. Little by little the distance between the *Argo* and the enemy ships diminished. The more her father's ships drew nearer, the more Medea grew pale. If these ships caught up with them, death was certain for her, for Jason, and for all his companions. Panic seized her. She wanted to live, live at all cost, live with this man whom she loved, live with the children she would have with him, *live*. A glint of folly suddenly crossed the enchantress' eyes. Jason alone noticed this dangerous light in Medea's gaze, this light ignited by fear and by the yearning for life. But he did not react. He did not shake her to bring her back to her senses. He let her follow her course towards madness. At that moment, Medea was no longer herself. She hurried to her half-brother and plunged a knife into his heart. Then she cut him into pieces and began to throw these pieces overboard, one by one. As the first piece fell into the sea, she howled in her father's direction: "There, *there* is your beloved son!" And she accompanied her horrific act with a madwoman's laughter. Her father let out a cry of agony and made his ships stop so that he might fish out the pieces of the dead body. Every time her father's ships approached, Medea threw one more part of her brother's body overboard. Little by little the *Argo* gained ground. It finally lost its pursuers, too occupied as they were recovering the body parts.

Among the Argonauts, a deathly silence had replaced the joyous atmosphere of victory. Everyone rowed without a word, frozen by the horrible crime that had just been committed under their eyes. After many long hours, Eurytus burst into tears. His brother Echion then gave expression to his own anger:

"Monsters!" he howled at Medea and Jason. "You are a pair of monsters! *How* could you have sacrificed Apsyrtus' life in this manner? He had not asked to come with you! He was the same age as I. And *you*, you witch, he was your brother! As for you, Jason, you are a coward; you did not hold back her murderous hand! I refuse to tell the rest of this story! May you be cursed by the gods!"

Medea's face remained contorted by folly, but her eyes had recovered their normal brightness. She simply replied:

"Without the death of Apsyrtus, it is you who would have been dead! We would *all* be dead, killed by my father, who would have caught up with us."

Jason lowered his head, ashamed. He *had* been a coward; that he knew well. This woman had saved them all by causing her own perdition. For he did not imagine that the gods would ever let such a crime go unpunished.

To be continued...

ΕΡΙSODΕ 89

IN WHICH ZEUS' ANGER IS UNLEASHED

*Previously: Gripped by terror and madness, Medea
has killed her half-brother and thrown the pieces of his
body into the sea. She has thus made it possible for the
Argonauts to escape their pursuers, who were forced to
stop in order to retrieve the body from the waters.*

From the heights of Olympus, Hermes had heard his sons' cries.
He rushed over and discovered with horror what had just
happened. He had been too naive to count on this sorceress for
the protection of the Argonauts. One more idea of white-armed
Hera's which had gone awry! Hearing a noise behind him, he turned
round: it was Hera, who had also been drawn there by the cries.

"Your sons are making quite a racket," she told Hermes.

"My sons cannot accept that a life may be taken, even if it is
to save another life," he replied, vexed.

"If you hadn't had this idiotic idea of making Medea fall in
love with Jason, we wouldn't be in this situation... Thank you
for this idiotic plan," she said.

Hermes was about to give a sharp reply when suddenly everything turned black around them.

"But it is not yet night, is it?" Hermes asked in astonishment.

"No," replied Hera, "it is Zeus, who is losing his temper, I think."

Enormous black clouds had just gathered in the sky. And instantly violent flashes of lightning streaked across it. Zeus had taken out his thunderbolt and he went relentlessly after the Argonauts. The *Argo* was tossed about in this tempest; it almost went under at every flash of lightning. Hermes anxiously watched his children clinging onto the mast. But Zeus' anger would not be appeased. Hera had gone away again: she was powerless before the will of the god of gods; her hero would have to manage without her. Jason did not know what to do any more. They could see nothing at all. Night and day became indistinguishable. After several days the tempest died down. But it was replaced by fog. Zeus would not relent. The ship no longer knew which direction to take. It was impossible to find their way in this thick mist. More days went by. Medea tried to establish the right course by means of magic spells, but she could not do it. Jason could feel that the gods and goddesses who had supported him until then were no longer on his side. His companions were no longer behind him either. Orpheus did not sing any more. Echion no longer spoke. Eurytus only wept.

One night, Jason decided to ask the talking oak for advice.

"Tree of wisdom, what must I do?" he murmured.

For many long moments the tree kept silent. Only the wind whistled in Jason's ears. Then it decided to answer:

"You have killed an innocent being. The wrath of Zeus is terrible. In order to appease him, Medea and you must go to the island of the sorceress Circe. Circe is Medea's aunt. She alone can purify you of this crime."

A voice murmured behind Jason: "We shall go."

It was Medea, who had got out of bed so she too could listen to the oak's advice. Jason looked at her. There was no trace on her face of the fear and the folly which had unleashed her savagery, just an extreme pallor which accentuated even more the coal black of her eyes and hair. Jason thought that she was beautiful and he smiled at her. It was for his sake that she had left her country, for his sake that she had betrayed her father, for his sake too that she had killed her brother. Without her he would never have recovered the Golden Fleece. He resolved to marry her as soon as they were back.

The following day, the veil of fog was torn asunder and the *Argo* made course for Circe's island. Jason dreaded the prospect of meeting this sorceress, and he was not far wrong. This was a woman of truly formidable powers. Circe lived alone on an island in a vast and comfortable house. She came to the doorstep to greet her niece, she bid her enter, and then she turned towards Jason, who was preparing to come inside as well, and said to him drily: "No, not you, you stay out. I am receiving Medea into my house because she is family. But I shall not receive assassins I have never met." And the door was closed once more.

To be continued...

ΕΡΙSΟDΕ 90

IN WHICH THE ARGONAUTS
ESCAPE THE SIRENS

Previously: Terribly angry because of the murder committed by Medea, Zeus has sent a raging tempest upon the ship of the Argonauts. In order to be purified of the murder, Jason and Medea have gone to see the sorceress Circe.

What happened in the palace of the enchantress? What pact was sealed between Medea and her aunt Circe? Jason did not know, but very early in the morning, following an entire night full of anxiety, he saw Medea coming towards him with a wan smile on her lips: "Don't be afraid, my friend, we may now take to the sea once more and try to reach your land safe and sound." The *Argo* left the island. Neither Jason nor Medea heard Circe's laughter which accompanied their departure. But they saw her tall, black form as she watched them go, from all the way up a cliff, and Jason could not prevent himself from shuddering.

Soon the ship came in sight of another island, whose name was not known to seafarers. But a sweet music came from this island, so sweet that even the most hardened heart melted upon hearing it. This music was accompanied by melodious singing. They who sang so divinely had a body that was half-woman, half-fowl. "The Sirens," murmured Orpheus. And his voice trembled with fear, for he had already heard of these fearful singers. The beauty of their music was such that any seamen who heard them were bewitched. They could not resist it, and they let their ships smash against the rocks of the island. Orpheus looked at his companions. Their faces were already ecstatic, they all seemed spellbound. He pounced on his lyre and he began to play in turn. He sought to bring out of himself the most vibrant music that he had ever played. And his song soared, overwhelming in its purity. Little by little, the Argonauts stopped listening to the Sirens, in order to hear Orpheus' beautiful music. They were snatched one by one from the lure of death; they turned themselves back once more towards the music of life, Orpheus' music. The more Orpheus' lyre produced its glorious sounds, the farther away the ship sailed from the Sirens. Once the accursed island had disappeared, only then did the exhausted young musician stop his singing. A strange silence ensued. Then a thundering applause burst out. The Argonauts were once more making their way towards life.

Their joy was short-lived, for black and sinister peaks protruded from the sea. "Charybdis and Scylla!" shouted the watchman. All seamen knew of the dangers run by any ship obliged to sail between them. A wind of panic swept across the crew. On one of the rocks there lived a monster called Charybdis. Thrice per day this monster swallowed vast quantities of the sea that surrounded her. Any unlucky ships which passed nearby were gobbled up at the same time. When the monster again spewed out the water it had swallowed, nothing but wreckage remained. Jason commanded each man on duty to brace himself against his oar in order to resist the current. For the monster was beginning its long suction. The Argonauts rowed, they rowed like mad. You could hear nothing any more except their panting breaths. Their every muscle fought against the current. Suddenly the sucking stopped: by resisting with all their might, the Argonauts had managed to come out of the whirlpool, they could sail away.

Yet once you had escaped Charybdis, you fell into the clutches of another sea monster called Scylla. This one had the body of a woman and was surrounded by six ferocious dogs which threw themselves upon the ships that sailed within reach to devour them. The dogs were already drooling when they saw the ship approach. Hermes, who was watching over his children from the heights of Olympus, had suddenly had enough of this. There were too many trials which made his paternal heart bleed. He asked Aeolus, the god of the Wind, to push the *Argo* away from Scylla's reach. Aeolus liked the messenger god a lot and he agreed to blow and save the crew. He blew so hard that the ship left at full speed the waters where Charybdis and Scylla lurked. Calm waters received them at last.

When night came, the Argonauts fell asleep, exhausted. Only Jason kept awake. It had been many nights now that he could not find sleep. He had snatched away the Golden Fleece, he was victorious, but this victory had a bitter taste. Would his trials end one day? Would he ever be able to bring his companions back to port safe and sound?

To be continued...

EPISODE 91

IN WHICH APOLLO LENDS
THEM A WELCOME HAND

*Previously: The Argonauts are still trying to return
to their homeland. They have just succeeded in
escaping the Sirens and the monsters Charybdis and
Scylla. But Jason does not feel easy in his mind...*

The Argonauts woke up joyful, glad to have been able to rest at last. They were going to alight on the island of Crete and already its shoreline was becoming visible. It was then that an enormous boulder of rock came crashing down a few feet away from the ship. As it fell into the sea, the rock raised great waves which drenched the ship's deck. Where had this rock come from? From a bright dot which seemed to be placed somewhere high on the island's shores. Jason shaded his eyes with his hand so that he would not be blinded by the light. And what he discovered was horrifying. A gigantic metal form was grabbing rocks and aiming them straight at them.

"It is the Giant Talus, the son of Hephaestus," murmured

Medea beside him. "He is the guardian of Crete. He is almost invincible."

Jason looked at Medea and, seeing the small grin on her face, he guessed that she already had a plan.

"*Almost* invincible? Why almost?" he asked.

"Because there is a flaw in his metallic body," answered Medea. "It is a little vein at the heel, in which his entire life force is hidden. If this vein bursts, Talus dies."

The young woman kept her eyes on the Giant's form. Behind her, the Argonauts trembled with fear. Medea was not afraid, she was concentrating. Soon she began to pronounce magic spells.

Talus suddenly saw men appearing before him, who grabbed hold of him. Livid with rage, he became agitated, chased them, thought he had quashed them, but others still continued to appear. Or perhaps they were the same ones, he did not know. And these men never stopped trying to climb onto him. They were visions, sent by the sorceress Medea. These visions drove Talus mad. He had no idea what he was doing any more. As he was kicking his legs right and left to get rid of his assailants, his heel struck violently against the edge of a rock. His life vein burst and Talus fell dead on the spot. The heavy colossus of metal crashed on the ground. Once more, the Argonauts had been saved by Medea.

A black veil fell across the sea. The sun disappeared and the Argonauts were plunged into the night. There wasn't a glimmer of light, nothing to steer the ship by. How could they advance in this total darkness without risking crashing into a cliff? They were seized by a great anxiety, as though death were on the prowl, coming to take them by the hand. Was the disappearance of the light a final trial? Would they ever come through this? The days went by in that same deep blackness and became indistinguishable from the night. Sometimes one of the seamen sobbed. There was nothing to eat or drink any more. It was impossible to find their way or to make landfall somewhere to replenish their supplies.

Jason did not know to whom to turn at this point. This was when with a rending cry he began to beseech Apollo, the god of Light. "O great Apollo, come to our rescue! Do not let us wander in the shadows like this. Our error was immense, we have certainly committed many errors, but please show us the way out of the night. I implore you, shed your light upon us." On Olympus, Apollo heard Jason's cry. In spite of Zeus' wrath, Apollo decided to send a ray of light to the unhappy crew. He hurled a shaft of flames which tore through the night. Thanks to their gleam, the Argonauts saw that they were approaching an island. They had been saved.

That night, Jason's companions slept on firm land. This time too Jason was the only one who did not sleep. He kept watch through the night.

To be continued...

EPISODE 92

IN WHICH THE ARGONAUTS PART COMPANY

Previously: The Argonauts have just escaped the giant Talus thanks to Medea's witchcraft. And Apollo has come to their aid by offering them a little light.

The voyage was approaching its end. The ship sailed fast and kept a straight course. When the shores of their native land appeared on the horizon, the Argonauts burst out with joy. Each one laughed, wept. They all fell into each other's arms. They had succeeded! They were returning to their homeland, victorious and alive! Even Jason was radiant with happiness. He had draped the Golden Fleece over his shoulder and could not take his eyes off the approaching shores. Medea alone kept herself apart from the general gaiety. She had abandoned everything so that Jason might return triumphant, she had betrayed her father, left her homeland, killed her half-brother. She regretted nothing, but she could not bring herself to rejoice all the same.

The reception of the heroes of the Golden Fleece was quite exceptional. Great celebrations were organized. People sang, danced, hailed the heroes. And already their adventures were spreading by word of mouth, like a legend. Having made the most of this triumphant return, Jason assembled the Argonauts one last time on the beach before the moored *Argo*. Orpheus played one last tune, Echion told the story of their long epic. They all listened in silence to the narrative of the conquest of the Golden Fleece. Hermes had taken advantage of the darkness in order to come close. He saw many smiles and many tears that night. A little before the day rose, Jason called each man in turn and held him tight in his arms, weeping. They had faced so many dangers together; this separation was painful for all of them. Each, however, had to follow his own path from now on. Hermes was proud of his sons. He looked at his children walk away in the distance, and he saw that they had become men.

Jason remained alone on the beach beside the hull of his ship, which had now become useless. It was then that Medea approached and laid her hand on his shoulder.

"There is one thing left for you to accomplish: recover your crown and avenge your parents. I can punish your uncle Pelias, if you wish it. It is because of him that you embarked on this adventure."

Jason did not have his heart set on vengeance. He sighed and said:

"Without that tyrant Pelias, I would never have experienced what I have just lived through; I would never have met my companions. And all these trials have made me into a different man."

Medea insisted: "Even if you have succeeded in the trial he forced upon you, even if you have brought back the Golden Fleece, Pelias will not give you back your kingdom."

Jason remained silent for a moment. Medea always knew his secret desires. He turned towards her and he said to her in a strangled voice: "Do as you wish."

To be continued…

EPISODE 43

IN WHICH A TERRIBLE
VENGEANCE TAKES PLACE

*Previously: The Argonauts returned
triumphantly to their homeland and then they
parted company. But Medea is preparing a
terrible vengeance against King Pelias.*

At dawn, Medea slipped inside Pelias' palace wrapped in a great red cloak. No one saw her shadow steal towards the rooms of the king's daughters. The young women were already out of bed and they were having fun together when Medea pushed their door open. They did not feel at all suspicious towards this long-haired woman. In a few words, they were completely seduced.

"Your father Pelias is growing old, isn't he?" asked Medea.

The young girls sighed: "Alas, yes, he is getting old..."

"I am an enchantress," Medea then said, "I can rejuvenate your father. With my magic herbs, I can restore youth to anyone who wishes it."

The young girls were innocent and gullible. They let out cries of astonishment. Only one of them, Alcestis, still kept back. Something about Medea's ways caused her fear, but she did not know what. Suspicious, she asked:

"Oh, really? Well, first of all prove to us that you *are* a sorceress."

Medea smiled and asked for a great cauldron full of water to be fetched and also for a very old ram. Once the servant girls had brought all these things, Medea boiled the water in the cauldron. The daughters of Pelias had made a circle around her, very excited. Medea closed her eyes and cast a few magic herbs into the cauldron. Then she killed the old ram, cut it into pieces and threw the pieces into the cauldron. Silence fell. All of them had their eyes screwed on the cauldron. Many long moments passed and then they saw a very young lamb emerge from the boiling water. Mesmerized, the young girls clapped their hands.

"I leave you this cauldron and the magic herbs," said Medea. "You only have to do the same thing to your father Pelias and then thanks to you he will recover his youth." With these words, she disappeared.

Furtive steps were heard along the corridors of the palace, where everyone was still asleep. They belonged to the daughters of King Pelias, who were going to their father's room. They loved their father and they could not bear the idea of seeing him soon grow old and then die. Medea's proof had convinced them. Only Alcestis resisted. She too had a passionate love for her father. But she could not resign herself to killing him, even if it meant that he would be reborn young by the process. And, what is more, she actually loved his wrinkles and the way his hair had turned white with age. Her sisters, however, would not listen to her. Which of them had struck the first blow? Which one had cut Pelias to pieces? Which was the one who cast the pieces of her father's body into the magic cauldron? No one can recall, for no one saw them act. Alcestis was sobbing in a corner of the room; the gleam of light shining in her sisters' eyes frightened her. Time passed. The young girls were staring fervently at the cauldron in which their father was boiling. But he was not being reborn.

Stunned, they continued to wait, without understanding. Alcestis then began to howl: "Madwomen! Madwomen that you are! You believed that sorceress! And she bewitched you! But now look, *look* at your crime. You have killed our father, and never shall he be reborn from this vile stew!" The screams and the wailings of Alcestis woke up the entire palace. The young girls, seized with horror at what they had just done, fled running. They left the island for ever. Already the frightful Erinyes were setting out to pursue them for the rest of their days. One could already smell the monstrous stench of these righters of wrongs. *Misery to all who kill their parents.*

All alone on the beach, Jason could not guess the appalling crime that Medea had once more committed for his sake. He had closed his eyes and had let this woman in love take action. The beautiful enchantress joined him silently. She simply whispered in his ear: "You have been avenged." Jason did not turn his head round to face her. He did not reply. He was thinking of his companions, and of his youth, which had just come to its end. He took Medea's hand in his and with his other hand continued to stroke the Golden Fleece on his shoulder. Hermes was looking at the couple formed by Medea and Jason and he could not help feeling worried about them. He had appreciated Jason's strength and bravery but he now dreaded his weakness and his cowardice. He had liked the passion of Medea but he was appalled by her cruelty. He could tell that she was likely to topple over into rage and folly.

To be continued…

EPISODE 94

IN WHICH MEDEA SINKS INTO
MURDEROUS FOLLY

*Previously: Medea has committed another
murder so that Jason can recover his throne: she
has killed Jason's uncle Pelias, who had sent
him on the quest for the Golden Fleece.*

Before leaving Jason and Medea, Hermes could not resist trying to find out what their future would be. He knelt down and threw his small pebbles into the water of a fountain. What he saw then confirmed his darkest forebodings.

An image appeared, that of a woman in tears kneeling before a window. This woman's back was turned. White hairs shimmered among her long, dark tresses, which fell in disarray on her shoulders. She raised her head and Hermes recognized Medea. Perhaps because he had never seen her crying, perhaps because of the few wrinkles that had fixed themselves in the corners of her eyes, perhaps because for the first time she actually seemed fragile, he was quite overcome to find her like this. The distress expressed on Medea's face was overwhelming. Hermes followed Medea's gaze to see what was causing her so much suffering. The window gave on to a garden. In the garden, a man was embracing a very young woman. That man was Jason. Hermes recognized him immediately, even if he too had silver threads among his black curls. He observed the blonde hair of the young girl whom Jason was kissing, he heard her laughter, saw her fresh and firm skin, and an infinite sadness invaded him. How could Jason be disloyal to the one who had sacrificed everything for him? Was his word of honour of so little substance that he could betray the woman who had made him into a victor? The voice of the young girl reached Hermes' ears:

"Daddy has told me that you have promised to leave your wife and marry me, Jason, is this true?"

"What Creon has told you is correct," replied Jason, smiling.

With a slight note of anxiety in her voice she continued: "But how will your wife Medea react to this?"

Jason's smile was extinguished. He made a gesture of annoyance: "She can say what she likes."

Upon hearing these words, Hermes turned his head sharply towards Medea, who was still by her window. She was no longer kneeling. Her tears had run dry. Erect and proud, she was looking at Jason. But in her gaze there shone a light so terrible that Hermes began to fear the worst.

In Medea's eyes Hermes could now only see hatred. He saw her take out from a great wooden chest a long white dress and pronounce some strange words; she then summoned her maidservants and ordered them: "Go and take this dress to the young girl in the garden. Tell her that it is a gift from me." She remained alone for a few moments. Then Jason entered her room. She lifted up her eyes and waited for him to speak. But Jason turned his eyes away and went out again without uttering a single word. Medea made a gesture towards him to retain him. He was already gone. Suddenly, piercing screams were heard. Then the noise of a stampede. Silent laughter shook Medea's body. At that instant, Hermes saw that Medea was no longer herself. She had the eyes of a madwoman.

Hermes saw then that the young girl had put on the white dress that Medea had offered her. The dress had instantly gone up in flames. She was now trying to wrench away the dress that burned her, but she could not take it off. She caught fire with it. And little by little the entire palace was overrun by the blaze. Hermes then saw the most horrible thing in the world, the thing he would never have wished to see. He saw Medea, devoured by madness, pounce on her children, the two sons she had had with Jason, and kill them with her own hands. She was howling: "*Jason*! Jason! Such is my vengeance! I destroy everything, everything! I destroy all that you hold dear! I destroy the flesh of your flesh since you have destroyed *me*!" Hermes shut his eyes. He blocked his ears. He did not want to see anything any more, nor hear anything. He threw far away his little pebbles which allowed him to read what was to be. Hermes wanted to have nothing to do with this particular future.

To be continued...

EPISODE 45

IN WHICH HERMES BECOMES
THE FATHER OF PAN

*Previously: By reading the future with his white
pebbles, Hermes has discovered the horrible
conclusion to the story of Jason and Medea. For
the first time Hermes hopes that his pebbles have
lied to him. Devastated, he returns to Olympus.*

Life holds many surprises in store, even for gods. And this
is how Hermes discovered that he had once more become
a dad. It was a morning with a sky so clear, so blue, that it was
a joy to behold. Having been warned that his companion was
about to bring a baby into the world, Hermes was hastening to
the place where she was to give birth. He had almost arrived
there when a great scream was heard. A scream of terror. Hermes
hurried quickly. He just had time to see the mother of his child
fleeing, running until she was gasping for breath. And there,
on the grass, wrapped in big leaves, was the baby, left alone
and whimpering softly. There was no enemy in sight, nothing

which could justify the mother's flight. Hermes approached the child. He gently folded back the leaves which enveloped it and gave a startled jump: the baby's body was covered with black hair, from its forehead protruded two horns and instead of human legs he had the two hind legs of a billy goat! This baby was monstrous. It was his ugliness that had driven his mother to flight. In discovering the baby, Hermes too recoiled instinctively. No, it wasn't possible, he couldn't be the father of such a monster! But the baby looked at him, grinning, with an eye that was full of mischief. Hermes remembered for a fleeting moment the birth of his brother Hephaestus, so ugly and deformed, that his mother had rejected him. So he took out of his bag a hare's hide, wrapped the baby in it and decided to bring it to Olympus.

When he arrived at the palace, Hermes appeared before the assembly of the gods. He set the baby down beside Zeus and declared:

"Here is my latest-born son!"

The baby was pulling faces. It stuck out its tongue and puffed its cheeks in such a funny way that, upon seeing him, all the gods broke into enormous laughter. And the more the gods laughed, the more the infant continued his antics. There had never been such gaiety on Olympus!

"We shall call your son Pan, which means 'all', because he has gladdened all our hearts!" proclaimed Zeus, laughing until tears came to his eyes.

But Hermes only half appreciated this massive, crazy laughter. He thought that people were making fun of his son, and he decided to keep him away from Olympus. He took the child to Arcadia, to the region where he himself had been born. Because half of Pan's body was like the body of a billy goat, he made him the protector of the shepherds and the flocks. It became usual to come across him galloping in the woods and the forests with a great shepherd's crook in his hand. If he was in a good mood when he met someone, that person would suddenly be overcome by mad, uncontrollable laughter. But when he was in a foul mood, Pan caused an equally uncontrollable fear in those who crossed his path. This is why we call this great fear a "panic".

Hermes had transmitted several of his talents even to this son, who was so very different from himself. He possessed most notably the gift of music. One day, Pan fell in love with a young nymph. Every time he came across her in the woods where she lived, his heart beat like mad. But the nymph did not like him the least bit. Every day Pan would return to her. Every day the nymph would flee, running. The nymph did not know any more how to get rid of this burdensome lover. So one day, as Pan was running after her once more in the woods, she decided to transform herself into a reed. "No! Don't do that!" cried Pan. But it was too late. The nymph had chosen to stay for ever beyond Pan's reach. In despair Pan cut the reed, so he could keep it for ever with him in remembrance of his fair maiden. He cut it in lengths, attached the lengths together and began to blow gently into them. This is how he invented the instrument that we call pan pipes.

Hermes, who had himself invented the first flute, felt proud of his son. He was content with his choice. Pan led a far happier life in the midst of the woods and fields than he would have had among the mocking gods of Olympus.

To be continued...

EPISODE 96

*Previously: Hermes has had a new son, called
Pan. This son is very ugly and deformed. He
causes frenzied laughter or terror and he
lives as a shepherd among the flocks.*

At the beginning of this month of May, as he did at the same time every year, Hermes went to pay a visit to his mother, because on his birthday he liked to hold Maia tight in his arms. Even if he had long ceased being a child, he would rest his head on Maia's lap and wait for the maternal caress of her hand on his cheek. He would go away happy, pacified. Stronger and more joyful than ever.

That day, the landscape that stretched below his feet was staggeringly beautiful. The light of springtime gently stroked the fresh green of the leaves. Each blade of grass quivered. Hermes' delight reminded him of the delight he had known on the day he was born, when he discovered the world for the first time right here. He had lived through many adventures, but his outlook on the world was still that of a child rapt with wonder.

Hermes was letting himself be carried by the warm air currents which enveloped him when his gaze was drawn towards a woman who was strolling through the poppy fields. She was blonde and her hair was coiled on her head in a gracious style. She was walking alone, a bow and arrows over her shoulder. But instead of hunting, she seemed to be breathing in the smell of nature. She would bend down to a flower to look at it more closely and then she would resume her meandering path. Hermes was so captivated by the young beauty that he had to get close to her, no matter what it took. While he was looking for a way to seduce this mortal maiden, Hermes noticed something stirring in the bush right next to her. A shadow was lurking behind the branches. "There is no doubt about it," murmured Hermes, "another admirer is waiting for her." He flew discreetly near the bush. Who was hiding there? Hermes discovered with surprise his brother Apollo. Busy as he was watching, Apollo had not noticed Hermes' presence. A blast of anger shook the messenger god. "Am I always to find my older brother on my path? Will he always be ahead of me?" The attractions of the young woman, combined with his jealousy, made up his mind for him. Hermes saw his brother turn himself into an old woman in order to get close to the beautiful stranger without scaring her. While Apollo was walking towards her at an old woman's pace, Hermes decided to pip his brother to the post. With two flaps of his wings he came right next to her. Startled, the young woman tried to run away, but Hermes touched her with his golden caduceus and she slipped instantly into a profound slumber.

When she woke up, she was lying on a bed of straw next to him and she no longer seemed scared at all.

"You are Hermes, the god of Thieves, aren't you?" she said, smiling. "I had no doubt that you would come to me one day. Because you love your sister Artemis, don't you, and they say that I resemble her. It seems that I am even more beautiful than she is..."

When he heard these words, Hermes was taken aback. He did not like boasting at all. "Who are you?" Hermes asked her.

"I am the Princess Chione. My father is the greatest hunter of all."

Hermes stood there staring at her. So what exactly *was* he doing next to her? Had he lost his head? When the afternoon came to its end, Hermes left Chione, promising her he would return. But he had no intention of doing so.

Hermes did not know that Apollo, trembling with rage, had not given up his own claim on the beautiful Chione. As soon as Hermes had flown away towards Olympus, Apollo approached Chione and won her in turn with his charm. Nine months after this crazy springtime day, Chione brought two children into the world. The first, Autolycus, was the son of Hermes, the second, Philammon, was Apollo's. How would Hermes react when he discovered this unexpected son?

To be continued...

ЄPISODЄ 47

During which Autolycus manages to get himself adopted by Hermes

Previously: Hermes has had an amorous escapade with a young woman called Chione. She was also seduced by his brother Apollo. Of this affair two boys were born, Autolycus, son of Hermes, and Philammon, son of Apollo.

Autolycus realized very young that he possessed an extraordinary gift: he was able to steal anything that came within reach without ever getting caught! The first time he discovered this talent, he was barely able to walk. His mother, Chione, was lying on a comfortable couch and had a plate of fruit placed beside her. She was chattering gaily with her female friends, talking as always of her incomparable beauty, which she considered to be superior to that of Artemis. Little Philammon had approached, had stretched out his hand towards the fruit, but Chione had refused him: "No, no, darling, these fruits are for my friends. Go and play elsewhere..." Philammon had left the room disappointed. It was then that his brother

Autolycus sneaked stealthily towards the plate of fruit. He took one; no one noticed him. He took a second. The women were not aware of anything at all. Emboldened, Autolycus emptied the entire fruit bowl in this way. His mother and her friends never saw anything whatsoever: it was as if he had become transparent! Having eaten to his heart's content, Autolycus left the room. Only then did Chione discover that the plate was empty. She suspected it was the boys' doing, but she was unable to find the culprit because she had not seen a thing. Since that day, Autolycus never stopped having the time of his life.

How different they were, Chione's sons! Autolycus was a tempestuous little boy, quarrelsome and a prankster. He never stopped teasing his brother. Philammon, for his part, was a calm and gentle boy, always daydreaming. He had inherited from his father Apollo a great beauty and everyone longed to be close to him and listen to his poetry. Every evening he recited poems at the centre of an admiring audience. Autolycus was jealous of Philammon's gracefulness. Why were all these people only interested in his brother? He decided to get even. All those who pressed around his brother would soon regret not having spared him a single glance... While they were in a circle around the young poet, Autolycus sneaked in among them and stole anything that caught his fancy: a gilt belt here, a pouch full of money there, or even a sheepskin cloak. He even succeeded in undoing the laces of sandals and in removing them without their owners ever being aware of anything. No one was able to catch the mystery thief.

The more time passed, the more Philammon was irritated to see his admirers being robbed like this. One day, he appealed to Apollo: "Father, father, I have never asked you for anything," he cried, "but today I would like a favour from you: can you try to unmask the thief?" From the heights of Olympus Apollo heard his son's plea and descended to see what was happening on earth. When he discovered young Autolycus, he was struck by the boy's resemblance to his own brother Hermes when he had been little. The same air of innocence, the same bewitching smile... There could be no doubt; he had to be the culprit. He went to see Hermes straight away. "My brother," said Apollo, "you need to do something about your son Autolycus. I fear that he may have inherited from you the same partiality to stealing! You need to sort this out."

Hermes had not chosen to have this child and he had no desire to take care of him. All the same, he promised to Apollo that he would go and take a look as soon as he could spare a moment. Time went by, and Hermes forgot his promise. Until one day a drama occurred.

The beautiful Chione boasted everywhere that she was more beautiful than Artemis, and in the end the goddess of Hunting grew vexed. "What a conceited woman! This mortal who dares to compare herself to a goddess must be punished: such is the law of Olympus." And she descended on earth. While Chione was out hunting, as she was accustomed to do, one of Artemis' arrows pierced her straight through the heart.

The two sons of Chione wept for their mother's death.

"We are orphans now," said Autolycus to Philammon.

"Not at all, we have our fathers," Philammon replied to him between sobs.

Autolycus answered: "Some hope! As far as my father Hermes is concerned, I have never even seen him. I do not exist for him."

While he spoke, Autolycus could not resist stealing a ring that his brother wore on his little finger and which he liked very much. Philammon of course did not notice anything. But someone had seen and heard it all, and that was Hermes. Forewarned by Artemis about Chione's death, he had finally decided to go and visit Autolycus. When he caught sight of him, he was really bowled over; this child resembled him so much: how could he not have recognized him as his own son? And, watching him in action, he suddenly smiled: there was no doubt—this little one was truly his own offspring. He decided to look after him from now on.

To be continued...

ΕΡΙSODΕ 48

IN WHICH AUTOLYCUS PROVES THAT HE DESERVES TO BE HIS FATHER'S SON

*Previously: Following Chione's death, Hermes
has come to meet his son Autolycus and
has decided to undertake his care.*

Many years had gone by. Hermes had kept his promise. A promise made to Apollo, a promise made to himself as well: he had kept an eye on Autolycus. But, for a father, he had a strange way indeed of undertaking his son's care: instead of preventing him from stealing, he had on the contrary offered his son an additional way to succeed in his thieving! This is how it had all happened. On the day that Hermes had shown himself to Autolycus for the first time, the latter had not jumped for joy. As soon as he had seen the winged sandals and hat, Autolycus had immediately recognized his father, but he had pretended not to see him. He had even turned his back to him! Embarrassed, Hermes had had to tap him on the shoulder:

"Er, ahem, good morning, my son..."

Without turning round, Autolycus had said: "So you remember you have a son now, do you?"

"This youngster is certainly full of character!" thought Hermes. Then he replied: "I ask you to forgive me. What if we tried to make amends?"

At that, Autolycus had flung himself into his arms. He was as full of pride and as impulsive as his father.

Hermes then said: "I saw you steal your brother's ring. And from what Apollo has reported back to me, this is not your first theft?"

Autolycus lifted up his chin defiantly. "And what about you, what were you doing at my age? I am not the son of the god of Thieves for nothing..."

Hermes did not know how to reply—and this was something that never happened to him! This son was clearly not to be trifled with. As he watched the petulant expression on his face, Hermes burst into laughter.

"Very well, you win. In fact, I shall make you a gift: I grant you the power to steal any herd that takes your fancy. From now on, any animals you steal shall change their appearance: they will no longer be recognizable to their rightful owners."

Autolycus' smile stirred Hermes' heart.

From time to time, Hermes came to see what his son was up to on earth. This is how he saw him sneak one night among his neighbour's herds and make away with some of his animals. Nothing could be easier for him, since he only needed to change a black cow into a white cow, a bull with long, curvy horns into one with short, straight ones, for the theft to remain undetected.

Several times, and full of suspicion, his neighbour had come to Autolycus' stable to verify whether his beasts were there. His herd diminished in number, whereas that of Autolycus increased. But of course he never recognized any of his beasts, and could therefore prove nothing.

One night, Autolycus had gone surreptitiously to his neighbour's property and stolen some cows. The following day, his neighbour knocked on his door, accompanied by several of his friends.

"Autolycus, you are a villainous thief," he was shouting.

Feeling sure of his ground, Autolycus replied: "But dear friend, please, do come and check my herd, you will not find any of your beasts there."

"It shan't be necessary. We have proof this time," snorted his neighbour. "I engraved on the underside of my cows' hooves the words 'stolen by Autolycus'. Look, all of you!"

And he pointed to hoof prints on the ground. Tracks of hooves with the words "stolen by Autolycus" at every step could be seen clearly on the muddy path. And these traces led straight to Autolycus' stable! For the first time in his life, Autolycus had been caught red-handed. Hermes laughed and did not intervene on his son's behalf. Because even though he was the god of Thieves, he also believed it was fair that once in a while theft should be punished as well.

To be continued…

EPISODE 99

IN WHICH HERMES BECOMES THE
GREAT-GRANDFATHER OF ODYSSEUS

*Previously: Autolycus, the son of Hermes, is
very skilful at robbing his neighbours. Even if
he is occasionally caught red-handed!*

The years passed. Autolycus grew up. He got married and had children. Then he grew old. One of his daughters went away to live on that small island called Ithaca. She is the one who gave birth to Autolycus' first grandson. As soon as Autolycus learnt the news, he hastened to the island. Deeply moved, Autolycus approached the baby. The wet-nurse who held it in her arms placed the child on his grandfather's lap and said: "It is for you to find him a name now." Autolycus hesitated and remained silent. As he was not very used to babies, he held him clumsily. And so the baby began to wail and wail! He was restless and he squirmed, and poor Autolycus, panicking and losing his wits, restored him hastily to the nurse's arms. Then, addressing himself to the child, he said: "You shall be called Odysseus! It means 'the one who gets angry'... and I hope that your anger will help you later in accomplishing great things." The nurse began to laugh, rocking the baby in her arms at the same time to soothe him. Autolycus then kissed Odysseus and said one more thing to him: "When you are old enough, I shall offer you invaluable treasures. Come to my house and take them, as soon as you are ready to come for them on your own." The nurse smiled. She promised to remind Odysseus about this.

Someone else had also arrived inconspicuously to greet the newborn and that was Hermes. He who never grew old, he who never died, felt nonetheless that he had changed over the years. And yet, for all that, he was greatly astonished to find himself already a great-grandfather. When the nurse had gone away he went close to the crib. Odysseus plunged his bright eyes into Hermes' eyes. Hermes could sense that this child had inherited the cunning of his grandfather Autolycus. He knew that this cunning came from him, from Hermes, and he felt a great pride. But what would Odysseus do with it? He decided to follow his destiny closely.

Odysseus grew up. He was not very courageous, he did not always tell the truth, and sometimes it even happened that he did some thieving here and there, but he was by far the cleverest of men. One day he was old enough to go to his grandfather Autolycus on his own. His nurse reminded him then of the promise made by his grandfather on the day of his birth. Odysseus set off right away. Autolycus was delighted to receive him. He kept his word and offered him a priceless treasure. Then, in order to celebrate his coming, he organized a great hunt on Mount Parnassus.

There was rich game on that day and the hunt was very fruitful. Odysseus did not kill many animals, for he was not very skilled in archery, but he took pleasure in accompanying his grandfather. All of a sudden, an enormous wild boar sprang out of a bush and charged straight at him. The young man was frightened. He did not try to fight it; he only sought to avoid it. But he did not manage to get completely out of its way, and one of the animal's tusks gashed his knee. The wound began to bleed profusely. His nurse, who never left his side, hastened to him. "What have you done to yourself now?" she cried. She was scolding him as though he were still a little boy. She treated his injury, bandaged it and the wound healed quickly. Odysseus was left from this adventure with a large scar on his knee. He always tried to hide it—to him, it was the mark of his lack of both skill and courage. But his nurse would laugh and say to him: "Odysseus, thanks to this scar, I shall always, *always* be able to recognize you. Even when you have become an old man, even if many years should go by without my seeing you, even if no one can recognize your face any more, even if I become blind, I shall always be able to recognize you thanks to this scar!"

Hermes, who had witnessed this misadventure, was concerned for his great-grandson. How would this clumsy boy manage to get through life?

To be continued...

€PISODE 100

IN WHICH HERMES TURNS HIS MOST
BEAUTIFUL INVENTION INTO REALITY

*Previously: Hermes has become the great-grandfather
of a child called Odysseus. This boy seems to be sharp-
witted but clumsy. Hermes is worried about him.*

I n order to set his mind at rest regarding the future of his
great-grandson, Hermes threw little round pebbles in the
limpid water and remained bent over the future life of Odysseus.
When he stood up again, he had seen one of mankind's most
extraordinary adventures. He had discovered that his great-
grandson would be one of the greatest heroes of all time. He
would experience a strife which would pit thousands of men
against one another for many years, the war of Troy. He would
take part in an immense and long epic, which would take him
to every sea, every ocean, and which would even come to bear
his name: the Odyssey. He would emerge victorious from all the
trials that awaited him and he would return to his homeland
covered in glory. And it would be thanks to this scar caused by

the wild boar that he would be recognized by his old nurse and recover his throne.

As he discovered this exceptional destiny, Hermes was filled with joy and with pride. He felt so very proud that he wanted to be certain that the entire world would hear of these adventures. But what could he do to keep a record of them? Men tell one another about the great events in their lives. Then those who have lived them die. Those who have heard the stories will retell them, but will also forget certain parts. Those who come after will forget even more parts. And so it goes, until death erases everything. And memory disappears. No, Hermes did not wish to allow the remembrance of the adventures that Odysseus would experience sink away into oblivion. He wished to see them recounted for centuries and centuries to come. He had to invent something which would allow their memory to be preserved for all eternity.

Suddenly an image stood out in his mind: the name of every human being was engraved in the cave where the Moirae spun the lives of men. The Moirae, then, had found a way of inscribing memory for ever and ever. This was where he had to draw his inspiration from.

Hermes had discovered fire; he had created the lyre with a tortoise and the flute with the help of a reed. On that day, it was the birds that helped him. He was lying on a beach and looking up at the sky. The light of the dying day tinged the clouds with pink hues. At that instant, he saw a majestic formation of cranes flying above. These graceful birds spread their long bodies in the air in a perfect geometric shape. Hermes slowly began to whistle through his teeth: "*Ffff...*" It was as though the shape that the birds had drawn in the sky had inspired in him the sound he was producing. "*Ffff*," repeated Hermes, looking at the birds growing more distant. And at last he found what he was looking for.

He leapt to his feet, seized his caduceus and began to trace signs on the sand. A different sound corresponded to each sign he traced. And the sounds placed together formed words. Hermes began to draw and draw. His eyes ran across the signs. Little by little, the signs began to acquire meaning: each group of signs became a word. And the words strung together formed phrases. And the phrases put together told stories. Hermes let out a great shout of joy. He had just invented the alphabet. Never again would stories be lost to oblivion. And people would be able to speak to each other without seeing one another; understand each other without ever having met; love one another across the centuries. Drunk with joy, Hermes fluttered around as on that first day when he had just learnt to fly. It occurred to him that Prometheus would have been proud of him.

As he was flying above the earth, he caught sight of Mount Parnassus. Antalia, Roxanne and Pausania, the three old nurses of the babies of the gods, were there. He heard the white sheets that they were hanging out to dry flap in the wind. He smelt the scent of the soap flakes. The three nurses gave a great wave of their hand.

"Thank you on behalf of the men of today," cried Antalia to him.

"Thank you on behalf of the men of tomorrow," Roxanne cried to him.

"And thank you on behalf of the men of yesterday," cried Pausania to him. Thanks to the alphabet, men would be able to read and write their present lives, their future lives and their past lives. Hermes turned three somersaults in the air and went away, bursting into enormous laughter.

THE END

PUSHKIN CHILDREN'S BOOKS

Just as we all are, children are fascinated by stories. From the earliest age, we love to hear about monsters and heroes, romance and death, disaster and rescue, from every place and time.

In 2013, we created Pushkin Children's Books to share these tales from different languages and cultures with younger readers, and to open the door to the wide, colourful worlds these stories offer.

From picture books and adventure stories to fairy tales and classics, and from fifty-year-old bestsellers to current huge successes abroad, the books on the Pushkin Children's list reflect the very best stories from around the world, for our most discerning readers of all: children.